W9-CTS-854

learning
fear

B. A. CHEPAITIS

ACE BOOKS, NEW YORK

LEARNING FEAR

This is a work of fiction. Names, characters, places, and incidents are
either the product of the author's imagination or are used fictitiously,
and any resemblance to actual persons, living or dead, business
establishments, events, or locales is entirely coincidental.

An Ace Book / published by arrangement with
the author

PRINTING HISTORY
Ace mass-market edition / January 2000

The Penguin Putnam Inc. World Wide Web site address is
http://www.penguinputnam.com

Check out the ACE Science Fiction & Fantasy newsletter
and much more on the Internet at Club PPI!

ISBN: 0-441-00696-5

ACE®
Ace Books are published
by The Berkley Publishing Group,
a division of Penguin Putnam Inc.,
375 Hudson Street, New York, New York 10014.
ACE and the "A" design are trademarks
belonging to Penguin Putnam Inc.

PRINTED IN THE UNITED STATES OF AMERICA

10 9 8 7 6 5 4 3 2 1

The novels of B. A. Chepaitis present the future of law enforcement in a society that has given up on justice . . .

In the aftermath of the Killing Times—when serial murder spread throughout the world like a plague— the Planetoid prison system was established. Jaguar Addams is one of an elite group of law enforcers working to cure killers of their murderous tendencies. Through empathic contact with her charges, Jaguar subjects them to their greatest fears.

Ace Books by B. A. Chepaitis

THE FEAR PRINCIPLE
THE FEAR OF GOD
LEARNING FEAR

acknowledgments

Some explanations and acknowledgments are necessary. First, I learned the term "bytelock" from Jan Finder, aka the Wombat, who coined it. Hey, Jan, thanks.

Second, if the university described in this book should in any way resemble the State University of New York at Albany, where I received my doctoral degree in writing and met some of my favorite people in the universe, that resemblance must be a coincidence, since this is obviously a work of fiction and the university at Albany is so obviously a real place. Of course, many places in the imagination do resemble real places, and so these little mix-ups are bound to occur.

Pay them no mind at all.

On the other hand, the Native American AIM leader Leonard Peltier, whose great-grandson appears in this work bearing his name, is a real man, and his situation is as I've described it. As of this writing, Mr. Peltier remains in prison for a crime that the U.S. government admits they don't know who committed. He has been denied retrial to avoid embarrassing the FBI and, I'm told, because some important people want him in jail. Call me naive, but I hate to believe that embarrassment or whim are more important than justice and freedom in what is supposedly a democracy.

In the book, I have written that Mr. Peltier ultimately goes free, in the hope that whoever listens to the stories will hear that one and make it come true. Many people are working for this to happen, and many more can help by writing to their congresspersons and senators, asking them to support executive clemency. You can get further information on how to help by writing Leonard Peltier Defense Committee, PO Box 583, Lawrence, KS 66044, going to Web site http://members.xoom.com/freepeltier/story/.html, or E-mail lpd@idir.net.

Finally, the Jaguars and Packers are real football teams. If the Jaguars have already won their Super Bowl, I want them to remember that I wrote this book long before it happened. Another dream waiting to come true.

To my teachers—Steve North, Judy Johnson, Harry Staley and Frank Sullivan—the very best.
And my students—you know who you are—the best and then some.

Teaching is the greatest act of optimism.

—Colleen Wilcox

Learning
fear

prologue

THE FIRST GENERAL FACULTY MEETING OF THE
cultural studies department was proceeding according to
all known traditions of faculty meetings.

Slowly.

On the agenda was a delegation of committee work,
with some argument over who would chair the dissertation requirement review committee, which nobody
wanted; who would chair the visiting speakers committee, which everybody wanted; some consideration of
how to handle current budget cuts; and an introduction
of the new on-line grading system, which half the faculty
objected to strenuously, and the other half ardently sup-
ported.

Professor Harold Smith, cultural linguistics, was ob-
jecting loudly and polysyllabically, stressing the risk of
hackers changing grades. His voice was lost in the theoretical moment of postmodernist Professor Dena Na-
lek's paragraph on technophobia and societal change,
and her words were subsumed by Yoruba expert Professor Samitu Laki's clear and cogent statement on the
dangers of Web snare.

"We've got a whole program established to keep our
students from falling into cyberspace—an innovative

and I might say progressive program that includes our on-line students. And after all the time it took to establish that, we put our faculty in a position of dependence on computers?''

"I agree,'' Harold said, his long gray mustache twitching with the impetus of his argument. "We've had enough trouble with webheads and the like. Why encourage it? I mean, why?''

Ethan Davis, dean of the cultural studies department, tapped a pen impatiently against the dark wood of the long table they sat at. "You may be right, but that's not getting us anywhere, is it? We can't go on bubbling in grades with number-two pencils forever, can we? What we have to deal with is reality, not rightness.''

Professor Emily Rainer, who taught Hebrew and Sumerian texts, clapped her hands lightly in his direction, her many bracelets jangling. "Bravo, Ethan. That's why you make such a good dean. Your sense of practicality is so much more finely honed than your sense of principles.''

He inclined his head toward her in acknowledgment of the truth. "But the real point is, the University has decided on the system, and we have to make sure all professors know the security procedures. Before this meeting's over, I want one of you to organize that. Understood?''

He looked around at them, making sure they did understand, and then nodded. "Good. Next on the agenda—what is it, Samitu?'' Ethan turned toward Samitu, who had tapped him lightly on the arm.

"Pardon my interruption, but I would like to add to the agenda. There is a new lecturer arriving, a woman whose résumé is rather sketchy, except that she comes here from the Planetoid prison system. Now, there is the general issue of the way these temporary hires are made behind the scenes without our knowledge—and the way they tend to become permanent," he said, looking pointedly at Ethan, who had started as a temporary hire.

"Some of our best faculty came to us that way," Emily said pointedly. Ethan's brief glance showed his gratitude, and her finely drawn mouth turned up in a smile, making all the features on her narrow face soften.

"Agreed. But in this case, I, for one, would like to know why someone from the Planetoids has been asked to teach here. I'm not sure this is appropriate, given our recent controversies."

"Very true, Sammy," Professor George Norton, resident expert on the Killing Times and their aftermath, stage-whispered, "but better not say it too loud. Our esteemed president might hear you from afar."

"Really, George," Ethan murmured, "That was uncalled for."

"It seems to me," Harold interjected, "that George has a valid point. We all know the Planetoids are rife with—well, you know. We *all* know. That's the point."

Ethan closed his eyes and leaned back in his chair. He had been hoping to run through the agenda in short order, and spend the rest of the evening in mutual enjoyment with the woman to his immediate right. Although she liked to show a tolerant attitude, he could tell by the way she jangled her bracelets that she was feeling impatient, and probably a lot of that impatience was due to the lack of attention he'd given her of late. He would remedy that tonight, if they could ever get out of here. Harold harrumphed his throat clear and spoke.

"I understand she's a—what do they call it— Teacher? Odd title for someone who works with criminals."

"Makes perfect sense to me," Dena muttered. The other professors smiled. "Is she here to find out what happened to the Gone Girls? After two years of no trouble, one would think we could put that incident behind us."

"No. She can't be doing that," George objected, with authority. "Planetoid Teachers don't do investigative work. They work with fear. Primal, core fears. Even before the Serials, as the prison system broke down due to overcrowding, the idea of approaching crime from its psychological base was—"

"A very bad idea," Emily cut in.

Ethan laughed. "Children. Let's try and stay civilized at least until the semester starts. The new lecturer is part of an exchange program that allows University professors to conduct research on the Planetoids. That's been a closed door until now, so we should consider ourselves fortunate."

"But what will she teach? Restraint procedures?"

"Some of our faculty could probably use such a class," Ethan commented, and laughter ensued.

"Really, Ethan," George said when it died down, "what's her field?"

"World religions," he said. "With a specialized field from her own background, which is rather rare. She's of the Mertec people."

Professor Leonard Peltier, who had been sitting almost invisible and silent, spoke up. "Did you say Mertec?" he asked.

Since he so rarely joined in the discussion at meetings, everyone turned to look at him.

"I knew a Mertec," he said. "Old man, though. He held a UN seat. But he knew the traditions. Not many left who do."

"Well, where'd they go?" Samitu asked.

"Killed by Europeans?" Emily suggested, looking sympathetically at Leonard.

"No," he said. "Europeans couldn't catch 'em. They just left."

The group stared at him. A light flush crossed Emily's face and left. Something like a smile crossed Leonard's face. He put it away, and let his gaze wander to Ethan and rest there briefly as if asking a question. Ethan returned the silent stare without any expression of approval or disapproval. Leonard turned to the others.

"Mertec share a language base and some ritual behavior with Tzotzil Maya, so it's hypothesized they're a related group," he said. "There's some evidence that they left the Maya cities well before the decline and returned to a nomadic way of life, traveling north. Their name means 'the people who walk,' and according to their own story, they were told in a vision to keep walking. They were sort of visiting singers and shamans for other tribes. Mostly they settled in with the tribes of the southwest. You'll see traces of Mertec tradition in a lot of different tribes, though."

Ethan nodded. "She's granddaughter to the man you mentioned. Not a full-blood, but apparently she knows her culture. She wrote her dissertation on it, and it's a fine one."

"With her name, it better be," Leonard commented.

"What's her name?" George asked.

Leonard and Ethan exchanged glances.

Leonard shrugged. "Jaguar," he said. "Jaguar Addams."

Emily tittered, then coughed to cover it. Someone could be heard to mumble something about no pets being allowed on campus.

"Jaguars," Ethan pointed out, "aren't pets. At any rate, the decision to send her to us was made on an administrative level. She's a temporary appointment, nontenured, assigned to teach a survey course and an honors seminar. And no matter what you've heard about Planetoid workers, she'll have nothing whatsoever to do with the History of Empathic Arts course, so we have no reason to worry or complain."

He looked around the table and saw mouths opening, all ready to contribute their opinion on the University's decision to run a course in the history of the empathic arts. He held up a hand to silence them, thinking that the problem with professors was that they were too accustomed to having all the air in the room to themselves.

"Not now," he said mildly. "There will be, I assure you, many many forums for dealing with the empathic arts course controversy. However," he continued, directing a smile toward Emily, who brightened visibly, "I would like to be out of here in time for dinner, and my reservation is for six, so if we could continue with the agenda?"

With a collective sigh, the professors expelled the unused air from their lungs and consented to follow the protocol.

1

THE MAN ON JAGUAR'S BED WAS THOROUGHLY
naked, and fully erect.

He crouched on all fours facing the foot of the bed,
his voice reverberating in a series of growls, groans, and
grunts, a long line of saliva seeping from his mouth
down his chin. Jaguar stood in front of him, draped in
a gray silk sheet, her hands on her hips, her head thrown
back in a howl of laughter.

"What a gentleman," she said, pushing her hand
against his face until he fell back. "The man who never
loses control."

He reared up and lunged for her as she took a step
back, and the image dissolved with a clatter and a buzz.
The viewscreen showed only snow.

"That's about it," Jaguar said to Alex Dzarny, her
supervisor on prison Planetoid 3, who had come over to
her apartment to view the tape of her interaction with
this prisoner. She pushed the remote to turn the viewer
off, stood, and stretched.

Alex drummed his fingers thoughtfully on his knee.

"What happened?" he asked.

"He started flailing, and I had to initiate restraint procedures."

"Then?"

"Then," she said, "the recorder was accidentally turned off. Like some tea?"

Alex raised an eyebrow at her, and she turned her back, walking into the kitchen area without waiting for a reply. He leaned back in his chair. The kitchen was open to the living room, and from this position he could watch her sift herbs from various jars into a kettle, hands moving gracefully through a familiar ritual, the silky cloth of her long loose dress moving like a green river to outline her lean and muscular frame. She had a dancer's body, and he enjoyed watching it in motion, though as he thought about it, stillness suited her, too.

The late-afternoon sun slanted into the window and poured pale swaths of orange gold over her, soft and warm, catching at the honey gold in her dark hair. A soothing setting. Beauty before and behind and all around him.

He wished his mood could match the setting, but it didn't. Not even close.

The tape Jaguar had played for him was not what the Governors' Board had in mind when they requested that she submit filmed records of her work with prisoners. It was, in fact, exactly what they didn't want a record of, and didn't want to know. She knew that, and she couldn't resist pushing their buttons, or Alex's buttons for that matter. This was the kind of stunt that landed her, repeatedly, on the wrong side of the governors who created policy for the prison Planetoid. Though he had to admit a little honest tape was mild in comparison to some tricks she'd pulled in the past.

"Jaguar," he called to her, "what did you want me to do with this?"

"I don't know," she replied. "Use it for training?"

He couldn't help himself. He grinned, and as she walked into the living room carrying a tray with a teapot and two cups on it, he saw that she was grinning, too. She set it down on the low table in front of the couch and poured. He reached over and picked up his cup, watching her as she took her cup, sat down on the couch, and curled her legs under her.

"Certainly," she said, "it would discourage the faint-hearted and the romanticizers from wanting to work here."

"Might encourage the freaks and pervs, though."

"True." She smiled up at him, the gold flecks of her sea eyes catching the colors of the sun and flashing fire. Nothing dangerous, Alex thought. Just a little fun. Though with her, a little fun could be the most danger-ous thing in the world.

"What'll I give Paul?" he asked. Paul Dinardo was governor for Zone 12, and he had almost begged Alex to get something from Jaguar that wouldn't embarrass them all.

"How about a kiss—from me." She lifted her hand, touched it with her lips, and breathed it toward him.

He shook his head at her. "It wouldn't hurt to co-operate a little, now and then, just for a change of pace."

"I am cooperating," she said. "They want tape. I have tape for them."

He put his cup down, leaned an elbow on his knee, and rested his chin in it. The problem was, he understood what she was saying when she made this kind of tape. The governors wanted something squeaky-clean to pres-ent to the world, and the work of Planetoid prisons just wasn't that. This tape was Jaguar's way of dosing them with truth serum, saying look at what we do here—what you want us to do, pay us to do, then pretend we're not doing.

The Planetoid system was created after the catastrophe of the Serial Killing Times left the urban centers of the home planet decimated. It became clear—too late to save the millions that died—that incarceration was neither effective nor affordable. In the aftermath of the violence, the burning, the horror, home planet citizens and politicians were both anxious to get criminals out of sight and willing to try a new way of rehabilitating criminals.

Now, the home planet had contained treatment sites for lesser criminals, and the Planetoids for the incorrigibles—those who refused treatment, or those whose first crimes were particularly heinous. Based on the premise that crime grew out of fear, and that criminals could be rehabilitated if they faced their fears, Teachers such as Jaguar created and ran programs to make them do just that. These programs took a variety of forms, from dramatic role-playing to what Alex had just seen on Jaguar's tape, and they were often risky to both Teacher and prisoner. If a prisoner successfully completed a Planetoid program, he either stayed on and was subsumed into Planetoid life, working in the service or the prison sector, or he went on to complete rehab on the home planet.

Although their recidivism rate was the lowest in the history of criminal justice systems, it wasn't pretty work, and no amount of PR would make it so. Jaguar liked to remind the governors of that now and then, in case they came up with any idea that they knew how to run the system better than she did.

Alex had been running interference for her since she'd been booted off of Planetoid One almost five years ago, so he knew how to deal with the governors in these matters. They were a cakewalk compared with dealing with her.

Especially on days like today, when he wasn't sure how she'd take what he was about to say.

"Jaguar," he said, "you've been asked to take on a special assignment."

She stopped stirring and placed her spoon on the table between them. "Tell me about it."

"It's part of an exchange program. We've got some University people coming up here to learn the system, and we're sending some of our people to the University to do some teaching."

"Who's bright idea was that?"

"Governors. Good for PR, and it gets some extra funding tossed our way. The University people here will be confined to interviews with exiting prisoners and reading open files, so that shouldn't be a problem. The Planetoid people on campus will teach courses in their areas of expertise."

"And what's my part in it? Confining the researchers?"

"Actually, you're being placed at the New York State University. Upstate campus. Cultural studies department."

She sat with her cup of tea poised halfway between the table and her mouth.

He continued. "It's a pretty light load. One undergrad survey-of-religions course, one honors seminar, three on-line graduate students. Research time."

"I beg your pardon," she said. "Did you say a teaching job? As in, a classroom? Grade sheets and ordering books and taking attendance?"

"I appreciate the irony."

Jaguar had spent some time teaching when she was a graduate student, but she'd never intended to work in a classroom. She'd gotten a degree to satisfy the requirements for work on the Planetoids. She said it was about the same job description as classroom teaching—long hours, low pay, and hard work with groups of people who would rather be somewhere else.

She sipped at her tea, a Cheshire cat smile visible over the rim of the cup.

"Quite a cover," she said. "Who's the prisoner, and what's the assignment?"

This, Alex thought, would be the difficulty. No way to say it except straight. "No prisoner. Just—research."

She put down her teacup, sat back, and folded her hands in her lap. Waiting.

Alex paced from the couch back to the window, and toward the couch again. Her apartment was, like her, clean and airy with a touch of the wild. Not too much furniture. Bentwood rocking chair which he knew had belonged to her grandmother. Shelves loaded with disks and books. Then, on the desk next to her telecom, a curved piece of wood intricately carved by busy insects, next to a clay pot filled with dried sage leaves. On the windowsill, a hawk's feather and two stones—one round and white, the other thin black obsidian. Fresh mint in pots, and dried mint tied in bunches that hung over the doorway to her bedroom.

He picked up the pack of cigarettes that was on the end table next to the couch and brought it to Jaguar, held the cigarettes out in front of her.

Jaguar stared at them, then took one out, lit it as he sat back down.

"Where's my blindfold?" she asked, breathing out smoke. "And which wall should I stand against?"

"It's not that bad," he said. "I just know how you feel about research jobs."

"I don't feel any way about them," she said deliberately, "because I never do them. I work with prisoners. Criminals. I'm a Teacher." She pulled deeply on her cigarette, flicked ashes into the saucer of her teacup.

"You'll be a teacher there, too," he said. "And the research isn't the usual. Just listen for a minute, okay?"

She unsettled herself in her seat, resettled, and showed him the green of her suspicious eyes. He supposed that was listening, of sorts, and he continued.

"The Board's been taking heat about psi work on the Planetoids. Apparently home planet opinion is moving to the right, and the media's decided we make juicy copy, so there's been more than the usual run of stories making us out to be freaks. The Board wants Planetoid people visible on the home planet as regular working folks. They want to shift some attitudes."

Jaguar rolled her eyes at him. "They might have a better chance if they could make up their minds about their own."

The Board was ambivalent about the use of the arts. They'd overturned the ruling that automatically discounted people with psi capacities from working on the Planetoids, but the codebook advised against use of the empathic arts. No specific punishment existed for using them, but Teachers could reasonably expect an absence of promotion if they were spotted as practicing. They knew use of the arts was extraordinarily helpful in the job, but they wouldn't support it as long as prejudice against it still existed on the home planet.

Like all good bureaucrats, they wanted to sit on any fence they could find, no matter how many pickets it drove up their behinds.

"Maybe a little learning on the home planet would help, too," he said.

"Go on."

"The campus you're going to is trying to set up courses in history of the empathic arts. Ultimately they'll add research courses."

Jaguar raised her eyebrows. "And wonders never cease. Will they have courses for practitioners? A sort of voc-tech for incipient empaths?"

"No, Jaguar. History only, for now. That's controversial enough."

"No shit. Anybody dead yet?"

"Not yet. The University president asked for someone from here who can spot trouble and let her know about it."

"The president? Is she—you know—one of us?"

"No. She just likes the color of the money she's getting from certain federal research organizations."

"Such as?"

"The usual. Military and Think Tank. That's part of the local controversy."

"Interesting," she said. "Am I to express support for the Pentagon while I'm there?"

"You're to discreetly track faculty feelings so the president can forestall any trouble. They're still trying to live down bad press over the disappearance of some sorority women a few years ago, and they want no more noise. But for the most part, you'll just be teaching your course and relaxing. I don't expect any trouble."

"How nice for you," she said. "But you won't be there, so it doesn't matter what you expect. What about me? Should I expect trouble?"

He folded his hands on his knees and studied them

before answering tentatively. "I don't think so," he said.

He felt the stab of subvocal communication from her. *Not so sure, are you, Alex?*

She raised her sea eyes to his, and maintained contact. He held her stare, watching the gold flicker in the green like sun on water. The sharp, clear aroma of mint curled from her to him. He saw the brief image of Jaguar, young and small, crushing dried mint in her hand. Her grandfather bent over her, nodding. Mint. Mint to cover the smell of rotting death, of bloodied bodies lying too long in the streets. Her grandfather, giving her mint, and outside her window, a group of vigilantes clubbed a woman to death because she wore a sage-green dress.

Color of empaths, color of healers. In popular lore, color of Satan. In fact, color of death for those who wore it, as the self-appointed Safety Squads ran the streets looking for anyone they could blame, anything they could do to control the terror of those times.

She gave him all this as easily as she would blow a kiss to Paul Dinardo. Then, just as easily, it was gone and she turned a cool smile at him.

"You're going to University campus in upstate New York," he said sharply, "not Manhattan during the Killing Times. This is not a big deal."

"This is a crock of shit," Jaguar replied just as sharply. "Putting *me* on a campus in the middle of an antiempath movement to do some discreet spying? Sounds like the Board wants me to get myself discreetly killed."

Alex frowned down into his teacup, swirling the leaves at the bottom. He knew an old woman who would have read the answer there, but he couldn't. Except that he knew Jaguar was right. It wasn't her job. Though they were both empaths, and though they both used the arts, Alex had learned how to do so within the bounds of Planetoid policy. Jaguar recognized only the boundaries necessary to accomplish the job at hand. She would get the job done at any cost—which is why her success rate, at 98 percent, was the highest in the system—but she was definitely a high-maintenance worker. On her last job she'd saved a few million lives, and cost a few million dollars when she decomposed an entire VR site. With her bare hands. Once she'd blown up a Lear Shuttle, just to save his life.

And that's why, Alex thought, she's going back to school.

Board Governor Paul Dinardo said her doctorate made her most qualified, and what he euphemistically called her special talents made her best suited to spot trouble. Alex said draw trouble was more like it, and Paul said maybe, but wouldn't it be restful to have her off the Planetoid, just for a little while? Maybe she'd like the job so much she wouldn't come back.

That's how all the governors felt about her, but they'd hand her the hardest assignments because they all knew that if Jaguar couldn't handle it, nobody could. Alex didn't know who to be angry with about that. Jaguar, or the conservative administrative body she tangled with. Sometimes, just for fun, he'd be angry at both simultaneously.

"If you could exercise a little discretion here," he said testily, "this sort of thing wouldn't happen so frequently."

"What? This is because I object to giving them tape? I will not have a bunch of tight-assed white men and blue-haired ladies setting the standards for my programs," she shot back at him.

He picked up his teacup and drank the remainder, setting it down on the coffee table a little too hard. He drew in breath and let it out.

"All right," he said. "The University president requested help in ferreting out faculty involvement in an antiempath movement, and the request seemed to mesh with the Board's desire to give you something dull and far away. It'll give them a break from your incendiary tendencies, and they can slap your wrists politely at the same time, hoping you'll come back properly subdued."

"The Board," Jaguar said, eyeing him coldly, "hopes I'll come back as a clean-cut white man who buys the system. Preferably, an Adept."

He shifted uncomfortably in his seat. The privilege of wearing a suit and tie, the privilege of a gut-level understanding of institutions were his. He was a white man, old enough to slap the backs of other white men, enough silver in the black of his hair that nobody commented much on the earring he wore, or the thin braid he could easily hide down the collar of his white shirt. And institutions tended to value the services of the Adept more than the kinds of arts Jaguar practiced.

His art was seeing future possibilities and manipulating present events to reach the desired end. Hers was—what? Blowing up technology. Singing herself into visions and the wisdom of the spirit world. Getting through the barriers that surrounded a shadowed soul. Seeing the world of the prisoners she worked with so clearly she could breathe on it, then wipe it clean.

Much of what she practiced didn't even have names yet. Chant-shaping, singing, walking in a world whose existence others didn't even acknowledge—they didn't fit into the dominant paradigm. His psi capacities were known quantities, and he used them quietly so the Board couldn't object.

And he couldn't do a thing to change either himself, or her, or the Board.

"Jaguar, give it up. You're not going to change the world today."

She unfolded her legs from under her and put her teacup down on the table. She stared at the smoke that rose from the cigarette in her hand, and then tamped it out hard in her teacup.

"A course runs fifteen weeks," Alex said placatingly. "The work is easy and interesting, and you get better pay. So why are you angry?"

She lifted her chin a notch. "Maybe I'm just tired of being treated like a wayward child. I'm not, you know."

"I know. What else?"

She lowered her head and raised it again, a gesture Alex had come to regard with the same caution as he'd view a bull making the same moves. When she raised her face, she let her green-gold eyes focus fully on his, and it took no empathic touch to read what was written there.

Infamy. Betrayal.

She was angry at—him?

"Why?" he asked, knowing he didn't have to say more. Not to her. "What did I do?"

"It's not what you did, Alex. It's what you didn't do."

"What didn't I do?"

"Talk them out of sending me."

She was right. He could have fought it harder. If he'd insisted, Paul would probably have backed down. He'd done that sort of thing for her in the past. Something stayed his hand this time, and she knew it. He wondered if she knew why, and wished that if she did, she'd let him know, since he didn't seem to have a clue. His confusion rippled into defensive anger.

"I don't see any reason why you shouldn't go. Christ—most Teachers'd jump at the chance."

"Since when am I most Teachers?"

"What do you suppose I could have done to change their minds?"

"How hard did you try?"

He scowled at her, said nothing.

She uncoiled herself and rose, stalked silently to the window, then back to the couch, looking somewhere over his left shoulder. She passed him, circled around to his back, and stood behind him. He sat still, feeling the hum of tension between them. Buzzing like lightbulbs in rain, he thought.

Then he felt her fingernail press into the back of his neck. It lingered there a moment before she raked it across his shoulder, delicate and deliberate, like a razor plowing flesh. Had she ever touched him like that before? Not that he knew of.

Her finger came to rest in the joint of his shoulder. He didn't move.

"Perhaps you haven't betrayed me, then," she said quietly, holding him still with her fingertip. "Perhaps you've betrayed yourself."

She stood silently behind him. Let the moment sink into him. Let time pass. She was so good at that.

"What the hell are you getting at?" he asked at last.

She answered, soft as silk brushing against his cheek, "Your fear."

She spoke into him now, easy as water, smooth as the blade of her knife.

Why are you sending me, Alex? What are you afraid of?

He was tempted to turn and let his eyes rest in hers, see what strange and wild creatures swam there. That's what she wanted him to do.

Give me your eyes.

To pull him into that compelling, and disturbing, place. And what would it show that he didn't know already?

Give me your eyes and let me see.

Nothing. There was nothing to see. He knew who she was and accepted it. What he saw on the tape with her prisoner. What he knew of her wilderness. Her untamable soul.

Then give me your eyes.

No. There was nothing to see. Once, he'd kissed her, but that was work. Kiss of life, given in the line of duty. Empathic energy and nothing more. It meant nothing.

Give me your eyes.

Nothing but the feel of her hair twined around his fingers. A blip of feeling, here and gone. It had nothing to do with what was going on now. Nothing to do with fear or wanting her to leave or wanting her. Or wanting her. Or wanting her to leave.

Then give me your eyes.

He lifted a hand and made a fist, brought it down hard against the table.

The teacups clattered. She didn't jump. Didn't say a word while he considered his fist, considered her touch on the back of his neck, considered his own reaction to her touch.

He felt her finger leave his shoulder, felt her eyes stop boring into the back of his skull. He was aware of her moving away from him like thunder heading south. He twisted around and saw her staring out the window, away from him.

"Right," she said. "What's next?"

He let his breathing and heart rate settle, asked his anger to dissipate, then he answered.

"Just the packing," he said. "The books are ordered and your syllabi were set by the department. I looked over the list. There's nothing on it you don't know."

"They ordered my books? Set my syllabi?"

"Apparently," he said, "they aren't taking any chances."

He did not say out loud that he couldn't really blame them.

"So," Rachel said to Jaguar, "have a good time. I'll miss you."

She'd come over to Jaguar's apartment on her way to work to say good-bye, see if there was anything else that needed doing in her absence. Rachel was a team member, working with Teachers on the programs they created, and working in the Supervisor's office with Alex when she wasn't on a prisoner assignment. She had once been Jaguar's assigned prisoner. Now she was her friend.

Jaguar turned from her bags to Rachel's concerned face and smiled a little tightly. "I'll miss you, too, Rachel. Stuck down there with a bunch of rat-fuck pencil pushers. I'll even miss Gerry."

Rachel bit her lip, trying not to laugh, a move she thought wouldn't be politic right now. "That's what I like about you, Jaguar. You keep that positive attitude working for you."

Jaguar ran a hand through her hair, let it rest at the back of her neck. "I'm positive this is a crock of shit.

What'm I forgetting?'' she asked. "You'll water the plants?''

"Check on the imaginary cats. Walk the invisible dogs. Assassinate Board members. Whatever you say. Got your notebook?''

She patted her shoulder bag, then her wrist. "Notebook here. Knife here.''

The tip of the red glass knife she carried up her sleeve made a brief appearance, then receded back under the sleeve of her red silk shirt.

"You shouldn't need that,'' Rachel said.

"Never know. Got a line you can't untangle—sometimes you need to cut it.''

Rachel shook her head and let it go. "Did you input all your codes? You'll need the office and my personal line codes. Alex said—''

"The hell with Alex,'' she said. "I'll file my reports—shit. My report code. I don't know it.''

She let her shoulder bag drop, opened it, and pulled out her notebook, which would have all the files for codes under which to report back to the Planetoid while she was away.

"Try file 75@HP.Univer,'' Rachel said.

Jaguar punched in the numbers, waited for the scroll to end, and stared at it.

"Rat fuck,'' she said. "Rat fuck rat fuck rat *fucked*.''

"What? What?''

Rachel scooted around behind her and looked over her shoulder. Then she blinked up at Jaguar. Even she couldn't find anything placating to say about what she'd read.

"They've got me listed on mandatory home leave, Rachel,'' Jaguar whispered.

"You have to tell Alex," Rachel replied. "He should—"

"What Alex should do is—never mind."

She fumbled with her bag, slipped the notebook back in. Then she performed an internal move that Rachel always referred to as Jaguar slipping into her catskin.

All signs of anger left her, fire blown out by a chilling wind. She became perfectly cool and still.

"Tell Alex I'm glad he's relieved me of the necessity of filing reports while I'm away. Tell him I hope he enjoys my rest leave as much as I will."

Then she picked up her bag and walked out, not even slamming the door behind her.

Rachel walked to the window and saw her walk fast down the street, three floors below.

Mandatory home leave. That wasn't good. When Teachers were given that, it made a nasty and large dark mark on their permanent files. It was used for Teachers who broke down, burned out, lost it under the pressure of their work. And that's what they'd named this assignment.

Rachel drummed her fingers on the window and tried to figure out why, but she couldn't. Tried to figure out if Alex had anything to do with it, but she couldn't imagine him doing such a thing to Jaguar.

She shrugged, and realized that trying to figure it was stupid. Unlike Jaguar, she found research more helpful than hypothesizing. She walked over to the telecom and punched the code for Alex's office.

"Supervisor Dzarny," she requested.

"Busy," the computer told her.

"Interrupt," she replied. "Code 5."

It was the emergency code, but what the hell. She felt a crisis coming on.

Alex's face appeared, looking surprised when he saw Rachel.

"What is it?" he asked. "Is Jaguar—"

"Jaguar's on mandatory home rest leave," Rachel said. "Sorry to code you, by the way, but I thought you should know before she comes over and kills you. Which is what I'd do if you did that to me."

Alex's brow creased. "What?" he asked.

"Jaguar's job. It's filed as a mandatory home rest leave."

"No, it's not. It's a research assignment."

"Check," Rachel suggested. "Got the file code?"

He nodded, and turned half away from the screen, worked his computer for a minute, then stared, the creases on his forehead growing deeper.

"Son of a bitch," he said.

"She said worse than that," Rachel noted.

He turned back to the screen, his face paler than it had been when she'd first seen it. "Rachel, I didn't do this. You know that. I wouldn't do this."

"You didn't stop it, either," Rachel noted.

She normally stuck up for Alex, especially when Jaguar was in one of her moods about him. But she wasn't letting him off the hook for this one.

Alex scowled. "What did she say?"

"She said rat fuck. A lot. Then she said to thank you for saving her the trouble of filing any reports. Then she said have a nice day."

"She didn't."

"No. She didn't. She said she hoped you enjoyed her absence."

He winced.

Rachel nodded. "I thought I should let you know. She left a few minutes ago, so if she's gunning for you,

you've got some time to leave the planet.''

''She's not. She'll leave me alone to feel my feelings. Dammit, Rachel, she thought I set her up before this happened.''

''And did you?'' Rachel asked.

''Jesus, not you, too. I swear I didn't—''

''Well,'' Rachel conceded, ''maybe not. But you always stuck by her, and you know the Board. You're usually smarter than this.''

He submerged his face into the palms of his hands briefly. When he reemerged, he looked tired. ''Okay. I'll do what I can. Thanks for letting me know.''

And then he was gone.

Rachel shook her head at the blank screen, then shook a finger at it. ''You should be nice to each other,'' she said to Alex's disappeared face.

And she wondered if they would ever begin to know how.

IN A BASEMENT, UNDER DEEP EARTH THAT LED to tunnels going anywhere on campus, a candle burst into flame under a careful hand.

"Woman of fire," he chanted, "call fire to fire and begin again."

She had arrived.

He sensed her palpable presence, shining flesh and blood walking the halls of disembodied theory. It had begun.

The planning and negotiation that brought her here was challenging and took a great deal of time and energy, but he was a patient man. He knew what he wanted, what and who she would bring to him, how valuable it would be. Now she was here, and the rest would follow if he continued to be patient. And he would, with her to amuse him.

He had started this project with a specific goal in mind, and he fully expected to realize it. But the more he knew about her, the more he realized that the journey could easily be as enjoyable as the goal. He would have the pleasure of knowing her, as well as the rewards of what she would bring his way.

He raised his hand over the candle, and the flame

followed, flickering and dancing in the cool, damp basement air. This hand would find her, and she would follow it as surely as the flame did. He would see to that.

He looked to his left, at the wooden door marked with the traditional glyphs for closure. Not that he believed in those old ways, but they could have a powerful psychological effect, particularly with impressionable students. Katia had been impressed. So had the others.

But this one—woman of fire—it would take more than glyphs to impress her. More than smoke and mirrors to outwit her. He'd learned of her years ago, and had filed the information away because he didn't need it at the time. Then, in his attempt to capture the one art he lacked, he'd stumbled upon her name again, learned how intimately she was associated with what he wanted. In fact, her name came up as the primary stumbling block to his goal, and he knew he'd have to remove it. That would be a challenge. He couldn't reach around or through her. Instead, he would have to utilize her. Play her.

He wondered what resistance she would use against his arts. He explored the possibilities, lingering over all he knew of her talents, her family ways, her gifts. He'd heard stories. About her red glass knife. About the mint she always carried with her and why. He'd heard she was an empath, a singer, something of a healer, and something of a killer. That she had the gift of clear sight. Not even the Pentagon had a list of her psi capacities because she'd avoided testing, but her history indicated all this, and more. Given what she did and who she was, he suspected she was also a chant-shaper.

A chant-shaper. He knew as much about that as anyone with his experience and background, but that wasn't saying much. It was an elusive art. The art of the elusive.

Highly visible, and almost impossible to grasp. Rare, and difficult of apprehension. Science wasn't ready to admit it existed, but there were too many years of stories about this art to ignore it. Her people were among those who laid claim to the ability to call on energies beyond themselves, assume those energies almost as a second skin, and walk within them.

The Mertec said it came from the spirit world, and that the chant-shaper was working with the spirit they shared soul with. That, like the glyphs on his door, he thought was just a pretty way of describing those who could control the motion of esoteric energies. Not that it mattered how you described it. What mattered was what you did with it. He thought he'd be able to find a use for the art, if he could find a way to seduce—or induce—her toward his desires. It would be new territory, but he felt ready to explore it.

He leaned forward and reached out a hand, pointing at the candle that stood flickering in the center of the largest table. The candle shivered, and the flame went out.

He pulled his thoughts in and narrowed them. The candle slid silently across the surface, stopping just at the edge. It lifted off the table and shot across the room, shattering as if it were made of glass.

A good warm-up. He'd achieved motion and molecular dispersion with the precision he wanted. Precision and speed. That was his value to the people he worked for, and they rewarded him well for it. In spite of their fears about his talents—or perhaps because of their fears—they'd give him anything he wanted, cover any indiscretion, help him set this project up, as long as he kept performing the rather mundane tasks they assigned.

He would try a few more warm-ups and then take a

minute to review some anatomy. He wanted to stay warm enough to work deeply, and serene enough to keep the pace slow.

There was every reason in the world to go slowly. He'd known a few winters, but this was the first time he was looking forward to the long nights of the semester ahead.

2

JAGUAR SHOULDERED HER BAG AND WALKED, face to the wind, up the cement steps that led to the rectangle of buildings where classes were held. She'd seen her rooms on campus, which were on the third floor of a two-hundred-year-old rambling Victorian house used by visiting faculty, spent a few hours tracking down the right offices to fill out forms for pay and parking and airvan service and meals, and found her way across the wide expanse of campus from gym to auditorium to health clinic to this central conglomerate of higher education.

She looked around at the buildings, which were white and arranged in perfect symmetry above and around a lower level of lecture centers and a central fountain. A wind circled the separate buildings—HUMANITIES, SOCIAL SCIENCES, BUSINESS, FINE ARTS, and more—each building exactly the same as every other, except for the small sign at the front.

"Cold," she noted as the wind sucked breath out of her and she tried to tuck her chin farther down into the collar of her raincoat. She'd forgotten how cold a rainy wind could be in upstate New York, even in early September.

But, as popular wisdom went on this part of the planet, if you didn't like the weather, stick around five minutes. It would change. The report she'd heard on the air shuttle said that the following day would be sunny and in the eighties.

She kept her pace fast as she moved past the fountain, where she could imagine students would gather to tan in nice weather, the Campus Center with its bookstore and food shops and meeting rooms, toward the humanities building where her office was located, paying little attention to the students who scuttled by her in groups of threes and fours. She had to acclimate herself to the place before she could do the same with the people. Both would take some doing. Unless her job demanded, she didn't spend a lot of time on the home planet.

She had gone last year with Alex, as they did every year, to look for the northern lights on the longest night of the year. Last year they found them pouring down magic over a snow-covered cornfield in Nebraska, where they stood and chanted the blessing for dreaming, and the gifts of darkness. She wondered what Alex would do this year, and whom he would do it with.

She'd also made her annual trip to New Mexico to take part in the sun rituals with Jake and One Bird, who had taken her in after the Serials when the rest of her family was killed. They had taught her how to walk the strange land of herself after she left Manhattan, an adolescent orphan with no idea what to do except follow the direction of the setting sun and ask repeatedly for Thirteen Streams, which was the name of their village. Somehow she had made it to New Mexico alive, and somehow, when she walked into a diner in Gallup in search of a glass of water, Jake and One Bird had been there, waiting for her. They continued to wait for her every summer, expecting her presence at the solstice ritual. She had a responsibility to share her gifts with the people who nurtured her spirit.

Taking part in the ceremonies was necessary for her as well. A time to renew her arts. A chance to sit in the sacred space of the mesas while the stones became a cauldron to cleanse her spirit and the heat a soundless pulse of rhythm to reset the beating of her heart. A place where who and what she was would be either taken for granted or valued, depending on the circumstances. Jake and One Bird's village was one of the places she could call home.

The University was not.

Learning itself was easy for her, but she was a strange and undomesticated animal sniffing the halls of academia, and she'd been glad enough to graduate and leave for the Planetoids, where everyone was a misfit or a criminal. A runaway or a throwaway. The place was almost as accepting as Thirteen Streams. And in spite of the Board of Governors, on the Planetoids she could even find people who understood what it meant to be empathic.

Alex, for instance. She frowned. Dammit. Damn him. Mandatory rest leave. Even if she was right about the particular bug he had up his ass, he still should know better than that.

If he wanted her to investigate an antiempath movement, he'd have to make it official. If he wanted to let the Board slap her wrist, she would act as if she was having her wrist slapped. Stay the hell out of it and teach her courses. Nothing more.

She stopped in front of a building and read the sign: HUMANITIES. Her office was on the third floor.

She walked up the stairs and down the hall, and

pushed the code key in 325, where her name was already displayed. She went inside and put her bag down.

It was a small space, long and narrow, but one wall had a bank of windows that looked out over the campus and toward the mountains. She went over to them and opened one, letting the cool air into the stuffy space.

The Adirondacks were soft and distant under a veil of cloud and mist. Between the mountains and the campus, buildings rose and fell with the rolling land. Pretty. Quiet and unpretentious and restful to the eye. She turned her gaze skyward and saw a hawk surfing the thermals over the road that encircled the campus. They would like it here, she thought. Probably they nested on top of the dormitory towers that stood like sentinels along the perimeter of campus.

She pulled the window shut and turned to her desk computer. The University kept their technology nailed down or built in to prevent theft, and she'd been told that any handheld equipment was her responsibility. She passed a hand over the sensor panel and watched the screen and keyboard elevate, listened to it beep on. It had been coded to recognize her hand. They were ready for her. She wasn't so sure if she was ready for them.

It had been a long time since she'd been in a classroom. She'd taught as a graduate student at the University of New Mexico and remembered liking it, feeling comfortable with the play of learning. She held authority in her hand loosely, as a ball of twine that unwound between her and the students, always prepared to slacken or tighten the thread in response to the way they tugged. She supposed she did the same thing on the Planetoids with prisoners.

Prisoners. Students. Fears. Education. What differences would she find? And what, she wondered, would it be like to work in a place where she could not be who she really was?

She smoothed down the lines of the gray skirt she was wearing. She'd gone out and bought herself suits for this job, and though she liked the look of them, she was not comfortable. She was used to clothes that fit as easily as skin and moved with her as she needed to in her job. Suits constrained her and heels made too much noise.

She took off her jacket and sat down at her desk. The books were on her hard drive, and she flipped through the list, stopping to read lines here and there.

"Pretty fucking cautious," she muttered as she read. None of her old standbys were there. Where was Post's *Unparticular Magic*? Rothenberg's *Symposium of the Whole*? Parrish's *Imagining the Witch*?

"Shit," she said. "Why didn't they just let the kids take a compu-course?"

When campuses reopened after the Serials, on-line courses were popular, and almost became the norm. On-line classes meant no possibility of violence in the dorms or the classrooms. No housing problems. Access for students who wouldn't otherwise have it. But once the fear wore off, students wanted to come back. They wanted to be social, learn to live in a community, with all its dissonances and harmonies. They wanted to be part of the eternal dynamic balance of the University, its astonishing mixture of rigid conservatism and radical progressivism. She supposed this year, with the empathic arts course, they'd have that in spades.

The University was being very careful about how they presented the course. It was listed as history, not science or religion, and they chose one of the oldest and stodgiest white male members of the history department to teach it. Everyone knew he had a real talent for taking an exciting topic and making it rigorously boring.

Still, the reaction of students, parents, and faculty had been immediate and explosive. An empathic arts course would promote activities and values we don't want our children exposed to, parents said angrily. Empath teachers can do things to our minds, students said suspiciously. Empathic arts are a fast slide into an anti-intellectual abyss, professors scoffed.

The press got in on it, and some students got noisy for them. Private Sanctions, they called themselves, and said their mandate was protecting the privacy of the mind. They made speeches connecting the course with the disappearance of four women a few years before. They signed petitions and chanted in front of offices, but the president wouldn't cancel the course.

It was the University's job to preserve old knowledge and generate the new, she told the press in a florid speech. She spoke of the need to overcome prejudice, mentioning the battles gays, blacks, and women had fought. Jaguar noticed she didn't mention the long history of denying Native Americans their religious rights, their sacred lands.

Her words did little to allay the fears of students or parents. Jaguar wasn't surprised. Every era has its own brand of witch-hunt, and her ancestors had often been cast in the role of witch. She'd be doubly suspect here, since she was both Planetoid and from a culture that was still inherently suspect in their spiritual and ritual practice, but that was nothing new. She just didn't look forward to cheating the hangman here, in uncomfortable suits.

She heard a knock on her office door and, when she

opened it, was greeted by a man who fit the description of tall, dark, and handsome stranger.

"Can I help you?" she asked.

"Dr. Addams," he said, "that's exactly what I'm here to ask you. I'm Professor Davis. Ethan. Dean of cultural studies."

He bowed slightly at the waist and offered his hand, which she took. It was firm, and very cool. "Good to meet you," she said.

"Are you settled in your rooms, and are they adequate? It's an old building, but it has a certain charm, and the advantage of being right on campus."

"My rooms are fine," she said. "Thank you for checking," she added, remembering her manners.

"Oh, it's nothing. We feel privileged to have you here. Your thesis on ritual space in the Mertec tradition was—well, seminal."

Jaguar found her face moving into a wry grin. "I'm not sure that's the word I'd use," she said, "since it concerned women's chant ceremonies."

He blinked his wide gray eyes at her, frowned slightly, then turned up one side of his mouth. "Ah," he said. "I see. How very male of me. Perhaps I should say your dissertation was ovulatory?"

The grin grew. "Don't bother. There isn't a word in your language to cover it."

He sighed, and held his hands palm up in a gesture of resignation. "If I can't get it right, I might as well make it worse."

Jaguar startled at hearing her own expression spoken from a man's mouth. "Pardon me?" she asked.

"Your dissertation was very female. Brilliant and cryptic and mysterious as the moon."

"Oh. Thank you, I think. Except I can't remember being cryptic anywhere."

"Page 78," he said, "the second paragraph. 'The practice of chant-shaping is too powerful to be contained within a worldview that limits itself to intellectual pursuits. It needs, by nature of its being, a circle of strength that allows for the physical manifestation of energy within the dynamic system of the spiritual world.' You go on from there to quote Paula Gunn Allen on the concept of the World of Power, and Lale Davidson on the importance of hiddenness in magic. Am I correct?"

"You have a good memory, Dean," she said

"My memory is photographic, Dr. Addams. A gift. Like chant-shaping capacities. I'd like to find out what evening you're available for dinner so I can get you acquainted with the other members of the department."

She studied his face. Definitely an alpha male, showing off just a little. Alpha males always forgot that cats recognized no hierarchical structure. But he was certainly handsome. Dark hair and eyes that seemed gray in this light, though they might change under the influence of sky or woods. His face was narrow and alight with the curiosity that signaled intelligence, and his broad shoulders tapered to a narrow waist, indicating someone who took good care of his appearance. He wore no gold band, which could mean nothing, but she would lay bets on him being single. Determinedly single. She had not missed the way his eyes strolled her body with the ease of someone who had experience in assessing the female form.

"I've got an intro class Tuesday and Thursday evenings, but the rest of my nights are free," she said.

"Then I'll see what I can arrange for later next week.

Perhaps Friday? I know a marvelous Indian restauraunt, if you like that sort of food."

"Yes," she said, "as long as you don't make any bad puns about currying favor."

"I wouldn't dream of it," he said. "And in the meantime do you have any procedural questions? Need to know where anything is? I can show you all the important places on campus—where to get the worst coffee, where students go to smoke pot."

"Do they still do that? I thought they only did cyberdrugs these days."

"My understanding is that pot is so cheap now, they actually prefer it. Especially since the cyber police are cracking down."

"Is it a problem on this campus?"

"Not too bad. Every semester we get our share of students snared by the Web, but it's gotten to be old hat with them. They're all off looking for whatever the next thrill might be. It's not that different from the problems we have with students drinking, or whatever else they choose to lose their minds with. If you want the lowdown on it, you can check our Web site." He grinned at her. "Ironic, isn't it? But I don't mean to keep you here chatting the day away. Let me be helpful or get out of your way."

"Well,"—Jaguar placed a hand on the control board of her computer and called up her University memos, scanned them briefly—"it seems I have to go to the registrar's office and pick up my RKN numbers. Do you have any idea what that means?"

"That's for your undergraduate students who haven't registered, but want to get into your class anyway. I'm headed toward the registrar's myself, so I can guide you if you're free."

Jaguar said she was, and picked up her coat, which he held for her while she put it on. Courteous, she thought. Old world. Alpha male, but interesting.

They chatted easily about the architecture of the building and its history as they walked down halls that were plastered with posters announcing conferences, lectures, fraternity rushes. They took the stairs to the lowest level of the building, and Ethan led her down another hall that looked exactly like all the others except for the graffiti, which she supposed was how students knew where they were. He stopped at a black metal door labeled in large print: TUNNELS LOCKED AT 10 PM.

He turned to her.

"I'm taking you through the tunnels, Dr. Addams. I hope you're not claustrophobic."

She shook her head. "Not at all. But—"

"It's quite safe. Just a shortcut. You'll find it useful in the winter."

He opened the door and waved her ahead. She stepped over the doorsill and looked around.

Great twisting water pipes and heat ducts snaked along gray walls, and the cement walk rolled ahead of them, curving downhill and back up toward an unseen corridor, creating the illusion of infinity. Recycling Dumpsters, piles of broken desks, laboratory animal cages in various states of disrepair, and drums of enigmatic liquids lined the way ahead.

A group of students in shorts and T-shirts jogged by. The white of their shirts absorbed the green-toned lighting, casting a slight phosphorescence around them. A young man slinging a backpack ignored the "No Rollerblading" signs and whizzed past, the sound of his wheels echoing off the walls.

Ethan, watching her, laughed.

"Surreal," he said. "but convenient. And once you understand that it's just a circular path under the buildings, with cross paths between, very easy to find your way around. Of course, it was meant for maintenance, not students or faculty, but the students figured it out right away—experts at the easy path that they are. Here"—he pointed toward a black door, "is actually a way to get from campus to your own building without emerging topside. Unfortunately, it's locked."

He gestured ahead of them, toward the upslope of the path, and spoke sotto voce. "It's said that the on-campus faculty houses all have access from their basements, so they can rendevous with each other at night."

Jaguar arched an eyebrow at him. "Romantic liaisons?"

"Nonsense. They roam the tunnels arguing about Nietszche."

She smiled. "And the ghosts—of course, there are ghosts."

"The souls of students who never managed to graduate. They linger here and torture first-years."

"What about faculty who didn't receive tenure?" she asked.

"Naturally. And part-time faculty, starved to death. But if you're afraid, you can take my arm."

Jaguar grinned. "I have ways of dealing with ghosts," she said, but she hooked her hand in the crook of his elbow, which he held out to her.

"Careful," he said. "Talk like that, and people will think you're some kind of empath."

Her arm jerked involuntarily, and she subdued it. Settle down, she told herself. He's teasing you. He turned to her and tilted his head. She kept her face smooth and smiling.

"You were warned of our campus ruckus, weren't you?" he asked. "Try not to worry about it. These fires have a way of drying up and blowing away if we don't pour gasoline on them. Though right now I wouldn't mind being an empath, if it would tell me what you're thinking. You have a way of keeping your face very neutral—or is it forward of me to notice that?"

"Probably," she said. "But forward is one of my favorite directions. I never was any good in reverse."

Dean Davis laughed, and gestured ahead. "Then let's proceed," he said.

Planetoid Three, Toronto Replica

Alex cast his line out once. Twice. Three times. The lake was silver, streaked with the bleeding colors of the setting sun. He heard the slap of a hand on skin.

"Whaddaya wanna do this for, Alex?" a voice asked. "Jesus—there's bugs everywhere. You'd think that if we made our own Planetoid, we could make it without bugs."

He turned and saw Paul Dinardo standing unsteadily in good shoes on wet sand, his hand moving frantically to ward off a whirling circle of blackflies.

"They're part of the ecosystem, Paul. You want real life, you gotta have bugs," Alex said, turning back to his line. "Though a few more lake trout might balance them out nicely."

"Yeah," Paul said, "But what'd get rid of all this sand?"

Alex laughed. "Seven maids with seven mops?"

"Huh?"

"Never mind. What brings you here, Paul?"

"Actually, I went to your office, and they said you

took the week off. Said you planned on taking a couple more. To go fishing.''

Alex drew his arm back and let the line in, then flung it far out into the lake. ''Not fishing, Paul. Just practicing my cast.''

Paul dug a toe in the sand, then pulled it out when a wave lapped too close to his foot. He took a step back. ''Yeah, well, I appreciate the need for R and R, Dzarny, but unfortunately, you'll have to wait for it. We got some University people coming our way, and it's your job to make sure they get what they need without getting in anyone's way.''

Alex continued to play with the feel of line and water as they pulled against each other. He took a step closer to the water's edge, then another. A boat sailed by in the distance, and he admired it, silently. He rarely took time off. Paul had no right to complain. Besides, he was feeling a little distracted, out of sorts.

''Look, you got some of these bugs up your ass by any chance?'' Paul asked.

Alex said nothing.

''Maybe you got a bug up your ass about Dr. Addams's assignment?'' Paul suggested.

''I have nothing to say about Dr. Addams. I don't have anything to do with her anymore.''

''What?''

''Someone sent her away on mandatory home leave. I can't imagine who would do that without consulting her Supervisor, but somebody did. And therefore, she's not working for me anymore.''

''Is that it? For Chrissake. With her reputation, it'll be safer for her that way. We list her as research, some-one gets into her files, they get nervous about what she's researching. But it doesn't mean anything. You know that. It's not like—are you listening to me?" Paul asked.

"No," Alex said. "I'm not at work, so I don't have to."

Paul made a noise like snorting. Alex didn't turn around to see which orifice he made it with.

He wanted time off, dammit. Time away from his office. There was something of the scent of mint around his desk, and he didn't like it. He needed to get away from it and think, without that feeling of always waiting for something. Without those great gaps in his day, when nobody showed up to swing a pair of discourteous heels onto his desk and spout imaginative profanities about people like—like Paul.

"Say something, dammit," Paul barked at him. "These bugs are eating me."

"That's what wild things do, Paul," Alex said. "They eat you. My advice—go home now while you still have some flesh left to call your own."

"Jesus, what is it with you?"

"You took one of my people and put her on mandatory leave without even letting me know. Isn't that enough for one day?"

"Alex, she can't be in there on research. The president nixed it. She said the students'd be on it like flies on shit. Like—" He slapped at his arm. "Like bugs in flesh. If they get wind of what she's there for, she's screwed, and we don't look too good either."

"She shouldn't be there at all."

"Why didn't you say that earlier? And why're you in such a twist about it now? I mean, I know people been sayin' for years that you're crazy about her, but—"

"Fuck you," Alex said.

Paul stopped cold. Alex cast his line out and said nothing more.

"Christ," Paul said. "Take your lousy time off and pout, but it won't change anything. She's still on the home planet, and you're still in charge of the University people here. Make sure they stay in bounds. I don't want 'em walking outside their own turf, and I'm counting on you to provide the leash. You wanna know why—because it's your job."

Alex drew his line in, cast it out.

"I'll put a memo to that effect on your desk. When you're at work, you can read it and remind yourself that you never heard a word I said."

The crunch of feet on sand told him Paul had walked away.

He reeled in his line and called it a day.

3

JAGUAR SCANNED THE THIRTY-THREE FACES IN front of her. A variety of shades of skin color. A variety of hairstyles. A variety of dress styles. A variety of genetic encodings reflected in round faces, angular faces, eyes that turned up or down, wide mouths, and thin mouths. An abundance of variety, except for one thing.

From the front row to the back, and from left to right, each set of eyes was both guarded and indifferent. She wondered if what they were guarding was their indifference. She pulled in breath, and let it out slowly. She'd taken attendance, made sure all the registration forms were in order, and given out syllabi. She'd have to make a start with them.

"Any questions about the syllabus?" she asked. Dull eyes stared at her. Disengaged. Every one of them. She sighed.

"Okay," she said, moving around to the front of the desk and pulling herself up to sit on it, swinging her legs, leaning back on her hands. "So someone tell me what you think the purpose of religion is."

Nobody moved.

"This is not a trick question," she reassured them. "You can't get it wrong."

Everyone continued not to move.

She pointed to a young blond woman whose curly hair framed a vacuously pretty face. "You there," she said. "Gracie. Just tell me what you think."

The young woman pointed to herself, then turned her head this way and that.

"That's right," Jaguar said. "You. What's religion for?"

"My name's not Gracie," the blonde said, her voice high and petulant.

The rest of the class snickered.

"Got your attention, didn't it?" Jaguar said.

The students murmured among themselves. A young woman with a broad and smoothly quiet face, dark hair and eyes, raised her hand. Jaguar nodded at her.

"Religion teaches people how to connect to the spirit world, and provides a basis for moral and ethical decisions," she said, her voice, like her face, quiet and smooth. The young man sitting next to her nodded in approval.

"Your name?" Jaguar asked.

"Katia," she said.

"That's a good answer. Basic and true. Where'd you get it?"

"I read a little in the text."

"Do you agree with it?"

The girl's face creased into a question and her shoulders went up and down a fraction of an inch. "I don't know what you mean."

"Is that what religion is for you?"

Jaguar turned the question toward the class as a whole, and saw Katia relax into relief at having the burden shifted from her. The young man sitting next to her put a hand on her arm.

"Anyone else?" Jaguar asked.

"Far as I can tell," a young man with spiked hair said, appearing to mumble the words to some point inside his own chest, "religion's supposed to keep people bored."

Giggles roved around the back of the class.

Jaguar tilted her head. "Bored?"

" 'S like school," he said. "You sit and listen a lot to stuff you don't understand and don't care about so you know how to put up with the boring job you're gonna have. And everyone's too scared to say anything about it, because God might get 'em when they die."

More giggles. Some murmurs of assent. Jaguar looked around at the lethargic faces.

"Is this a required course for you?" she asked.

They turned to each other, as if asking permission to speak, and heads began to nod.

"I see. Okay. Let's try this, then. Do what I do."

She picked up her syllabus and held it in front of her. They all did the same. Slowly, starting at the center, she began to tear it in half, taking the two halves and putting them together, then tearing it again and again, then tossing the pieces into the air in front of her.

The students muttered to each other and passed glances to their buddies.

"Well," Jaguar said. "Go ahead. It's your turn."

A young man in the rear of the room said what the hell and ripped with gusto. Others around him followed suit. Then they all tore joyously—except for Katia, whose motions were tentative, and the young man next to her, who sat still as a stone.

There was always one, she thought. No matter what you did. She smiled at him. He was an attractive young man, with sandy hair and a face that had the shadow of childhood freckles.

"Got a problem with this?" she asked.

The young man looked at Katia and shook his head at her rather than at Jaguar. "It's nothing, Katia," he said in response to the concern in her eyes. Then he smiled at Jaguar. "I just like to play by the rules, and if I tear this up, I won't know what they are."

"Good point," she said. "Since we've disregarded this particular set of rules, we'll have to come up with some new ones. Your name is . . . ?"

"Steven," he said. "Steven Haigue."

"Okay, Steven. What rules do you want?"

A black woman at the back shouted out, "Everybody gets A's." Hoots and cheers followed.

Jaguar held her hands out. "Yes? Is that the class rule?"

"No," Steven said firmly. People groaned.

Jaguar held a hand up for quiet. "Why not, Steven?"

"Because," he said, "it's not fair. The people who work for A's should get A's."

"And how do you work for an A in a class that's about matters of the spirit?"

"By learning the material and doing good on the tests."

More groans ensued. Jaguar couldn't quite hold back her grin, and he noticed. His face furrowed into sullenness.

"What's so funny?" he asked.

"I was just thinking about what it might mean to pass a spiritual test."

"Oh man," the black woman said, "you gonna make us walk on hot coals or—or whatever you did on them Planetoids?"

"Be quiet, Selica," someone hissed at her.

So, Jaguar thought. They knew. She wondered what stories they'd heard about the Planetoids. What stories they told themselves to get a delightful shiver of fear on dark and stormy nights. She was about to respond when Steven spoke again.

"This is a class about world religions. Not spirituality. To try and teach spiritual matters in class would be . . ." He paused.

"Inappropriate?" Jaguar suggested.

"I was going to say dangerous."

"I see," Jaguar said, and she did. She saw that she could spend the rest of the class, and probably the rest of the semester, engaged in argument with him, or she could try to teach everyone else. She decided she was tired of argument. She'd rather teach. She smiled at him.

"Well, I try to avoid danger at all costs, so let's start with a religion. Everybody stand up."

They murmured. Frowned. Laughed nervously.

"What're you waiting for?" she asked in response to their immobility. "We're starting in China, with the concept of Chi. Can't learn about that without moving around."

When they began tentatively to shuffle out of their desks, she laughed and held her arms out wide. They were no different from her prisoners. Terrified of seeing who they were, and being it. And it was her job to make sure they faced that particular fear, and overcame it, so they'd have room to learn what the rest of the world was like.

"Up," she said, at full voice. "On your feet and let's get started."

• • •

When class was done and the students filed out—some stopping to ask questions about the assignment and some stopping to ask more questions about the concept of Chi—Jaguar made her way down the halls to the Campus Center.

She had to pick up a few essentials at the campus store. Bath salts would be in order, since the best part of her rooms was a large antique claw-foot tub, and plentiful hot water from the University's very efficient solar heating system. And she wanted a sketch pad for class so that she could draw some of the concepts that eluded words.

She took her time, getting acquainted with the tunnels between class and Campus Center, letting her energy levels settle back to normal after fielding the many energies directed at her in class. Steven's truculence. Katia—whom she took to be Steven's girlfriend—and her serious eyes and quiet face. Selica's outspokenness. Taquara's hair. Joey and Jesse's whispers to each other. And great hulking Glen, who spoke gruffly but giggled when he tore up his syllabus. They seemed like an interesting group so far.

She stopped and read notices on the bulletin board. Notices of meetings for student groups. Gone Girls Memorial Fund Dance. Gone Girls—that was the popular name for the disappeared sorority women, her files said. Rooms for Rent: Conveniently located near all bars. Some things, she thought, never change. Gay and Lesbian Campus Coalition meeting on Wednesday. She thought of getting in touch with them to see if they were any friendlier toward empaths than the majority heterosexuals. They should be, she thought, given the similarities in the ways each group was seen and treated.

Like gays, you couldn't tell if someone was an empath

by looking, but you could make a guess based on certain gestures, habits of dress, speech, and manner. A sage-green item of clothing. The earring in the left ear, the kind of stone indicating the kind of empath. A tendency to either avoid or maintain heavy eye contact. Certain catchphrases. Any of these might tag you as an empath, whether you were or not.

But empaths, who were inclined to keep under cover, didn't have coalitions. They didn't identify their talents except in very specific situations and for very limited circles with other empaths, who were also busy keeping quiet. There was some safety on the Planetoids, and within certain groups like Jake and One Bird's village, where what Jaguar did was considered normal. But in mainstream society, empaths were still seen as objects for either derision or fear or, oddly enough, both, though Jaguar never understood how you could ridicule some-thing and at the same time take it seriously enough to be afraid of it.

She made her way to the ladies' room and found a stall, entered it. As she did so, she heard voices, heels tapping, laughter.

Bits of conversation floated to her.

"I think it's neat," one voice said enthusiastically. "I mean, at least we'll be doing more than just sitting there and falling asleep."

"Yeah. We'll be busy making sure she doesn't mind-fuck us," came the response.

"Come on," a voice protested. "You don't know that about her."

"Get a light on. She can wear the suit, but it doesn't hide the earring. Obsidian. Left ear."

She felt at her earlobe. Great, she thought. Every

teacher's nightmare. Stuck in the stall while her students talked about her.

"So drop the course," the first voice chimed in. "You got your diversity requirement covered, don't you?"

"I'm gonna drop it. I just thought you should know. Be careful of her. The president's probably got plants around campus for the course."

"You are so paranoid, Celie."

"Maybe. But I sat in a few Private Sanction meetings, and they know about her. They got her Planetoid records."

Voices paused, and Jaguar could almost see the young woman pointing upward. Toward the Planetoids they couldn't see, but could and did imagine.

"What're you talking about, Celie?"

"Ask anyone. They're all over the Planetoids. I read about it. Don't you ever *read* anything?"

Giggles. "Is it required?"

"Only if you want to protect yourself," the voice said, and retreated from the room.

Jaguar heard the door creak open and click close, then counted a minute of silence before she emerged from her stall.

She stopped at the mirror, considered her face. It was tight, holding anger and some fear.

Then she shook her head at herself. "Maybe your students are afraid to be who they are for a reason," she said to her reflection. "Maybe they know it just isn't safe."

Planetoid Three, Toronto Replica

Rich Forrest put his briefcase down on his desk and slid a hand across the surface. Nice, he thought. Built-in computer and telecom. Everything at his fingertips, and the rest of it a sleek and shiny mirror in which he could see his face. Which looked a little disgruntled.

He hadn't wanted this assignment and told Lieutenant General Durk it was a bad idea. First of all, Alex knew him. They were on the same cleanup unit in Manhattan during the Serials.

Durk said that wasn't a problem. Forrest was ten years out of regular army work and into research on the academic circuit. Alex couldn't possibly find any remaining association because it was all under Blackout Code. Besides, Durk wanted someone who knew Dzarny, might be able to call his moves before he made them.

But Rich didn't like it. Durk didn't have to hang out feeling trapped on this sky island. And he hadn't worked with Dzarny ever. Rich had seen Alex in tight spots, and saw how he could get out of them.

There was the time they were checking on some kids who had a camp set up in a Dumpster. They were in the alley, and the kids scattered, but a man crawled out from behind the Dumpster and pulled a rapid-fire on them. Alex hadn't skipped a beat. He walked right into the barrel of his gun with those strange eyes of his blazing.

The guy didn't fire.

Another time a woman jumped them from behind. She had a meat cleaver in her hand. Alex caught it by the blade in the palm of his hand and flipped her on her back. Forrest remembered the sound of her skull cracking against the cement. He remembered thinking that Dzarny seemed like such a quiet kind of guy. He liked having Dzarny on his unit, but he wouldn't want to have him on the other side, as he was in this operation.

He opened his briefcase and pulled out the disk with Alex's file, popped it into his personal computer, and read through it one more time before erasing it entirely. He took another look at Alex's photo. It was almost twenty years since Manhattan, but Rich would recognize that bony face, those slightly slanted deep-set eyes, that set of chin, even if Alex had changed enormously. And he hadn't. He was in good shape, not carrying any spare flesh on his large frame. His hair had more silver in it, but it was still thick and inclined to be riotous, and he still wore the earring that signified the artist. Practitioner of the empathic arts.

He'd heard some stories about Alex since he started working the Planetoid, and especially since he buddied up with that Addams woman. They'd developed a reputation as a formidable team ever since they'd taken down the Division for Intelligence Enforcement. And the last job they did—Rich had to admit it was pretty spectacular work. Dzarny was good, and he heard she was holy hell, and born damn lucky with it.

Empaths, he thought, were a pain in the ass. They could do good work, but they didn't take to the chain of command at all. After a certain point they were simply unmanageable. Like their specialist on campus, which is why he was here in the first place. To do a job for the specialist on campus. He didn't know who the specialist was, except that he worked takeouts and communications. Very valuable. He could get into coded net rings and play them like a piano without a trace. The Pentagon would do just about anything rather than risk losing the special services of the specialist on campus.

So here he was, stuck with a lot of Ivy League types who thought they were here to profile exiting prisoners and study treatment efficiency data, waiting for whatever Durk would tell him to do next. It could be anything. Durk was known for setting private agendas. He was a heavy, clumsy man with a wooden hand, but his mind danced more delicately than a ballerina *en pointe*.

He hoped somebody knew what they were doing on this one.

He read through the rest of Alex's file, hit the delete code, and watched it disappear. Then he closed up his briefcase and slid it across his desk. The others would be arriving soon, and the job would begin.

4

''BYTELOCK,'' JAGUAR SAID POINTEDLY. "Dammit."

She sat at a row of computers reserved for student use, trying to get a message through for Rachel to remind her to repot the mint before it got root-bound. But her message kept bouncing back to her, and she was advised, in computer terms, to stay in line and wait her turn. There was a bytelock and it would take time to clear.

She supposed the lines got pretty crowded at the University. Every seat there was occupied and students hovered at the door, waiting their turns. She would use the computer in her office, but something was wrong with it. Every time she touched it, it turned itself off. That sort of thing often happened to her when she interacted with electronic technology, and she couldn't always tell if it was mechanical trouble or the machine responding to her particular charge, which was an unfixable problem. She'd have to get it checked, but in the meantime she had work to do.

She was finding it impossible to get work done in her office, anyway. Yesterday she'd had visits from George Norton and Emily Rainer, just asking if she needed any-

thing, but George leaned his butt on her desk and talked
for an hour about whose promotion was likely and
whose wasn't, who was sleeping with whom, whose theory ruled department politics, and how long that would
last. Emily Rainer came, jangling her bracelets and making deliberately tolerant observations about the value of
nonacademic work such as Jaguar's, while she put as
cold an assessing eye on Jaguar as Jaguar had ever
known. Rainer stayed for a long time, and left Jaguar
believing that she was the only faculty member who had
work to do.

Then Katia came by with a question about the home-
work, which was an obvious cover for what she really
wanted, which was apparently to apologize for Steve's
argumentative nature. He meant nothing by it, she said.
He was just passionate in his opinions. Jaguar liked Katia well enough, but she thought it was a bad sign when
a woman carried the burden of apology for the man in
her life.

"Don't worry about it," Jaguar advised. "I can take
him."

Katia looked a little shocked. "Oh. I don't mean he's
dangerous or anything," she had amended.

Jaguar had to explain that it was a joke. She'd forgotten how seriously undergraduates took themselves.
"It's okay," she reassured her again, "You're supposed
to argue in class. You can argue with me, too."

But that notion seemed too far out of Katia's realm.
She said something about having no arguments and left
for her next class.

Then Ethan tapped on her door to ask if she was free
for dinner next week, Wednesday. He'd managed to
make arrangements after all. He stayed to chat about the
difference between materialist and nonmaterial feminist

theory, neither of which meant much to Jaguar on a daily basis, though she had to admit she enjoyed his banter and the appreciation his eyes showered on her. His words were all about gender egalitarianism, but his eyes were all about bed. She didn't hold that against him, though. She just hadn't made up her mind if she'd take him up on it. But now she was behind in her work, and hoping for a chance to catch up.

No such luck.

She tapped impatiently against the side of the computer, sitting with her chin in one hand. It was just a little message, and she had a lot of other shit to do. Too much to sit here waiting.

"Damn," a voice behind her said. "Bytelock."

She lifted her head and turned around.

The man standing at her back was tall and broad as a mountain, with a face like the crags in the side of a mountain and a ponytail of dark hair that went all the way down his back. He wore a plaid flannel shirt under his sweater and jeans over his boots. One hundred percent Skin, she thought. Native all the way.

He stuck his hand out to her and she took it, the spreading warmth of it encompassing hers. Bear hands. He had big bear hands.

"Dr. Addams," she said, "Cultural studies department."

"I know. I'm Leonard Peltier. "Sioux culture and history. You got bytelocked, huh?"

"Looks like I'll be here awhile. Did you say Leonard Peltier?"

"Yup."

"Any relation?" she asked.

He grinned. "Great-grandson from my mother's clan. You're the first person here to ask that."

She wasn't surprised at that. It was the kind of story everyone wanted to forget. The first Leonard Peltier was a leader of the American Indian movement who was arrested for the murder of two FBI agents in a shooting at Pine Ridge Reservation. He didn't do it, but somebody had to pay and it ended up being him. He served over twenty years in prison for a crime everyone knew he didn't commit. Jaguar had a vague memory of seeing her grandfather raise his own large hand and make a fist to shake at a world that imprisoned men like Peltier. Though she was very young at the time and didn't understand what it was about, the force of his gesture impressed the name in her mind.

Peltier had been a political prisoner in a country that supposedly was free, whatever that meant. But certain key officials in the Justice Department took a dislike to him, and had the power to make their feeling into his continued imprisonment. Or so the inside rumors said. It took thousands of people and the retirement of certain key officials before he was granted executive clemency, but if Jaguar was remembering right, he was sprung in time for the millennium. His name became synonymous with endurance, with Native rights.

"Good blood," she said. "I don't think I would've lasted a week in prison. I can't even stand five minutes of bytelock."

"Yeah, well, my grandmother told me old Leonard cursed like crazy if he got stuck in traffic."

Jaguar grinned. Sure he would. "How'd you get his name?"

He held up one of his meaty paws. "My family name's Tom Bear Hand, but ever since I was a kid the old people called me Leonard Peltier. After a while nobody called me anything else. They said I had his face.

Later on they said I had his elk medicine."

Jaguar wasn't sure how to take that. Elk medicine
meant good with women. Very good. He seemed to be
joking more than he was bragging, though, and he didn't
seem the type to engage in the sort of smooth seduction
Ethan would attempt if she gave him half a chance.
Something about his presence was warmer, more about
listening and less about talking. But then, she thought,
listening can be the most seductive art of all.

"We have a few students in common," he said.

"Which ones?"

"Steve Haigue and Jesse Goodman. Peter Pesetto and
Katia Stone."

"Quite a few students, then."

"Small department. Sooner or later we share everything. Colds. Gossip. Bad jokes."

"And even so, nobody knows who you are?"

"Same to you," he said, and pointed to her name,
written out at the top of a student paper she had in front
of her. "That's the name of someone who's supposed
to meet with trouble."

She startled and tried to cover it. What did he know
about that?

"I met your grandfather," he said in answer to her
unasked question.

That was a sweet and sharp surprise. "You—how?"

"He came to ceremony with us a few times when I
was a kid. He talked about ways of keeping our people
safe during the Killing Times. He saw it coming. You
knew that?"

She knew. He met her in the lobby of their apartment
building. The walls were gray and white. Disinfectant
mingled with the smell of death, which she already recognized as a distinct scent, burning the nostrils. He bent

down and put his large hands on her shoulders.

It's not safe, he said. *Not safe to be here alone*.

But when they returned to the apartment, the killer was already there, waiting for someone—just anyone—to kill. His vision had failed them, abandoned them both.

"Yes," she said, shaking off the memory, "Jake told me. Jake Silver and One Bird at Thirteen Streams. I lived there when I was little, and I went back after my grandparents were killed."

"I've heard about One Bird. She took in a lot of city Skins during the Killing Times. Made a village. It's still going, right?"

"That's right. My mother was born there. So was I."

He nodded, as if he knew all about that, and more. "Well, he was a good man, your grandfather. His vision helped us get through the bad times. He had lots of power."

Yes, she thought. He did. In Manhattan, he'd put her on his shoulders and stride the city streets as easily as he did the mesas, stepping out with such ease that the crowds seemed to part before him. She thought he was one of the spirits. A thunder being, striding the sky.

"Mm," Leonard said, keeping a careful eye on her. "Sometimes it still hurts."

"Sometimes," she agreed, "it does."

"He talked about you. That's how I know about your name. He must've been around right after you were born, because people were talking, said he shouldn't give you such a big name. But he said you'd need it, with the trouble you'd find. He said you were gonna be a real beauty, too." Leonard nodded at her. "Guess he was right on both counts."

"Maybe," she said, "about the trouble part, anyway."

"Both," he insisted, then asked casually, "Finding any trouble here?"

She saw the quiet in his eyes that masked concern. Empath, she thought. An empath who knows a lot about me.

"Not so far," she said. "Should I expect any?"

Leonard shrugged. "There's the usual cyberdrug thing. See a student looking a little too happy in class and hugging his computer, you gotta report it. And there's Private Sanction, the group that's making all the noise about the Empathic Arts course. You got a couple in your class."

That was no surprise. "Steve," she guessed, "and Katia."

"Steve," he agreed. "Katia's trying to figure it out, but Steve's her boyfriend."

He lifted his large shoulders and let them fall. Jaguar understood. Katia was caught between the search for love and the search for truth. As if the two were ever separate. She sighed. She was glad she wasn't eighteen anymore. The age had too many questions and not near enough answers.

"She's a smart girl," she said. "She'll catch on."

"Probably," Leonard said. "Maybe she could use a little help with that."

What did that mean? His face stayed quiet, but he was asking her for something. Making assumptions that they were of one mind. And she supposed he was right. After all, she recognized his name when nobody else did. And if he was an empath, they would seek each other out. Share ritual with each other in a world that didn't necessarily make space for them. That's what she and Alex had always done on the Planetoid. Intertribal, Interempath unity.

But not here. She was here against her wishes and she wouldn't do anything beyond the letter of her contract, much less be an empath for a student involved in Private Sanctions. If Alex or the Board had an agenda for her other than that, she wouldn't fulfill it. And if Leonard was asking her to get involved with a student's emotional dilemma, he was going to be very disappointed. Starting now.

"I don't know what I can help her with, Leonard," she said. "Besides her papers."

He rubbed at the back of his neck, then pointed at her screen. "It's open," he said.

"What?"

He tipped a nod at her computer. "Your bytelock. It's open. You can send your message."

"Oh," she said, turning to the screen. "Thanks." She punched in the command and watched it go. While her back was still to him, he spoke, his voice so subtle an intrusion she couldn't tell at first if he was speaking empathically or not.

"If you're really your grandfather's girl," he said, "you'll find out what you can do for her."

She felt her back stiffen. That was direct enough. But what the hell right did he have? She turned and raised her eyes to his, looking deep enough to read him, but not enough to be read. As she did so, she was flooded with sensation. Something tingling in her hands, behind her eyes, and pressure at the base of her neck. Tingling in her skin.

The sense of being touched, reached for, wanted. The sweetness of it, and the fear.

Close down, she told herself. Close down, and don't let him see.

She turned away and fumbled with her papers, gathered them up, and stood. She opened her mouth to say something neutral. *Look at the time. Gotta go. Nice to meet you. We'll talk again.* But no words would come out.

He put a hand on her shoulder. It was warm, and warmth spread through her shoulder, her neck, her face. Warmth like a hotpack on sore muscles.

As it spread through her, he made words she didn't know. Whatever they were, her jaw opened up again. His hand slid off her shoulder.

"Well," she said, "look at the time. I gotta go, but it's nice to meet you. Let's talk again."

She clutched her papers to her and left.

He continued standing at the computer, shifting his weight from one foot to the other and back again.

Jaguar made her way back to her rooms, stumbling and still shaken as she climbed the three flights up and closed herself in.

She leaned against the door as if to block out whoever was waiting, though she knew no one was. She stayed there and breathed until she could find a way out of the fear. Breathed it out of her. Let it go. Whatever the hell it was, let it go. She let it run out of her with her breath, and shook it out of her arms and legs.

Then she got out of her coat and flung her papers down on the bed and ran her fingers through her hair. Every muscle in her body suddenly ached, as if she'd run five miles with rocks on her back. Maybe she was catching one of the ubiquitous flus the students passed around like answers to exams. Maybe that would explain what she felt, what she was feeling.

"A bath," she said to herself. "I need a long hot bath."

Her rooms at the top floor of this old Victorian house were small. She had to be careful not to knock her head against the slanted ceiling of what had once been an attic. When she cooked in her dinette, she kept slamming her hip into the corner of the cupboard as she turned from stove to table. And her sitting room fit a small love seat, a small table, a small lamp, and nothing else.

But the tub was a bonus and she used it as often as she could.

She ran water and poured oils into it, stripped quickly, and lowered herself into the steamy scent of rosemary and mint. Already she was better, muscles untying themselves from the knots they'd gotten themselves into. Though she wasn't sure from what, because she wasn't sure what happened. Had Leonard made a subtle empathic contact, and was she feeling the residue of his presence?

No. This was more than just presence. It felt intrusive, and he didn't seem intrusive. She let the hot water flow over her skin and empty it out of her, whatever it was. Maybe something to do with being in a room full of computers. Sometimes she had a funny reaction to the energy that technology emitted.

She watched steam rise from the water, clouding the window at the side of the tub. She could see a thin crescent moon riding high in the night, seeming to cup a dark sphere within its own belly. It would set soon, dipping under the surrounding pine trees where crows sat and talked to each other, dropping feathers for her to collect and stick in her hair and shock the students with. She lowered herself in the water and gave herself a better view.

Under this moon, she had only to be Jaguar.

A Teacher. A cloaked empath. A woman on her own,

which is where she was most comfortable, thank you very much. In the Mertec tradition, she was a traveler, bringing her gifts to where they might be needed. And in the Mertec tradition, she sought sacred space wherever she went and, if she couldn't find it, relied on what was within her.

She ran her hands along her neck, across her breasts and belly. Right now this was her sacred space, her only grace contained here, in this skin, which was warm and smooth under her hands. It was a good body. She knew, from seeing Ethan's eyes gather her in, from Leonard's studied perusal, from Alex's approving glances, that others found it beautiful. For herself, she approved its capacity to endure, as well as its ability to respond to pleasure.

Alex once told her she had animal grace. Animal grace, and animal tact. Going directly for the jugular whenever possible. She'd corrected him, saying that jaguars bit through the back of the skull, not the jugular. It wasn't as messy, and it was safer.

She pulled a washcloth from the ring on the wall to her left and soaked it in warm water, pressed it against the back of her own neck, and rubbed, letting the muscles loosen and let go of the job of hiding. Since she got here she had remained adamantly closed against any empathic contact. She didn't want Alex poking at her, trying to explain, apologize, manipulate her into cooperation with the current scheme. She didn't want involvement in any of the currents of emotions she might pick up in her students or the faculty. But staying closed as tightly as she was took effort, and she was feeling the strain of it. Maybe that's what was wrong with her. Too much holding on. Too much hiding. Maybe she should let the walls down some and relax.

She would take a surface read of her environment. Nothing too deep. Just a scan of campus energy. She flexed her hands, stretched long fingers out in front of her, and let herself open.

First she felt small, vibratory movements under the earth. The motion of little thoughts, little actions, smooth and without tension. Just a feeling. Just a feeling of hearts beating, and whispered thought like eddies of water in the streets after rain.

She opened further, and let her thoughts travel to a specific place. Her students. Their faces in front of her, becoming less guarded, less indifferent as class progressed. Nervousness, shaded with interest. Glen. Jesse. Selica. Katia. Steve.

Katia's face, staring at her with large, dark eyes. Leonard said she needed help, as if he knew something. As if she should know something, should do something. She could go into those eyes, searching her. Into them and through them, because they were like tunnels, leading her somewhere. Long tunnels into unfamiliar rooms. All she had to do was search them.

She pulled back. Nothing too deep. Just a scan. She swirled her hand in the water, making spirals in the bath oil that coated the surface, and asked her thoughts to move away from her students, and to continue searching the place. The tunnels, going underground from building to building. Those would be good to know. Ethan said they led to her own house, to other faculty housing, to the dorms, though those corridors were locked after one too many parties held there, one too many incidents reported after the parties.

Easy. Easy to slide through the tunnels and sniff the dead air, the presence of many anonymous people she didn't have to know or care about. She let her thoughts

follow the sloping paths up and down, circle the buildings, sniff at the old equipment left to molder, the new
equipment being transported, the strangely curling paths
leading to black doors that went nowhere.

Vision began in pulsing white shaded into gray, taking
slow form.

She wasn't alone.

Someone walked with her. No face. Just the rhythm
of breath and

Hands.

White hands, reaching.

Hands white and cool, glowing like ice.

This was—what? Memory?

There was a gun. She saw a gun, and surgical gloves
on the hands that held the gun. The gun that killed her
grandfather. The gun held to her head while those hands
stripped her and held her down and raped her. The hands
smeared with her blood, the bleeding of a little girl, at
eleven too small for penetration but these hands didn't
care. Hands and her blood and her grandfather's blood.

Memory—now? Why?

Her heart pounded in rhythm to the old fear, not a
current fear, not a now fear. She stilled herself and
brought the image to focus. Hands. She saw hands.
Memory shifted, but she still saw hands.

Not memory.

Hands, but these hands held no gun. They weren't
encased in surgical gloves. They were silky cool.
Smooth as laughter. Not memory. Not past. These hands
were now, and they wanted her.

Wanted to touch her, know her, explore her.

Hands moving over her body. Hands wanted her.

Desire pierced her, skin tingling with longing. Desire
growing like a jungle in very deep places.

What do you want?

With her question, desire moved into pain deep inside her chest, squeezing at her heart. Who? Who was it walking with her who knew her, could contact memory desire and pain without pause.

She sought a face to go with the hands. Peered through the glow of white ice and looked for

Saw.

Who?

Alex? Alex? Is that you?

Her hand slapped down into water and she sat up hard, pulled herself out of contact fast.

"Jesus Christ," she snapped, "cut it out."

She deliberately slowed her breathing as she reentered the space of her room in this time. No more opening, she told herself. Something was wrong.

She pulled up a handful of water from the tub and poured it onto her face, which was tingling uncomfortably. Her hands tingled, too. Odd. She lifted them from the water, letting them drip and steam and tingle.

It was Alex's face, Alex's voice inside her, but the touch she felt wasn't his. She'd had enough empathic contact with him to know the shape and texture of his touch. Besides, he was too busy running away from his guilt over betraying her, and she was too busy making him feel worse about it for contact between them to have anything in it except confusion, defensiveness, and fear.

She pulled herself up out of the tub and grabbed a towel, wrapped herself in it. Steam rose from her skin like mist in the morning. She walked to the window and looked out, pressed her warm hand against the cool glass.

Someone had pulled memory and desire and pain and his face from her and made her feel them as connected.

So who was it, and how the hell did they manage that when she was only scanning the surface of her environment? Contacting and combining many points at once was an advanced sort of empathic trick. She knew how, but not many empaths did. Alex did, but it wasn't his touch.

This felt . . . alien seemed like the right word to her. It lacked the warmth she associated with empathic contact. It lacked the pull of Adept space, and the fiery stroking tongues of a chant-shape. There was something cool in the touch. Something detached, but highly charged.

But Alex was the only man she knew who could find her that easily, and that deeply. He'd followed her into the land of the dead, pulling her out of a Death Walk when she'd gone too far. She ran a finger across her lips, remembering the feel of his lips on hers when he'd given her the kiss of life, transfer of empathic energy from him to her, an infusion of his life. He'd done that, and now he'd thrown her into the academic boxing ring out of foolishness and fear.

And what about your own foolishness and fear? she asked herself. Memory and desire and pain, all wrapped up in his face.

No. That was a connection someone was trying to force on her. It was Alex's burden, not hers. She wanted nothing except to go on as they had, without emotional entanglements, without the heat that could be so potentially explosive. She wanted no involvement.

She went to the bed, lay down, and stared at the young moon resting in the sky, cradling her own darkness within a silver crescent of light. There were no answers in that lady tonight. Nor could she currently find any where her only power was hidden, kept safe, within the confines of her own body, her own thoughts, her own heart.

Planetoid Three, Toronto Replica

Alex sat at his desk in his apartment, staring at his computer screen and scowling. It was late at night, and tomorrow he had to go back to work.

In the past three weeks he'd taken a lot of walks. Gone and looked at Jupiter through the telescope situated at the top of the weather tower. Walked some more, and read a lot. Rachel called him a few times, tried to get him to go to dinner with her, but he politely declined. He spent some time sitting at the Silver Bay with some whiskey and Gerry, techno-poet and guitarist for the band Moon Illusion that Jaguar sometimes sang with. Used to sing with.

Gerry missed her, he said. Where the hell can you find someone who can howl in three octaves the way she can, he wanted to know. Alex couldn't tell him, but he decided he'd take his whiskey at home after that.

The last two days he'd spent at Ecosystem 4, a tropical environment where they lowered the deflection screen once a week for people who wanted to view the earth's phases. But when he stared at that beautiful blue planet spinning in space, something in his chest went hollow and indeterminate. He found his eyes seeking only one spot on that great globe, as if he could see. As if seeing would bring him understanding. As if understanding would chase that hollowness away.

He came back to his apartment, determined to read and sleep and do nothing else. He still wasn't sure why he was sitting here at his computer, surfing the Univer-

sity Webs, looking for news of a certain campus in upstate New York.

He was angry at himself for doing so, and angry that
so far he'd found nothing of value. The lines were
crowded with students trying to make cyberlove within
the safety of electronic air, but there was nothing about
the antiempath movement other than a few bad jokes.

What do empath's call sex?

A real mind fuck.

*How many empaths does it take to change a light-
bulb?*

None. They just wait for the bulb to see its own light.

The topic must be hot or else there wouldn't be jokes,
but that didn't tell him how Jaguar was coping.

He had telecommed her twice, and left messages, but
she'd only responded via computer with two words.

Back off.

Apparently, she was still angry.

Alex flipped to the student interpersonal network,
which at least had the advantage of occasionally being
interesting reading.

*"But do you think Hanifin's bisexuality is reflected in
her bitextuality?"* Burhasa asked Jamie.

*"How could it not, and aren't we all bisexual/bitex-
tual? Wish I was bilingual, though. In a literal kind of
way,"* Jamie replied.

"Sounds like fun to me, too. Want to have dinner?"

He scrolled rapidly forward.

"Going to the Gone Girls Dance?" Carla asked Mariah. *"David'll be there, setting up for it."*

"Depressing," Mariah replied. *"All those speeches
about safety take the edge off. How do you know David'll be there?"*

"He's on the memorial fund committee, stupid. Re-

member the dinner? The speech he gave with his fly down?''

Alex paused. The Gone Girls. Local name for the sorority women that disappeared. But that was old news. He moved on through the messages, finding nothing more of interest, and then opened his own mail. He expected that by now he should have received at least one response to a message he had posted two days ago, offering information on the best way to spot an empath.

Don't let the University bend your mind. Learn how to see the empath in the professor. For more information, use network Private Sanctions 1–85@futureworld.

His telecom showed three responses. One was from a nervous student asking if he knew how to tell if your girlfriend was ''one of them'' and explaining in great detail why he thought his might be. The second was a student offering herself as personal secretary on the networks for a rather exorbitant fee which suggested her duties would involve more than keyboard skills.

The third was more helpful.

Campus survey group seeking information about the following professors. Jibhul Alka, mathematics; Don Porter, history; Jaguar Addams, cultural studies; Beatrice Feda, languages; Ameda Blancorth, physics; Harrison Fish, fine arts. I've got some info on one—Jaguar Addams—because I'm taking her class. She makes radical gestures and talks about the unspeakable. Probably an easy A, but not very safe. For more info post reply Private Sanction 5–8@futureworld.''

''Doesn't that just figure,'' Alex muttered to the screen. Radical gestures. She'd been there four weeks and already she had a reputation as a radical. Couldn't she stay out of trouble anywhere?

He glanced at the clock and saw that it was late, saw

that he had been working more than four hours over his regular day. He would go to sleep, as soon as he completed two more tasks.

The first was to set his computer to work gathering any available information on all faculty and staff of the cultural studies department at the State University. He collated it so that names would be matched to previous employment and personal histories. By morning he would have results. Then he picked up his telecom and punched in her office relay line, which would transfer automatically to her campus housing if she wasn't in the office.

There was no answer on either line, and he left a message for her to call him back, though he had little hope that she would. Dammit, he just wanted to warn her.

A small and honest voice that emanated from somewhere very near his center chided him, reminding him that he sent her there in the first place, with no backup, no real information, and the official blacklisting of the Governors' Board.

Not much he could do about any of it, either. Except maybe the backup.

He could get someone else down there. Someone to just be there, in case of trouble. Not that he expected any. Of course not. But just in case.

He picked up his telecom and punched in Rachel's code. Her machine answered, and Alex remembered that it was late, and he was being rude.

"Rachel," he said, "if you're there, pick up. If you're not, call me when you—"

The blank screen was replaced by her face, looking puffy in sleep. "What?" She yawned at him.

"Listen," he said, "do you know anyone who'd want

to do some continuing education on the home planet?''

She blinked at him, and caught on fast. ''I can pack my bags tonight. Leave in the morning.''

''No,'' he said, glad he didn't have to waste time bringing her up to speed. ''She'd know I sent you. Somebody less personally involved, I think.''

Rachel looked disappointed, then chewed on her finger. ''You're right. How about Brad?''

Alex's face brightened. ''Brad Deragon,'' he murmured. ''Perfect.'' He'd put in a request for school leave for the spring. Why not let him start a little early with a trimester course and some independent study. The paperwork was in process already.

And he was reliable, almost impossible to unnerve, so if Jaguar caught onto why he was there, he'd just smile it away. Brad would be perfect.

''Thanks, Rachel.'' Alex said. ''Do you think we can get it started?''

''I'll push the paper through. He'll need—let's see, I guess a Z20, and fund coding. It might take a week, if you want to do it without anyone noticing.''

''I'd like it kept quiet. I'll talk to him about it myself. Go as fast as you can, Rachel, without raising a wake.''

5

''HOW ARE YOU LIKING YOUR STUDENTS?''
Emily Rainer asked, her smile deliberately friendly as
she reached for the raita, the sleeve of her embroidered
muslin shirt catching in a bowl of curry sauce.

"They like a little shaking up, I think," Jaguar said,
handing a napkin over to her. She hadn't gotten the hang
of Emily yet. She was always making friendly gestures,
indicating that they were comrades in arms—women of
the same age in the same situation—but her eyes remained cold and the baseline emotion under her deliberate friendliness smelled to Jaguar more like fear.

Emily laughed and wiped at her wrist. "Shaking up?
Dr. Addams, they're already horrified because we ask
them to actually *think*. Isn't that right, Ethan?"

"Alas, yes." He smiled, and offered the bottle of
wine to Jaguar, who took it.

The semester was in its fourth week, and the welcome
dinner had finally become possible because they were
past the crisis atmosphere of start-up and settling into a
rhythm, which would build to near crisis for midterms,
settle again, and reach critical mass at end of term, after
which everyone would collapse and go on break, only
to start again next term. University educators, she

thought, were energized by the cycle of disaster their year represented.

Not all faculty members were present at the dinner, partly because Jaguar had nothing to offer them in terms of career advancement, and partly because not all of them were speaking with each other. Ethan had managed to secure five and so far none of them had indicated any desire to hurt the others.

"I heard you were behaving in a radical way with the poor innocents," George Norton offered. "Tearing up the syllabus. Having them jump around in class and so on."

Jaguar kept her smile in place as she waved these words aside. "Attention-getting devices." She turned her gaze to Emily. "They work."

"I'll bet," she said. "Try the papadum? It's very good here. Any trouble students so far?"

"Trouble students?"

"You know," Samitu said, licking at his thumb and making a fist, which he punched in the air, "Boxers. The ones who enjoy a fight more than an answer."

"Steven Haigue," she said, without stopping to think.

"Steve," Ethan said. "He's in my Rhetoric and Principles class. Very intense. Likes to go by the book. Always stops after class to continue discussion."

"I had him last term," Emily said. "He was pretty broken up over the Rodriguez incident, wasn't he?"

Jaguar looked around questioningly.

Ethan leaned across the table to her. "Doris Rodriguez. One of the women who disappeared. The students, exhibiting their usual penchant for bad taste, call them the Gone Girls."

"I know," she noted. "I see the memorial notices."

"It was pretty bad," George said. "Four young

women just vanished. One right after the other. The press was howling, the police were crawling up our pant legs and out our ears, the parents were frantically withdrawing their darlings. Did anyone mention it to you?''

''Mention it?'' Emily broke in. ''George, we've spent two years working as hard as we can to develop amnesia about it. A semester of sheer hell while they dropped off the face of the earth, then a year of worse than hell when their faces were plastered on telecoms and beer bottles—*beer* bottles, if you can imagine. Some local brewery's idea.''

''Yes, and just when we think we can settle back into our dull routine, we lose the dean.''

George Norton leaned toward her and tapped at his chest.

''It was a heart attack,'' he said to Jaguar. ''Totally unexpected. He was more fit than anyone at this table, I'd venture to say. And only fifty. Maybe it was the stress.''

She bit back a comment about their definition of stress. ''Terrible,'' she said sympathetically.

George shook his head. ''Never found out what happened to the Gone Girls, either. Oddly enough, all four were cultural studies majors. Police tried to make something of that, especially with poor Leonard, who had all of them in his class.''

Jaguar looked to Leonard, who shook his head and remained silent. He was being very quiet this evening. Barely visible. She wondered if that was intentional.

''Like great-grandpa?'' she asked.

''Almost,'' he replied.

''What?'' George asked.

Jaguar and Leonard exchanged very quiet smiles. ''Nothing,'' Leonard said. ''Family story I told Jaguar.''

"Oh," George said, "well. If you say. At any rate, they finally chalked it up to some elusive, and probably off-campus psychotic when a few more women in town disappeared. I hate to say it, but I was glad of those disappearances."

"I still think it was a cyberspace jump. Ought to keep these kids off those damn computers," Samitu said. "They should be out rolling around in the grass making love with each other, not hooking themselves up to machines and making words do what their bodies won't."

He tapped the back of Jaguar's hand with a spoon. "Lips should be locked together in passion, not laser overload. Don't you agree?"

"Really, Samitu," Emily said, "leave poor Dr. Addams alone. You'll terrify her."

He shook his spoon at her, spraying droplets of soup around. "Not her. One can tell at a glance that *she's* not bloodless, or easily terrified." He said this in such a way that Emily could easily have taken offense, especially as he scanned her from the top of her deliberately casual hair to the bottom of her appropriately heeled shoes. Ethan intervened.

"Samitu is right that some of our students get their heads stuck in a VR unit with disastrous consequences to their GPAs. But I don't think any of the young women in question were involved in that. The police would have turned it up."

"Yes," Emily said, "exactly. And I wish the whole thing would blow away, since it's pretty dried up by now. Ethan's been wonderful in implementing that process, of course. We were very fortunate to have him step in for the dean, and we're all hoping he'll take it on for the next term." She leaned in toward Jaguar and added, with deliberate lightness, "Somebody's got to keep the empaths under control."

Jaguar laughed, with what she hoped was deliberate indifference. Emily leaned away, but kept her friendly eye on Jaguar, who ducked her head down to a plate of chicken tandoori.

George lifted his glass. "Count on my vote," he said. "Now, I've heard something interesting. That the president's hired a professional empath to check faculty response to the new course. Have you heard anything about the empath investigator, Ethan?"

Ethan frowned. "No. I heard no such thing."

"I heard it, too," Emily chimed in, "From a rather reliable source. It's all being done very discreetly, I'm told. Someone disguised as a secretary or a professor or something. Between that and the empath course, we'll be crawling with them, Dr. Addams."

Jaguar had the sudden sensation of being in an elevator that had lost its cable and was careening down toward a hard landing. She wasn't sure if it was her paranoia, or if Emily, Ethan, and Leonard were all watching carefully to note her response. She held on to her smile.

"The course is a big issue," she noted in what she hoped was a detached and academic way.

"Well," Emily said, "not so big as an elephant, but about twice as messy, if you know what I mean. Honestly, though. A course in empathic arts? You can imagine what these young and very impressionable people will make of it. They've grown up on a steady diet of virtual reality and holodisk infusion. They'll be wasting hours trying to bend spoons with their minds and see through some first-year student's clothes or—well, inventing dangerous sexual rituals. We'll end up with our own version of the Serials on a small scale.''

Jaguar felt her jaw begin to tighten, and asked it to relax. Just relax. This was nothing to do with her. All she had to do was keep her mouth shut and in a minute they'd be fighting fiercely over the ludic nature of reconstructionist movements. She told herself this, but apparently she wasn't listening.

''The empathic arts weren't even named as such until after the Serials,'' she said. ''I've never been sure why people insist on attaching the two.''

Emily's fork stopped between plate and mouth, and her face began to pinch in. Apparently, Jaguar thought, her friendliness wouldn't cover disagreement.

''You're right, Dr. Addams,'' Ethan said quickly. ''To establish a causal connection between empathic practices and the Serials is the height of non sequitur. At the time nobody was even discussing psi capacities as a scientifically established phenomenon. All we had was pseudopsychics on TV. However,'' he continued, smiling down Emily's scowl, ''that doesn't mean we should run a course in either ritualized psi work, or ritualized killing.'' He let his smile drift from Emily to Jaguar, including them both in his good graces.

Nicely done, she thought wryly. A little intellectual ménage à trois, and now everybody's friends. If only she could keep her mouth shut, which she apparently couldn't.

''But doesn't it make more sense to allow study of an issue?'' she said, speaking to Ethan rather than Emily. ''Let all the relevant voices speak to it, instead of trying to pretend it doesn't exist.''

George picked up the water pitcher and poured into her glass. ''But the ethical implications are too complex for students, much less their parents, who pay the bills.

We can't give the appearance of condoning something as morally ambiguous as the empathic arts.''

Jaguar took in the faces circled around her at this table. They were part of a system she didn't know how to work, or even understand. She once thought University was about learning, but it seemed to be much more about grappling for positions of power on ground as ephemeral as theory. Or what they called power, which she thought was merely control. She could make them very uncomfortable. She could tell them the truth about herself and her work.

"Are they?" she asked quietly.

Everyone paused, waiting for her to complete her sentence.

"Are they what?" George asked, when she didn't.

"Morally ambiguous. The arts. I never saw them that way myself."

George and Emily clamped shut on their surprise, Leonard's forehead creased, and Samitu raised an eyebrow, but Ethan leaned back in his chair and laughed. "Oh, come on, George. There's no moral issue here. The problem is we're scared to death. We've kept this stuff confined to primitive lore, forensics, classified military files, and social misfits for centuries. If we admit it's worth legitimate study, we're changing the way the whole world looks. It's revolutionary. Like Galileo, only now our church is rational theory and there are more people to excommunicate."

Interesting, she thought, the way he saw the many sides of the issue, and seemed to agree with all of them. It was an art she'd never learned.

"What's the matter with theory?" Emily asked.

"There is none," Jaguar responded before Ethan could. "That's the trouble."

Emily turned to her, her less than friendly eyes glittering. Maybe, Jaguar thought, what she hid under her deliberate friendliness was more anger than fear. And maybe the friendliness was a lot more fragile than Jaguar had realized.

"I beg your pardon?" Emily asked, her voice as brittle as her eyes.

"There isn't any matter in theory," Jaguar said. "It needs to be grounded in something physical, or kinetic, or emotional. Theory has to integrate with the rest of learning."

"You see," Samitu said enthusiastically. "I told you. This is a woman who likes to be touched for real. None of this airy fakery for her, yes?"

Jaguar inclined her head toward him.

"Indeed," Ethan said, laughing lightly. "So you believe a course would ground the problem?"

"I do," Jaguar said. "It would at least take the fears out of the closet where they could be examined, instead of abstracting them into nothing, so that they seem to be everywhere."

"One does wonder," George said, "how many closet empaths there are. Or—they're called cloaked, aren't they?"

"Cloaked," Emily said, and waved a dismissive hand. "Best they stay that way rather than overwhelming our students with foolish notions."

"Isn't that what they used to say about gays?" Jaguar noted, keeping her voice light and her smile high while she saw how the color rose to Emily's cheeks.

Ethan leaned over and tapped her hand. "Check and mate for Dr. Addams. Did you know that Emily's brother is director of the New York City Gay Coalition? Or did you take it from her mind, empathically?" He moved closer to her and waved his fingers in her face. Without pause, she caught them, stopped them, and just in time remembered not to twist.

Now what? she heard herself asking herself. You pull out your knife and slit his throat?

She called up a smile, then a laugh. "What do you think it is, Dean? Research, or empathic arts?"

He pulled his hand back from hers and regarded her with pure and unadulterated lust. "I think only further investigation would determine that, Dr. Addams."

Jaguar thought she might suffocate in the the palpable stoppage in conversation that followed, or be bled to death by Emily's eyes boring into the side of her face.

"Jaguar?" a voice asked politely. She looked up and saw Leonard, the only one at table who used her first name, regarding her with very serious eyes.

Empath eyes, she thought. Without a doubt. This was followed by the quickened feeling of empathic contact. She stayed closed against it.

Leonard's forehead creased in thought. Then he smiled broadly. "Could you pass the bread, please?"

Taking a piece out, she handed the basket to him.

"I understand you'll be doing research while you're here," Leonard continued. He was helping her out, she knew. Reestablishing comfortable conversation around the table. She let him.

"I've been doing some work," she lied. "Comparison of tribal funeral rituals." Now where, she wondered, was that from? She had no intention of saying anything specific.

Leonard nodded as if he already knew all about it. "Any particular aspect?" he asked.

Again her words ran ahead of her thoughts. *"Tzok-ol,"* she said, using the Mertec word for soul thieving.

She blinked at him. Soul thieves. People who prevented the passage of a spirit from this world into the spirit world. Or people who were able to intrude empathically into the gifts of other empaths. People who could take a gift from someone. She didn't mean to say that.

"I know a little about that," he said. "Maybe we can talk sometime."

She turned to Ethan, who was searching her face with an unexpected intensity. He lowered his face and went back to his food, but not before she felt the blood creeping warmly into her own face. Next to her, she heard Emily sniff.

Jaguar smiled at her. "Can anyone explain to me," she asked, letting her voice sound querulous, "how one manages to get disk copies made without spending a small fortune?"

The laughter was general, since the exorbitant copy fees charged on campus was one of the most contentious issues within the department, and for the University at large. Conversation moved in easier ways after this, with Jaguar continuing to lead them away from topics of controversy and toward the necessities of University life. When they rose to leave, Ethan hung behind and Jaguar took the opportunity to thank him for the evening.

"My pleasure," he said, taking her hand and holding on to it.

"I hope," she said tentatively, "I didn't say anything out of turn."

"You had your moments," he admitted. He ran a slim and elegantly smooth finger along the skin at the back of her hand, and she felt a shiver of something running over her skin. Not unpleasant, she noted, though a little stronger than she would expect. "You do seem inclined

to stir things up. I'd love to do it all over again, only
with less of an audience."

"You have my number," she said to him, reclaiming
her hand.

"Dr. Addams," he said, bowing to her, "I certainly
do."

Jaguar, looking over his head, could see Emily watching. Ethan watched where her gaze went, and smiled first
at one woman, then the other. He shrugged lightly,
turned, and went back to Emily, whose casual hand on
his arm had something of a grip to it.

Jaguar was glad not to be a fly on their bedroom wall
tonight—if they were sharing walls, which she assumed
was the case. She let them get ahead of her by a few
minutes, and when she left the restaurant, since it was
close enough to the University, she decided to walk over
and check her messages before going home.

She walked alone, a fine cool mist against her cheek
to remind her that autumn would turn to winter with
alacrity around here. A campus security car trailed by
her, then sped away when she waved, indicating that she
was fine, and carried no weapons. At least none that they
could spot. Reflexively, she felt for the glass knife at her
wrist, and was comforted by its presence. She'd learned
to get at it quickly, no matter what coat sleeve or shirt-
sleeve she wore. She walked up the road, taking the
quarter mile to humanities and her office rapidly, then
stopping for a minute before she entered the building.

Quiet. All quiet. The evening classes were over by at
least a quarter of an hour, and everyone except the maintenance people were gone. The building doors were still
open, though, and she went inside, took the stairs to her
office, took her key out for her office door.

Then she stood still.

The halls were dimly lit this time of night, but she saw someone at the far end. Someone who stood. Watching?

"Hello?" she asked.

"Just me," a voice said in response.

She realized she was tense when she felt herself relax.

"Leonard," she said. "Working late?"

"Forgot a bunch of papers I need to go over. You?"

"Just checking my mail," she said, and bent over to put the lock in the key.

But she didn't need it.

The door was open already. A crack of light showed through. She straightened up and frowned at it. Leonard, reaching her, stood looking over her shoulder.

"Uh-oh," he said. "Expecting company?"

She put a hand out, pushed at the door, watched it open.

Her office was empty, but the lights were on, and her computer was humming. She walked over to it, and checked the screen, which was open to the faculty bulletin board.

There, written in a fanciful font, boldface, and eighteen-point, were four words.

MIND FUCKER GO HOME.

Then, in parentheses, *unless you want to end up like the gone girls*.

Leonard peered over her shoulder. "Damn," he said. "That's not good."

And of course there was no return address because it was typed as an unsent outgoing message right from her computer rather than sent to her from somewhere else. Ironic, she thought, when it was actually safer to be physically present at the scene of a crime than to be at your computer.

Anyone could have done this. Keys to doors were so easy to get hold of, and there was a master key in the main office that hung on a hook in the open for anyone's use, since faculty were so frequently losing or forgetting their own. It could have been any faculty or student, or maintenance staff or stranger.

She let her hand hover over the keyboard, hoping to pick up residual information from the hand that touched them. But they were cold and lifeless. Nothing to read there. She let her finger drop onto the delete button, and the message went away.

"Hey," Leonard said. "Don't you want to—"

"Want to what?" she cut in, more harshly than she meant to. "Tell someone? Show someone? Draw a little more attention to myself? That seems like a bad idea to me."

She hit the off command. "Right now all I want to do is go to sleep. So if you'll excuse me, I think it's time to say good night."

Leonard stepped out of her way, let her get out and close her door, but he remained standing in the hall, shaking his head as her back retreated into the night.

Planetoid Three, Toronto Replica

The research offices, in a building two down from where Alex worked, were humming with genteel activity. Alex walked into the reception room and gave his name to a young woman who worked at looking studiously attentive. Then he took a seat on a plush mauve couch and stared at a generic abstract designed to match the color and style of the carpet.

People walked in and out, ignoring him. He waited and stared, trying to see beyond the tinted window that kept him from fully viewing who and what moved in the office behind the receptionist. A particular form caught his eye. A man, about his age, about his height. He turned, and Alex saw his face. He could put a name to it.

"Rich?" he asked nobody.

He stood up, and walked to the door of the office, going behind the receptionist and ignoring her when she said he couldn't do that. He rapped sharply on the door and opened it. The three men and one woman in the room turned to him.

One of them opened his mouth and gaped.

"Rich Forrest," Alex said, extending his hand. "Nobody told me you were with this crowd."

"Jesus Christmas," Rich said, moving to him, taking his hand, and pumping it. "I didn't know either. Jesus Christmas," he repeated. "What're you doing here? Sit down. Sit down."

He motioned Alex into a seat and waved to the others. "Oh—Sally, this is Alex Dzarny—Sally Manta. Roger Harrison. Zach Ulesti. Harvard, New York U, and Berkeley respectively. We were in the army together. Way long time ago, right?" He slapped Alex on the shoulder.

"Nice of you to put it that way. What're you—Ivory Tower now?"

"Yeah. Well, the army put me out to pasture about ten years ago, and I had to go somewhere," Rich said. "I teach psychology to spoiled Princeton kids. And you're—"

"Supervisor for Zone 12. You're on my turf, Forrest. I'm your boss."

Rich's mouth dropped open again. "You work here? On this pie in the sky?"

"That's right. And everything you do, I get to know about. Like old times, isn't it?"

"Just like it, buddy," he said. And the two men laughed.

"So—where do you start with us?" Rich asked. "Want access to our files? Our women?"

Alex smiled hard. "Not yet. Maybe, if I find out too many of you are Pentagon types."

He paused for laughter, which took a moment to work itself up. Interesting, he thought, and went on. "Today, I'm just supposed to see if you need anything, how you're settling in."

"Oh, we're fine. You know what our research is?" Ulesti joined in.

"Profiles, I was told. And comparative gender stats."

"Yup. That's two areas. There's two others. You want the tour?"

"Sure," Alex said. "Love it."

Ulesti nodded at Rich, who did not nod in return. Alex thought more was said between them than just who would lead the tour, but he was suspicious of ex-army on principle, so it might just have been his principles acting up.

"Tell you what," Ulesti said, "can you come back after lunch? We're just finishing up a meeting here, and then we've got some interns to deal with."

"Fine with me," Alex agreed. "Three o'clock?"

"Three o'clock," Ulesti said. "Rich?"

"Great. Alex, I can't tell you how pleased I am. Nice to work with you again."

"My pleasure," Alex agreed. He grabbed some door and left the room more thoughtful than when he'd entered, because now he had something to think about.

He walked back to his office, went right for his telecom, and waited for Rachel's face to appear.

"Rachel—how's it going with Brad?"

She seemed startled. "He's gone."

"On his way?"

"As we speak."

That was good. "Rachel, can you do me a favor?"

She laughed. Whenever he had work for her, he said this. As if he didn't pay her for her work. "I can do you a favor," she admitted.

"Okay. I want the records for our University visitors."

"Professionals, or personals?" she asked.

"Both, and all of each," he said. "Where they've worked. Who they worked with. What they like to eat, and who they like to eat it with."

She whistled. "That'll take some doing. There's about a dozen of them if you include interns."

"All right," he said. "I'll give you a hint. Pick your shovel up and follow the ones that lead you to the Pentagon. Then put it down and start digging."

She lifted her face and widened her eyes. "Really?" she asked.

"I am very much afraid so," he replied.

6

BRAD DERAGON STARED AT THE MAP HE HELD
in his hand. It must make sense, he knew, and he was
pretty good at reading a map. It was just that everything
was too damn symmetrical here. He wondered if it was
true that the toilets each had two flush handles, as he'd
heard it joked.

He'd gotten in three days before, set himself up in a
dorm as a transfer, and was lucky enough to be in the
same dorm hall as one of Jaguar's students—Steven, his
name was. In fact, Steve's suite of rooms was just across
the hall from Brad's, and he'd come over to say hello,
ask him if he needed anything. They had a good long
talk about the professors here, and Brad felt he'd hit the
jackpot on his first try. And he could pursue the connection even further.

If only he could find the humanities building.

He peered from the map, across the podium. The
fountain was turned off, and the field-sized shallow pool
surrounding it had been drained for the coming winter
months. Students hustled by, hunched over armloads of
books. Humanities should be to the right, and diagonal
from where he stood. He inclined himself that way and
walked. A group of pretty young women passed, and he

let his eyes feast on them, enjoyed the sounds of giggling. There wasn't a lot of giggling to be heard on the Planetoids, and not a lot of young women who looked like these. Open. Unafraid. Unwounded.

Nice assignment, he thought. Easy, undangerous, and with perks. Maybe it was time to come home. Go back to school for real. He'd been on the Planetoid for three years, and he felt ready for a change.

Maybe he could even come here. He'd be getting credit for a criminal justice course he was taking—an easy A after working the Planetoids, where all tests were a little more visceral. Steve also told him the teacher he was taking it from was a cream puff. Two exams, one paper, and attendance not required.

When Brad asked how he knew that, Steve nodded knowingly, and said, "I know a lot. You interested in learning more?"

Brad said he was. He expressed concern over being on a campus where they were offering a History of the Empathic Arts course, said how he hated all that mind-control crap, and that he wasn't sure he'd matriculate if they did offer it. He'd even heard rumors that a Planetoid worker was teaching here, and did Steve know anything about that.

Sure. He knew everything about it, and said not to worry. The teacher he was talking about would be gone by next semester, unless she bailed out early. Which, he hinted, she might. There were ways of applying pressure, he said. Especially with professors like her who were obviously—you know.

Brad said he didn't know. Obviously what?

Steve cast a glance around quickly and then whispered to Brad. Mind-fuckers, he said. Empaths.

Brad demonstrated the appropriate mixture of horror

and interest. He asked how could the University possibly let people like that teach. He swore he'd do anything to help get her off campus. If there was anything he could do, that is. But weren't empaths dangerous?

They were, Steve agreed, but they were also stupid. Arrogant. He knew lots of ways to get over on them, and he knew people who were teaching him more. He had help. Lots of people wanted to help. Brad could go to a meeting if he wanted to.

Sure, Brad said. He'd love to.

And he wanted to get there on time.

If only he could find the humanities building.

Jaguar found the cheap halolighting in her office irritating and uncomplimentary to the amber in her skin. She'd purchased two small kerilamps, which shed a softer, less intensely rose-colored light on her face. She sat under their glow, gazing plaintively at the pile of student papers she had to read, wondering if there was any empathic art that could make it smaller. She turned her attention to procrastinating about the reading by going through her on-line messages.

They included a message from Alex that read, "Have you managed to destroy your telecom, and so quickly? We need to talk."

"Glad you sent me here, yet?" she asked it. It did not respond.

And neither would she. She hit delete and expunge. The message disappeared.

There was a light tapping on her door. She resisted the urge to respond, "Abandon hope," and instead called out, "Come in."

The door opened and Emily Rainer stood inside the frame. Her face and clothes were just as carefully casual as they were last night, her blouse and flowing skirt just as pressed, and her shoes just as appropriately heeled. Jaguar was of the school that believed that heels should either be stiletto and therefore a weapon, or just gotten out of the way. The in-betweens that Emily wore seemed pointless to her. That, she scolded herself, was no reason to delete and expunge the woman herself.

"Hello," Jaguar said, and sat up at her desk. "It's good to see you. I'm looking for a reason not to read."

She indicated the pile of papers and Emily smiled. "Horrible, isn't it? If only they could form a coherent thought and hold it long enough to make a sentence."

"Actually, their writing is fine," Jaguar said, "It's my reading that's off." She waved Emily toward the other chair by way of invitation.

"Dinner was lovely last night," Emily said, seating herself but not exactly relaxing. Jaguar saw that her eyes had that glitter, like the surface of a lake coated thinly with black ice. For the first time she thought maybe it wasn't emotion. It could be drugs.

Ethan told her that Emily was having a grueling year, seeking tenure, pushing her research toward completion, taking on extra committee work. Maybe she was taking retrorem, which simulated REM brainwaves so she could keep up with the extra load on less sleep. It was a great drug, except for the side effects like extreme emotional instability, a leaping back and forth between exigent sorrow and exigent fear and uncontrollable rage. Retrorem would go far to explain Emily.

"Nice for me, too," Jaguar said, smiling brightly. "Let's do it again sometime."

Emily laughed. "That's what the dean said to you, isn't it?"

Jaguar made her face still. So. That's what the visit was for. A little boundary setting.

"Is that a problem?" she asked.

Emily's hand went to her collar and fidgeted. "Problem? No of course not. Only—" She leaned forward and spoke confidentially. "Well, don't take the dean too seriously," she whispered. "He's a bit of a flirt."

"He is, isn't he?" she replied.

Emily nodded. "I know it's been a while since you were at University, but you'll find it hasn't changed much. Men are still men."

"And a kiss is still a kiss," she said.

"What?"

"Nothing. Just an old song."

Jaguar felt a twinge of guilt. She and Emily were two of four women in a 25 person department. She could spend more time with her, and less time letting Ethan lean on her desk and—well, flirt with her. But between the nervous tension she felt moving under Emily's deliberate friendliness, and her comments last night about empaths, Emily made her twitch. She wanted something from Jaguar, kept trying to get it without asking for it, and that made Jaguar want to push her away. Ethan, on the other hand, Ethan soothed her because he was consistently cool and sedate and slightly detached. Or maybe Emily was just enough on the edge to remind Jaguar uncomfortably of herself. Too complicated, she told herself. Leave it alone.

"Oh," Emily said. "Well. Actually, I came by because I've been fielding some questions about you."

"Questions?"

"Yes. Students who have you as a Teacher are apparently a little afraid to broach the subject, but they know you're from the Planetoids and—well, as you were saying, sometimes open discussion of these things clears the air remarkably well."

"They haven't mentioned anything about it to me," Jaguar noted.

"As I said, they're a little afraid." Emily waved her braceleted wrist dismissively. "You know how they get these notions in their heads about who people are and so on."

Jaguar knew she was being asked to do something, but she wasn't sure what. "Do you want me to talk to them about it?"

"Actually," Emily said, "I thought maybe you could give an open lecture as part of the speaker series. About working on the Planetoids. It would make sense as part of the exchange program, and I know a lot of the faculty also want to know."

Jaguar thought of the last tape she had made for the Governors' Board. If she had thought ahead, she would have brought it along and shown it, then fielded questions afterward.

"Did I say something funny?" Emily asked, when she saw the grin on Jaguar's face.

"No. Not at all. I'm just flattered at your request. It's a shame there's certain confidentiality rules I couldn't possibly break. I don't think my office would allow it."

"Oh," Emily said, disappointed. "I see. But—are you sure?"

"I could check, but I'm reasonably sure."

"Well, if you find out different, let me know and I'll arrange something."

Arrange to make me a nonmoving target, Jaguar thought. She didn't know if Emily was actually involved with Private Sanction, or if she just spouted the bigotry of the general public when she talked about empaths, but she must know that giving a lecture about the Planetoids, as a Planetoid worker, would mark Jaguar for all eyes.

Emily said nothing for some time. Her mouth twitched and her glassy eyes peered over Jaguar's shoulder, out toward the distant mountains. Jaguar watched her, saw that her emotional ground was shifting, and something interesting was waiting to rise up from the epicenter.

At last she spoke. "About Ethan," she said, and then stopped, fidgeted with her bracelets. "I feel obligated to let you know that he's perfectly free to see whom he wishes," she said, and sighed deeply.

"I don't have any particular interest in any kind of—of relationship," Jaguar said.

"I know," Emily said, speaking more sharply. "That's what makes you so dangerous."

Jaguar pulled back in her seat and brought her chin up. "Dangerous?"

Emily leaned forward and pulled her gaze into focus, turning it on Jaguar. The force of it was astonishing. "When I first came here, I believed in the University. I thought it was a place where you could live your ideals. Teaching, learning, guiding young people, and following the call of enlightenment. I was wrong. It's a place of pettiness. Petty greed. A pretense of power to ward off fears of impotence. Petty men grappling for the biggest piece of a rotten potato. They think it means something. I thought it meant something. I was wrong."

There was enough fire in her eyes to burn the building down, and she reached over and put a hand that felt like a talon on Jaguar's arm.

"And you—you come here as if you can get away with living as you please. As if you don't have to get caught in the web of all the relationships, all the needs and feelings and grapplings and gropings. As if you're above all that. But you're not. You'll see. You can act like nothing will stick to you, but you'll come out as bloody as the rest of us.''

She held up a hand like a claw. Held it high, laughed at it, then dropped it back into her lap and stared out the window, away from Jaguar, who waited to see what might happen next.

Emily stood, smoothed down her skirt. ''Well, I won't keep you,'' she chirped. ''But let's have lunch some-time. Shall we?'' She gave Jaguar a hand to shake, and left the office.

''Well,'' Jaguar muttered to the door when it closed. ''Wasn't that fun? And yes, let's do it again sometime, when one of us is a little more sane.''

She picked up her student papers and riffled through them absentmindedly, thinking about Emily, about the message left on her computer, about the glassiness of Emily's eyes. As she ran her finger over the edge and listened to the paper make its small music, a printout of an Internet article floated out and down to the floor. She scooped it up midair, and held it in front of her face, reading.

''Shit,'' she said.

It was an article about the murder of two Wiccans. They were performing a ceremony for Samhain when someone bashed their heads in, pinned notes to their tongues. ''Mind-fuckers,'' the notes said.

Jaguar put the article on her desk. Did it go with someone's paper? She sifted through, looking for Wicca. Discrimination. Samhain. Anything resembling this ar-ticle.

Nothing.

Without thinking, she ran a hand over it to feel the last hand that had touched it. Such a natural gesture for her. Her hand stroked the paper, and she felt for signs of life. At first there was nothing. Then a sense of her students. None in particular. Just their faces, their eyes, passing by hers like lights past the window of a speeding car. Eyes, looking to her. Eyes, wanting something from her. All their eyes. Then, Steve. And Katia.

Katia, eyes deep and dark and frightened. Katia's eyes and her mouth forming words. Her eyes, a tunnel to fall into, and Jaguar fell to the feel of cool hands running her skin and pressure at the base of her neck.

A cool hand touching the back of hers. Pressure at the back of her neck. Something cool and firm and highly charged moving through her. In her.

Down into her belly and her groin.

Fast. Whoever was doing this was fast. She pulled away from it, getting nowhere, stuck in the hands that surrounded her held her down talked to her.

You want him. Want him. Call him. Not safe here alone.

She struggled against it. Breathing hard and rough. Want who? Want—

Alex.

Want him. Call him. No, she wouldn't. Breathing was a chore. She fought for breath, felt a strangling at her throat, brought her hand up to grab it, keep it away.

Call him. Not safe alone.

No, she thought. Not right. No breath in her. No breath and no way out of these hands jesus what was this her body moving without her volition and she couldn't pull out of it couldn't pull out close down get away too much.

She crushed the article and pitched it away from her.

Then she leaned forward, put her head down on her desk and listened to the humming of pain in her head as it passed from her.

When she was aware of herself and her surroundings again, the only thoughts in her brain were her own. Whatever she'd been caught in, she was out now.

No contact. No more contact. Stay closed. No messing around.

A hand at her shoulder brought her up sharp.

She lifted her head, and her arm followed to ward off whoever was there. Leonard caught her wrist and held it, regarding her in silence.

"Jesus," she said, "you scared me."

He loosened his hold and she pulled her arm away. Shook herself and ran a hand through her hair. Tried to gather herself back to normalcy.

He stared at her with his empath eyes. "You okay?"

"I'm—fine." She cast a glance at the door. "How'd you get in?"

"I knocked, and you didn't answer, but I heard you in here. So I went to the office and got the master key. Told them I locked myself out. You sure you're okay?"

She nodded, tried to smile lightly. "I guess I fell asleep. Ever doze over papers?"

He frowned, recognizing the lie. "All the time. But I don't talk in my sleep like you do."

"Bad habit," she said, and shifted in her seat. "Did I say anything interesting?"

"Nothing too bad," he said. "But I'd watch it if I was you. With your job, I don't think it's a good idea to keep a high profile."

"I'm here to teach a course," she said carefully. "There's nothing high profile about that."

"Is that why they sent you?" Leonard asked quietly.

She turned her face up to his, held his eyes with hers, asking her face to be a solid and blank page for him to read. "They? You mean the Board?" she asked.

"No," he said, "Not Supervisor Dzarny either."

"I'm here to teach," she said, clipped and angry. Too angry to think about how he knew her supervisor's name. "If you heard anything else, you heard wrong."

"Okay. I heard wrong." He smiled agreeably. "It happens."

She reined her temper in. "It does. Do you mind telling me who you heard wrong from?"

"A few people, I suppose. Emily has some ideas, but you already know that, don't you?"

Jaguar frowned. His voice had emphasis. Carried warning. "I know. She was here earlier."

"Yeah?" he asked. "What's she got to say to you?"

"She says don't mind the dean. I guess that's her personal tenure search, right?"

Leonard grinned. "About right. And I don't think it's going too well."

His massive shoulders lifted and fell slowly, like boulders moving their way down a mountain. He had such a capacity for quiet one tended to forget he was a big man. He had a face that listened. She wondered how he managed on this campus.

"Are you looking for tenure here?" she asked.

"Not me," he said adamantly. "I'm a temporary appointment. Special visiting professor. Next year I'm back home on the res. Right now I'm doing Intertribal Unity work with the Mohawks at Kanatsiohareke. They're like One Bird's place—a traditional community, not on res land."

Jaguar knew. They'd done well, as had the reservations since the Killing Times. They'd escaped the trou-

ble of the cities, as Leonard said, partly because they
had warnings from men of vision like her grandfather.
It was the only time the Natives made out better than
the white man's world. A time during which she was in
exactly the wrong place to have the rare advantage of
her people.

"Y'know, Katia's a Mohawk," Leonard continued.

He was as bad as Alex, still trying to pull her in, she
thought. "I didn't know," she said.

"She did an independent study with me on it. You
get to talk with her much?" he asked.

"Just the usual. She stops by my office sometimes.
She's pretty closed, and," she added deliberately, "I
don't like to pry when a student isn't ready for it."

"Right," Leonard said, catching on. "Sure." He
sighed, and moved himself toward the door.

When he got there, he turned around and looked at
her. "Be careful around here, okay, Jaguar?" he said.
"When you walk, walk soft."

Walk soft. In her language, that was a reference to
the chant-shape. Walking in power, but inaccessible.
Elusive. Silent and, if you wanted to be, invisible. What
was he trying to tell her? She decided to ignore it. Pretend she didn't understand the implication.

"I'll be careful," she promised.

He opened the door and stepped out. "Good. I'll call
you, and you can come over to my place. I'm right on
campus, too. We'll talk about your research, and I'll
cook you an injun dinner. How's that sound?"

"That sounds good, Leonard. That sounds very good.
Right now I'd better—great Hecate's cloak. I'm late for
class."

She fumbled with her book bag, grabbed her coat, and
made a dash for it.

107

"Dinner," Leonard yelled after her, standing in the hall. "I'll call."

"Great," she shouted over her shoulder.

She avoided knocking anyone over on her way down the stairs and managed to find the right turn in the tunnels to her classroom building. When she arrived in her classroom, she found the students whispering among themselves.

She looked up at them.

"What? What's going on?"

"Nothing."

"Something," she said.

Glen pointed to the blackboard behind her.

She turned. Written in large white letters, the same words that were on her computer.

MIND FUCKER GO HOME.

So far, her day was going like hell.

She used a minute of studying it to keep her face away from her students. Then she put a hand on her hip. "I always thought 'mind-fucker' was a hyphenated word."

Some laughter from the back. Some shifting in seats. Discomfort. She picked up an eraser and started wiping it away.

"Is this going on a lot?" she asked as she erased.

"Yeah," Glen said morosely. "All over campus. It's the Private Sanction group."

"It's about the course, right? History of the Empathic Arts?"

"We shouldn't waste class time on this," Steve chimed in. Katia gave him a dark look.

"What should we waste class time with?" Jaguar asked. "A theoretical discussion of religious persecution?"

"This," Steve said, "has nothing to do with religious persecution. The empathic arts are not a religion."

She put down the eraser and went over to the table where her lectern stood perched and pointless. She never used it. She swung herself to sitting on the table and regarded the students.

"They are to the practitioner," she said. She let that settle in. "That message on the board—would Private Sanction mean that as a personal affront to me, or just a general directive to whoever happened to walk in?"

Shifting. Whispering. You say something. No, you say it. No, you.

Katia, finally, speaking up. "Dr. Addams, I think it's because you worked up there." She pointed toward the ceiling. Up there. With the bats in the belfry.

"Everyone thinks that if you work up there, you're—well, we hear all kinds of things about Planetoid Teachers," Jesse Goodman told her.

Jaguar ran a finger down her nose, let it tap thoughtfully against her lips. "What kinds of things?"

"Like you're here to investigate the Gone Girls," Selica said. "That some professor snuffed 'em, and you're gonna find out who did it."

"And," Taquana piped in, "that you're setting us up so we'll take the new course. At least, that's what Private Sanctions says."

Jaguar grinned. "Between teaching and papers and investigative work and mind-fucking, I'm pretty busy. How do I find the time?"

Murmuring. A little appreciative laughter. Katia nudging Steve, mouthing "I told you so" at him.

He pulled away from Katia and addressed the class, his voice high and loud. "Y'know, you guys' favorite religion is apathism. You're all apathists. You don't care and you don't think you have to. There's been a lot of trouble here. At least Private Sanction's trying to do something about it.''

Jaguar turned her attention to him. Caught his eyes and held them. Felt Katia's dark stare move toward her with his. Remembered at the last minute to make no empathic moves here. Keep herself contained. Closed. And knowing this was necessary made her even angrier.

''So are the people who work on the Planetoids,'' she growled.

He tightened his lips and said nothing.

''The Planetoid prison system was created in response to the Killing Times—the Serials. Ten million people killed—that's a problem. How many people did you see killed, Steve?''

He kept his eyes, cold and belligerent, on hers. A band of pressure formed at the base of her neck and she twitched it away.

''I know. You weren't even born yet,'' she said. She shouldn't be doing this. It was very unteacherly of her to lose herself in anger. But the force of it was bigger than she was, tightening with the bands at the base of her neck, the pressure at the back of her eyes, hands reaching for her that she didn't want reaching for her. Dammit, she'd make it go away. Stop this shit.

She saw that the rest of the students were gaping at her. She was shocking them. They were used to her being easygoing. Tolerant. She included them in her speech.

''It's so much easier to find convenient targets for your fears than to face them, isn't it? Just get rid of the empaths, and all those dark and horrible years, the memories your parents carry that they insist on telling you about, the fears you carry—that'll all just go away. Except it won't.''

She strode to the middle of the room and wrote on the board in large letters the word WITCHES.

"Lots of these were killed in the Middle Ages, along with the cats people said were their consorts. Only thing is, with the cats almost extinct, the rat population grew. And then—guess what? The plague overran Europe, with not a healer in sight to do a thing about it.''

She wrote in even larger letters the word JEWS. "Getting rid of them sure helped the Germans fix their economic problems, didn't it?'' she said.

She wrote on the board again. GAYS. INDIANS. BLACKS. WOMEN.

And finally, all in capitals, the one word she was afraid to write most. EMPATHS.

"Somebody tell me what the hell the difference is?''

Steve's mouth clamped shut, and Katia put a hand on his shoulder. He shrugged it off.

Then she turned back to the class, quiet again, already ashamed of her outburst. Her anger settled in the room around them. She lowered her head and rubbed hard at the back of her neck. The pressure dissolved as quickly as it had risen.

Murmurs rose and died away. She dropped her hand and looked up.

"Look,'' Glen said, "not everyone here thinks those things. That attitude—it's just in the air.''

"I know,'' she said more quietly. "But why do you have to stand downwind and breathe it? You're here to learn the difference between the smell of truth and the smell of—of shit.''

She sighed. Facing the truth. Getting the dearly beloved illusions out of the way. Teaching. This wasn't rest leave. It was more of the same job, with the danger included.

Gone now, that pressure at the back of her head, in her eyes, but she didn't know when it would occur again. Didn't know its source or intent. Didn't know anything. Just knew danger when she smelled it. Like truth, it had its own scent.

"That don't mean we have to take *your* truth," Jesse pointed out.

"You're right," she agreed. "But how will you find your own?"

"It might be easier," Selica said, "if we knew what we were talking about."

"How's that?" Jaguar asked.

"I don't even know what the hell the empathic arts are, except like it's some gypsy shit about people who tell you your future and read your mind."

"We shouldn't be talking about this," Steve growled. "It's not right."

She turned to him. He stared at her, silently. No, she thought. I won't fight with him again. She turned back to the board and began writing.

"Empathic arts is a general term that includes a number of psi talents—scientifically identifiable states of consciousness," she said as she put terms down on the board. "They include empathic touch or the ability to directly experience or share someone's emotions, memories, and thoughts. Also telepathy, which is a subvocal reading or projection. Clear dreaming and clairvoyance—receiving knowledge through dreams or waking visions. The capacity to see events and objects that are distant. There's esper—long-distance touch, and the art of the Adept, which is visions of future possibilities. Unfortunately it's rarely specific enough to give you the right horse.''

The students laughed at this, and the tension lessened some.

''There's others, but what's known abou them is anecdotal. Shape-shifting, Protean change, the Greenkeeper, and the chant-shaper all have stories, but no hard evidence. Questions?'' she asked.

''What about telekinesis?'' Katia asked.

Unexpected question, Jaguar thought. ''The ability to move an object without touching it,'' she filled in. ''That's a little different than the others. Everyone is born with some capacity for telepathy or empathy, and skill beyond that is a matter of practice. Telekinesis is inborn.''

Glen chewed on his lip. ''That sounds kind of cool. How far away can they work? And how precise can they be?''

''Depends on the Telekine. How much they practice. They can make great surgeons, though.'' She didn't tell them that she knew a Telekine, a woman who could probe the inside of neural matter as if her fingers were lasers. She was one of the few people who knew why she was so good at her job. Jaquar had also had a prisoner who was a Telekine, with a slight gift for empathy as well. He'd chosen to give up his gift because he didn't trust himself. Jaguar was the only Teacher who knew how to help him do that.

She put her chalk down, brushed her hands off.

Steve leaned forward and raised a hand. ''Dr. Addams? You leaving something out.''

''What?'' she said, looking to him.

''Mind fucking,'' he replied, dropping the words into the classroom like a gauntlet on the floor.

She picked it up. "Actually, that comes under a different heading."

"Yeah? What?"

"Advertising," she said.

The class hooted, and Steve's face flushed over with red.

"Or," she added, "education. Or even religion. We've all got something we're trying to sell. And it's up to you to figure out what you want to buy."

They nodded appreciatively.

Enough, she thought. That was enough, and she hoped it wouldn't get her in more trouble than she was already. So far she wasn't doing very well at keeping the hell out of it.

"Had enough lecture for one night?" she asked. "Steve?"

He glowered at her and shook his head. "You have a right to your opinion."

"And you have a right to yours," she agreed. "Let's talk about something less frightening."

"Like what?" Jesse asked.

"Ghosts. Vampires. The undead."

"What?" Selica inquired.

"Halloween's coming up," she noted. "Who knows where the ritual started, and more importantly, what're you all gonna be?"

Talk turned to familiar ground, and everyone relaxed except Steve, who stayed sullen; and Katia, who stayed watchful; and Jaguar, who found that Halloween carried its own set of unexpected memories and tensions for her.

Tonight was the harvest moon. She couldn't help but wonder what Alex was doing without her.

Planetoid Three, Toronto Replica

Alex didn't have to go far to speak to his ancestors.

Lakeshore was good enough, as long as he was willing to be chilly, feel the wind and damp around him, and watch the harvest moon rise and set. Tonight was set aside for honoring the ancestors.

He'd done this ritual with Jaguar since the year after she arrived and they realized that they could share their knowledge of the arts with each other. In fact, they'd done all the seasonal rituals together. Solstice and equinox, harvest and planting—even though they rode a sky island that was only partly composed of earth, the ceremonies still needed to be performed.

As he lit a small fire and began the song of welcome and thanks, he felt anger rising in him.

She should be here. And dammit, she would be here if she wasn't always getting herself in trouble, wasn't so wild and insistently raw.

He groaned to himself. This was not the right mood to start with. He needed gratitude and an open heart if he was to listen to the ancestors, hear what they needed from him. He moved closer to his small fire, and focused. Breathed. Felt the play of space opening around him.

His ancestors—people who trekked cold northern countries in search of sun. People who crossed the landmasses that formed an ancient bridge, seeking sun. Going south.

Seeking war. Seeking stories. Seeking sun. Always, seeking light and sun and heat and fire.

They were here tonight, the many lives it took to make his.

He could hear them nearby. And they were all laughing at him.

Laughing at him.

He turned his face from the fire he'd made, to the sky, where the stars burned hot and the moon, that grandmother, did her job of pulling at water and earth without visible force.

"What did *I* do?" he asked plaintively.

But he already knew the answer to that.

If he didn't get at the truth in himself, he wouldn't find any visions, because all his energy would be focused on maintaining an illusion. That was just the way it worked, or didn't work, as the case might be. Even when he was a teenager, and first started having visions, he knew that.

He was thirteen the first time he'd seen a vision. He was playing a game with a Ouija board when the room disappeared and he was walking in a place he'd never been, talking to creatures he didn't even know how to name at the time. He remembered how it frightened his friends when he kicked the board across the room and wouldn't tell them what happened. They looked at him a little differently after that. He looked at himself differently, too.

For a while he thought he was going mad. Unlike Jaguar, he had very little cultural context to understand and explore what was happening when he fell into Adept space, or found himself in the mind of a friend, or felt knowledge pass directly from an object into his hands. He stumbled through on his own, learning what he could from reading books and watching shows on TV. And he learned to hide. In fact, one of the earliest capacities he realized he had was the ability to block knowledge of his presence from other people's minds.

He could, for brief periods of time, be invisible. Handy tool, that.

In college, he studied psychology, the nervous system, physics, and non-Western religions, practicing on his own with a polyglot of traditions as his guide. By the time he was in the army, he knew how to utilize most of his gifts, including the Adept space, though he didn't know the names for them yet. Then, in Manhattan, he'd met Sophie, a woman left on the streets in the upheaval. He'd found her shelter, and she'd recognized the empath in him, took him on as a student. He learned a lot in very little time. Continued study and meditation taught him more.

Then there was Jaguar. She was nineteen the first time he saw her, and already profoundly capable in the empathic arts. He could still feel the shock of her presence the first time they met, as if his oldest vision had suddenly appeared in the flesh and sat calmly across the desk from him, asking how to get work on the Planetoids.

She had to go back to school, get a degree first, and another nine years passed before she came to work in his zone. But the feeling was the same. The shock of recognition. The shock of the known, always known.

He didn't know her so much as he remembered her.

She was part of the first vision he'd ever seen, at the age of thirteen, while playing with a Ouija board.

He stood in a rain forest. Steamy, rain forest all around with the call of insects and night birds. Click and buzz of wings close to his ear. Heat swathing him like a second skin, and he walked toward a river that uncoiled itself through the land like a serpent eating earth and moving on. The texture of it was part of him in the same way his blood was—there, beating in his arteries and providing knowledge, unremarked by words or conscious volition. It was a blood texture, thick and wet and warm.

At the bank of the river he stopped and considered how to cross. A log floated by and he hopped onto it. It carried him downstream and across the wide water to the middle, where he saw a golden-spotted jaguar swimming the serpentine currents.

When his log drew parallel to her, her eyes called him like moonlight and he fell into them.

I choose you. I choose you.

Eyes pulling at him. Choosing him. Asking for his eyes.

He said yes.

At thirteen, he said yes easily, with no effort, because he didn't know any better. He didn't understand the danger. He only knew the pleasure of that complete union.

How could he choose the same now, or say yes to that wild union, consent to the force that was drawing him into her, allow himself to fall into her eyes?

How could he choose something so wild and avoid either domesticating it, or being eaten by it?

How could he?

The fiery eyes tugged at him, and he felt the warmth, the pleasure in going there. Felt his terror at letting himself fall into that.

He kicked sand at the fire and listened to it hiss. "I can't," he insisted. "I can't. I can't."

A sigh of disappointment. Small laughter. Knowing laughter. He stood by a dying fire, staring into a moon that was falling away from him, into the darkness of space, over the horizon and gone.

He stood and rubbed at his legs, which were cramped

from squatting for—for however long he'd been there.

This was all he'd get from his ancestors tonight.

As he walked home, he wondered if Jaguar was faring any better than he was on this day of the dead.

IT WOKE HER FROM A SOUND SLEEP, AND tossed her into terror.

She was asleep.

She was awake.

Something was happening to her body. Something like what happened in her office, only worse much worse. Convulsing it with pleasure and pain, pain and pleasure, waves sweeping her from dreams into waking.

Sleep. Was she sleeping? Bands of pressure wrapped her head, then stopped. Something like fire spread through her legs and into her groin.

"No," she gasped, watching her body as if it might be on fire as if she might be dying or making love and she couldn't tell which it was.

She tried to lift her hands to press at her belly, her breasts, her vagina to feel the source and intent of the fire, but her hands were glued at her side. Tried to call out for help, as if anyone else in the house would hear or respond except if she yelled fire. Fire. Fire.

Fire. Woman of Fire.

Fire, choking her, moving through her swift as lightning, like lightning searing her to pleasure and pain and she couldn't breathe, felt strangling at her throat.

Hecate, I was sleeping. Just sleeping. Not open not doing anything.

She'd chosen not to engage in ritual tonight. It was too dangerous, with something ready to slip into her whenever she dropped her guard. Let Alex take care of the ancestors. She'd come home from class, crawled out of her clothes and into bed, to sleep.

Sleeping is open enough. Open to dreaming. Open to be who you are in the place where you can't hide who you are.

Can't hide, Jaguar. Nowhere to hide. Nowhere to go. Nobody to help.

She lay glued to the floor. How did she get on the floor? She was on the floor, naked, body on fire with pain that became pleasure just as excruciating because she didn't ask for it had no control over it as it moved from breast to clitoris, nipple to lips, thighs to breasts.

Close down, she told herself. Cut off contact.

But she couldn't because she didn't know the source or intent who or why or how and it had gotten into her gotten into her.

Need help, Jaguar? Call him. Call him you want him call him.

No. No contact, she told herself. That would make it worse. No contact. No Alex.

Call Alex.

Help. She needed help. Couldn't close. Couldn't close. Hands like lightning grabbed her, sliced at her brain. Hands like lightning held her and the charge coursed up and down her veins, stunning her with an ecstasy of pain. She struggled, the charge coursing through her.

No. Struggling was no good. Panic was no good. Stop

fighting. Can't close, then open. Can't make it better, then make it worse.

She gasped for breath, feeling the absence of air in her lungs, and let go of struggling. Let go of fighting pleasure pain anything let it wash over her as her thoughts turned to one place left only sacred space left to her sacred and safe safe safe in the most dangerous of ways.

She opened, and called to what she knew best.

Aiweeo. Aiweeo. Gaiwato. Gaiwato.

The words had no translation. They were the sounds of her heart and would work for nobody else.

Aiweeo. Aiweeo. Gaiwato. Gaiwato.

Then she felt it. Unmistakable.

Old friend. Shadow creature. Stalking the curled edges of time and space. Growing out of the preverbal beginnings of her people, of herself. Self and not self. Spirit and not spirit. Dream and not dream. Matter and immaterial. It had been with her from the start. From the moment her grandfather chose her name.

She was being called into her power. Into a chant-shape.

She knew how to do this.

She let her body roll onto itself, curved herself over and over into the shape required, sleek and inaccessible, falling into the earth, the darkness, the silence.

I myself, spirit in flesh, speak.

As space opened around her, she felt the whispering of motion. Attention turned to her, waiting to see what she would do next.

I myself, spirit in flesh, sing to you.

Thought disappeared from words into being, and she felt her body go limp. Her impulse was to struggle, keep her strength. She resisted the impulse, and let herself fall into being. Attention focused on her more keenly as she fell.

I myself, spirit in flesh, say yes. My people, come to me.

The skin of the night stretched out around her, into the shape of what she had always been, the one she shared soul with. Those eyes, a golden holocaust, met hers, welcoming her home.

The skin of the night took her back to that place she had issued from and she felt her birth with those eyes, that skin around her. Felt her birth in fire and singing. Knew the places she had sailed the air and earth and all the skimming laughter of those journeys. She understood the language of this wordless song.

Knew the origin of her clearest eyes, her abundant voice, her killing hand.

We are here, the Old one said. You have need of this.

Yes, she said. *Yes.*

Old friend, sending her knowledge wordless and direct. Something so old it had never been named. Speaking in the language of fur rippling along a spine. The language of scent and moon song, telling her things. The oldest friend she had poured through her and she poured through it, into the realm of spirit where she would walk now.

She would know the scent of the moon. The knowledge of trees. The heart of the earth. Grace falling like stars into her and into her and into her. Body brought back to spirit. Spirit in flesh, flesh in spirit, walking in her power. Walking in beauty. Walking in a word that had no translation, but meant beauty and power and they were the same.

You will walk here, the Old one said.

Yes, she replied. *Yes. I will.*

Wordless agreement seeped into her. The night folded back on itself, returned her to normal space and time, to normal body and thought, and she lay naked on the bedroom floor, with the light of the moon shining on her face, and the new skin she wore invisible, even to her.

She lay still a moment, feeling the cellular tingling of ecstasy. This art was an ecstatic one. It would give her a joy almost as dangerous as love—the kind that made her forget all need for safety or self-protection. But unlike love, it would protect her while she wasn't looking. Still, her body would take a beating from it. Tomorrow she would ache all over.

"Hecate," she murmured, and she sat up. She turned her wrists and ankles, felt at her joints, and pressed her hands against her organs. Everything seemed to be working. And she was Jaguar again. Not hiding. Not holding back. Not needing to. From here on in, she'd be led. The chant-shape would stay folded around her, and whenever it was right, she would walk within it. The only trouble was, she didn't necessarily get to decide when that occurred.

This gift was yours only if you relinquished control. That was the paradox of chant-shaping. You let go of the need to do and know, in return for the chance to be.

And how, she wondered, could she do that in this unsacred space?

This art was reserved for the most contained of ritual settings, and never sustained for more than a few days. It was about a world of spirits, about needing to jump the track from normal to liminal space and let the spirits take you for a ride. Jaguar took that world for granted as a normal part of life. Once a year at Thirteen Streams, Jaguar assumed the chant shape and wandered the realm of spirit to gather visions and bring them back to the people of that village. But here at the University, she wouldn't have the safety of the village, or Jake and One Bird's presence to help her if she fell in too far and couldn't find her way back. It was an ecstatic art, but it wasn't an easy one to practice. She'd never done so alone.

In chant-shape, she had to breathe in energies the human body wasn't built to sustain or contain. She would relinquish conscious control for that power, which would be directed only by the deepest workings of the truth. That power could batter the body that carried it. And acting only according to the truth of the heart was a dangerous way to live. Especially here. She had no idea if she'd be able to carry on her normal tasks. Could she continue teaching? Would the spirit she shared soul with let her? Or would she start taking bites out of the bloodless legs of the academy, end up arrested or disgraced or dead?

And, she said to herself, what are your options?

She stood, found her legs steady enough, and went to the window, pressed her hand against the cool glass. No matter what happened in the chant-shape, it would be better than what was happening without it. She would welcome the spirits. Thank them.

They were here to save her life.

She breathed deeply, in and out, making room for what would become. As she felt the hum of energy rising around and within her, she let her voice rise and fall in the twining and spiraling chant of her people.

Her song would wind through the room all night, and it would start with the greeting to grandmother moon, who had somehow heard the whispering questions of her heart, and sent her what she needed.

7

BRAD SAT IN EMILY RAINER'S OFFICE, AS
nervous as he was in first grade when he was called up
to the board to do math. Something about this woman
reminded him of his first-grade teacher, come to think
of it. She smiled nice enough, but her eyes seemed ready
to see any mistake almost before it happened.

He cleared his throat. "I was wondering," he said,
"if you could tell me about your course."

"Undergraduate, I assume?" she asked. "I'm teaching two."

"Well," he said in his most friendly way, "why don't
you tell me about both?"

She handed him two pieces of paper. "These are the
syllabi," she said, and leaned back in her chair, eyeing
him like he was a lab specimen. As he read the syllabi,
Brad was relieved that this was all for show. All for
report. That he didn't really have to take a class with
her under any circumstances. Most of the words he read
looked like English, but they didn't read like it. English
didn't normally have so many hyphens and slashes, and
what was a "culturally (de)constructed/rehypothesized
norm" anyway?

He had come to see her at Steve's advice, who had

declared her trustworthy. In Steve's terminology, that
meant she was against the empathic arts course. In fact,
at the Private Sanctions meeting Brad attended, he'd
handed out a list of faculty names divided according to
where each professor stood on the issue, along with a
shorter list of faculty who were believed to be practicing
empaths. The list was in alphabetical order, which is
why, Brad supposed, Jaguar's name was at the top.

Other than that, the meeting was a lot of hooey, Brad
thought. Kids trying to act big. He'd like to put them on
the Planetoid for a week and see if they felt so big after
that. Or felt so sure they knew what was right. It was
one thing to pump up your ego sending anonymous
memos and plastering walls with rude graffiti, and another to really look at the way something worked, where
it was working.

But he'd gotten some useful information out of it. He
already had a good report for Alex, and if this meeting
went well, he'd have an excellent one. He'd insinuated
to Steve that he had a friend who needed help. Someone
getting involved in that mind stuff, and where could you
go for advice on that. That was when Steve told him to
see Emily. She might be able to guide him.

Brad handed her back the syllabi. "This is very interesting," he said.

"Three-forty is closed," she noted, "and besides,
that's for people who're interested in doing some real
research. Upper-level students." Not, her words implied,
snot-nosed puppies like him. If this went on, he thought,
he could see getting angry about it, even if it was for
show. "And 240 is a required course for majors. It fills
up fast." She smiled at him in a friendly way.

Okay. She didn't want him nohow. So, move on. He
assumed an expression of proper humility. "That's too

bad," he said. "I heard it was a great course. Do you keep a waiting list?"

She relented under flattery and handed him a pen, pointed toward the wall behind him. "Put your name and ID there. Show up the first day of class, and I'll see what I can do."

He stood and did so. "That's great. I hope I can get in. I mean, I'm new here, but everyone tells me how much they love your course. And there's another one they keep talking about. Intro to world religions. Dr. Addams teaches it. Do you know her?"

Her expression consolidated itself briefly into anger and was quickly recontained.

"I know her," Professor Rainer said, not friendly, but not unfriendly. Just informational. "She's temporary. She won't be here in the spring."

"Oh," Brad said. "Um, Professor, I have another question, but it doesn't have to do with class. Another student—Steve Haigue—he said you'd be able to help me out."

Her attention shifted at Steve's name. She put on her listening face. Brad sat back down, put his hands on his knees, and stared at them. "It's about Private Sanction. Steve said if I wanted a—um—deeper involvement in the issue, you'd be able to steer me right."

"As a faculty member, I'm not personally involved in student organizations, though I'm aware of the issues surrounding something like Private Sanctions, and do my own work as I see fit."

"Sure," Brad said. "Sure."

She breathed in and out deeply. "How deep an involvement do you want, and of what nature?" she asked.

"It's—for a friend," he said.

"A friend?"

"That's right. I'm worried about—her. She's been doing things. Trying things. With her mind. I think she needs help. Steve said you know someone around here who can help."

Emily looked over her shoulder at his name and ID number, written on her waiting list. "Brad," she said, "that's a very delicate situation, and it takes a great deal of experience and discretion to deal with it. You're aware of that?"

He swallowed hard and nodded vigorously.

Emily said nothing for a long while while her hard eyes nailed themselves to his face. He held eye contact with her, hoping he looked sincere and stalwart. Then she wheeled her chair away from him.

"I'll see what I can find out for you," she said abruptly. "If it seems feasible, someone will contact you."

Understanding that he'd been dismissed, Brad stood up, shook his pant legs down, and left.

Jaguar drew up the collar of her wool coat, and wrapped her purple woolen scarf around her head as she walked down the line of stores and boutiques, carrying a bag that contained both her favorite material and some of her favorite colors. Loose-fitting sage-green pants and top, batiked with dancing salamanders in fiery orange. Tight black jeans, black turtleneck, and a pair of black leather boots. She was as content as a hunter hoisting a twelve-point buck, and didn't even care that the sage green would tag her as an empath.

Halloween had turned the corner into November, with ice that might become snow, might become rain. Icy pellets bit at her face, and she felt them, but they didn't bother her either.

The chant-shape was moving in and around her with a surge of energy. The feeling of it was better than drink. Better than sex. Well, better than any sex she'd had so far, at any rate.

She lowered her head and walked on, bumping into a young woman and stopping to apologize.

"Clumsy of me," she said, then looked at the face. "Oh. Hello, Katia. What brings you out walking on a day like this?"

Katia smiled nervously and stepped back. "Window-shopping," she said. "There's a really cool pair of boots in the window at that French boutique. I keep hoping the price'll go down."

"The joys of the student budget." Jaguar smiled, remembering that herself. Then, on an impulse, "I was just about to get a cup of coffee. Want to join me?"

Katia looked around nervously. As if she'd like to, but didn't want anyone to see her. "Sure," she said, "I guess. There's this little place right up a few stores. They have good waffles, too."

They found seats easily since it was postlunch hour, and after they'd picked from the menu, they sat and sipped at their mugs of steaming coffee.

"You're a junior, aren't you?" Jaguar asked.

"Yes. I graduate next year. My friends from home thought I couldn't do it."

"Are you from around here?"

Katia shook her head, dark curly hair bouncing around the frame of her pretty face. "I'm from this really small town like right across the Canadian border. It's like—well, everyone was really shocked when I said I was going to college. Why not be a data coder? they said. There're lots of jobs in that." She laughed.

"You know," Jaguar said, "what they're really say-

ing is that they'll miss you if you go. They know that
even if you come back, you'll be different, and that's
frightening.''

Katia's expression darkened. "I always was different.
That's why I left in the first place.''

Jaguar made her face inquisitive, in a detached and
teacherly way. "Different?'' she asked.

"Oh, you know. Couldn't fit in. Just—I don't know.
I had friends, and we did lots of fun stuff together, but
what they thought—'' She broke off. Nervous again.

Jaguar felt the motion of a song inside her, telling her
things. Knowledge would come to her that way in the
chant-shape, wordless and direct, unexpected. Katia was
an unpracticed empath. Young and alone. Afraid of herself, with nobody to tell her that her gifts were natural
and could be directed. Nobody to teach her how to use
them.

As the information moved through her, she saw that
Katia was frowning at her. She took a good breath, and
smiled. Try and stay in the world, she told herself. Give
it your best shot.

"You live very close to the Mohawk reservation?''
she asked.

"Oh yeah,'' Katia said, shrugging the moment off.
"My mother was from there. She's part Mohawk. She
had some relatives there, so we used to spend time, although my mother was kind of funny about it. I guess
she couldn't decide where she lived. You know, like in
her heart?''

"I know,'' Jaguar said. "Not sure where you fit in.
You must enjoy Professor Peltier's course.''

"Sure,'' Katia said, going underground. "He's teaching me a lot.''

Maybe she wasn't so unpracticed after all. Maybe she

had practiced when young, then, as so often happened with girls in adolescence, had given it up. Too much power. Scary. Time to change the subject.

"And way up north there," she asked, "did you ever see the northern lights?"

Katia smiled. "Aren't they the best? I took Steve out once, and he even liked them."

"Now, that is truly amazing," Jaguar noted, grinning.

"I guess—well, Steve's wonderful, but you see how he gets tense."

"It happens," she said. "People get tense when they don't understand."

"Yeah." Katia sighed, then ducked her head down to her coffee cup, took a sip, looked up at Jaguar with a mixture of apprehension and daring. "I was wondering. Do you have, you know, like, someone you're seeing. I mean, maybe I shouldn't ask, but I was—I guess we all wondered about that."

Jaguar, not sure if Katia was referring to a ritual elder or a doctor or a lover, tilted her head quizzically. "It's okay. You can ask, Katia. Only, you have to use a few more nouns."

Katia laughed and leaned back in her chair, keeping her coffee cup held protectively against her chin.

"Like, a man you're seeing," she tried tentatively.

"Not a woman?" Jaguar asked mischievously.

"Well, we thought—I mean, you seem—well, it doesn't matter, either way. It's just that everyone sees how beautiful you are, and some of the kids think you're here, you know, getting away from someone. Like there was someone up there."

Someone up there, Jaguar thought, forcing her lips to curl back on the smile they were trying to form. Alex appeared unbidden in her thoughts, his dark eyes blazing at her. She shook him away, and saw that Katia was regarding her with sympathy.

"Is he handsome?" she asked.

She opened her mouth to say no. It's not like that. But the words that fell out when she spoke weren't those at all.

"Yes," she said, "Very handsome. Dark hair with silver in it. Dark eyes. Tall, and broad across the shoulders. His face—it's one of the oldest I've ever seen."

"That's good?" Katia asked uncertainly.

"I mean old as in from another time. From the beginning of time." Jaguar told herself to stop talking. Shut up, dammit. Just don't say anything if you can't make sense. But when she saw the look of supreme satisfaction on Katia's face, she felt relief. She'd given them all something else to talk about. Something to take their minds off empaths and Planetoid workers.

"What do the other kids think, Katia? The ones who aren't writing romance novels."

Katia returned from her reverie and shrugged off their opinion even before stating it. "Don't worry about them. They're just conservatives."

Okay. That was pretty clear. "And you're not?"

"I think people should just be who they are. As long as you're not hurting anyone, what does it matter, right?"

This said with dark intensity. Jaguar waited, hoping silence would encourage her to say more. It did.

"I mean, some people get all over me because I spend time with my professors. With—Professor Peltier or Professor Davis. But why shouldn't I?"

"I don't know," Jaguar said. "Why shouldn't you?"

"There's no reason. Just because they get this thing going about the Gone Girls. There's no evidence. Steve and I had this sort of argument about it. He thinks—''

She broke off abruptly, and Jaguar waited for some time before she realized that the girl's words had stopped completely. Katia picked up a packet of sugar and ripped it open, dabbed her finger onto it, and licked.

Jaguar reached across the table and stopped her hand. "Rot your teeth, girl," she said.

And in the touch, she felt the fear. Fear of her own art. Empath and—something else. Some other energy moving in her. She feared it.

Katia pulled her hand back. "Steve thinks Professor Peltier's a cloaked empath. I told Steve he was wrong," she said definitively. "Because he isn't hurting anyone. And empaths—it hurts, Dr. Addams. They hurt people."

Jaguar marveled at the statement. "Who told you that?"

Katia shrugged. "Lots of people. And there's Steve's dad—I guess his dad left. Went off with some guru and said he had to be himself. Said he could see things. Then, he killed himself."

That went a long way to explaining Steve, Jaguar thought. And of course Katia, having her own fears, would be drawn to his, which were at least easily named. "But that doesn't mean he was an empath, Katia. Maybe he was ill, or just confused."

Katia's face grew dark, and she leaned back into herself. "How do you know the difference?"

Now, there was a question. Jaguar was so used to seeing the exotic as normal that she forgot what it meant to ask that question. Or maybe she had been taught her art at such an early age by people who knew how to do it so well that she had answered it long since. Katia didn't have that advantage.

"You know by the feel of it, Katia," she said. She

put a hand to her temple and rubbed. "When something's wrong, you feel it, and you trust that even if it all looks good. And when something's right, you feel that, too, and you trust that even if it all looks a little off."

Katia scanned her, looking hard, eyes glittering. "You mean you figure it out?"

"No. It's like I said in class. You learn the difference between the smell of truth, and the smell of shit."

Katia's hand twisted around her cup and held it hard. "What if you don't know? What if you can't tell? What if you're—confused?"

Jaguar looked at her hard, saw her eyes glittering. She was confused and afraid. Jaguar instinctively reached out to soothe her, reached out with her mind to say it's okay. It takes practice and if you get it wrong you'll learn to put it right. Without thinking, she opened.

No. Stay away. Stay back.

Her vision turned double, blurred, went out entirely. She breathed in, pulled into herself. A flock of hands, reaching for her, fluttering around her. Tightness in her neck, around her eyes. Then, the soft feel of night falling into her, around her. Old friend, standing guard.

"Dr. Addams?" Katia was saying, and Jaguar saw her. "You okay?"

"Fine," she said quickly, recovering herself. Strong stuff here. Strong stuff in Katia. "I was just thinking about what you asked."

"Oh. Oh. Well. I mean, it's nothing really."

"No," Jaguar said. "It's an important question. I think if you're confused, the best you can do is wait for the confusion to clear."

"What if it doesn't?" Katia asked.

"Oh, it will," Jaguar assured her. "One way or another, because everything changes."

"And what do you do in the meantime?"

"Stay alive, and await further instructions."

Katia turned her cup around in her hand, examining the motion of the liquid left in the cup. She wanted something more. Jaguar wished she had something more to offer—to Katia, and to herself. But she didn't.

"I'd better get back to campus," she said. "There's a general faculty meeting tonight and I'm told I have to be there. You remember we're not meeting in the class this Thursday, right?"

"Oh. Yes. I remember. We're meeting at Cutters Bar and Grill, at seven."

"That's right." She wanted these kids to do some fieldwork. Connect their intellects to the world, starting with what they knew best. "Should be a nice break," she said.

"It's—different," Katia agreed.

"Just another ritual, Katia," Jaguar said, standing and putting her coat on. "Like faculty meetings, only a little more fun."

And about that, she was right. The meeting was a boring recitation of budget issues and procedural emendations that meant nothing to anyone outside of administration. Jaguar noticed that Emily was conspicuous in her absence. She's ill, someone said. The flu.

More like a sudden attack of wisdom, Jaguar thought.

After the meeting, Ethan helped her on with her coat and slipped her wool scarf over her shoulders. "That was dull," he said. "Can I make it up to you with a good dinner?"

He placed his hands under her hair and lifted it carefully from her coat collar, smoothing it across her shoulders. She kept her back to him and bit down on her lower lip to still the frisson that ran along her spine. Such a lovely gesture. Intimate and courteous at the same time.

He would be a skilled bed partner, she thought, and her body was calling to her. Wanting touch. Wanting the kind of touch he promised—intellectual and cool and practiced, with a minimum of emotions that could slip like diamonds to the bottom of a wind-tossed lake.

And why shouldn't she have what she wanted? There was nothing stopping her from that. No prisoners. No Board governors looking over her shoulder like old ladies. No disapproving glances or comments from ex-Supervisors.

"That is," Ethan said, "if you're free."

"I'm free," she said. "As always."

Professor Davis's house was high-ceilinged, old, and filled with wood. That, at least, was Jaguar's first impression. The wood, she thought, made the house seem dark. A fireplace crackled in the living room, causing the soft shadows to leap about the room, but everything else seemed very still, as if it had been still for a long time. She noticed that alongside his shelf of modern disks, there were two shelves filled with books. Everything from Homer to Poe, Parrish and Maclean, Ramjerdi and Davidson for fiction and poetry. Then a large section of the philosophers, next to a wide array of scientific tomes. *Gray's Anatomy. Phelps's Neuroanatomy. Oxford Unabridged Encyclopedia of Neurophysiology.*

"An eclectic library," she said to him.

"I like to know everything," he said. "At least, everything I can know."

He served her a delicate and well-planned dinner of veal Marsala and risotto with asparagus, good bread, and good wine. As they ate, they talked books, and food, and winter weather. Nothing important. Just the most pleasant surface items on the agenda. She was glad of that.

They didn't even talk about school until they got to the after-dinner wine, and were seated in front of the fire.

"Have your students been behaving for you?" he asked.

"Behaving? None of my students behave. I don't encourage it."

He laughed lightly. "I remember you said something about Steve being a pest. Is he still?"

"Steven—he's different."

"If he's a problem, I can talk to him. I have some influence," he said, pouring more wine into her glass.

She swirled the wine around, watching the patterns that formed and dispersed along the sides of the iridescent glass. "And he'll listen?" she asked. "It doesn't seem to be his strong point."

Ethan stopped pouring into his own glass and raised his eyebrows at her. "My dear, he quotes you so frequently I assume he's listening much more closely to you than he is to me."

So. They had discussed her. Not much surprise there. "I can imagine what he says."

He finished pouring his wine and joined her on the couch. She found couch conversations uncomfortable, because it was difficult to turn properly to see the full face of the person you were talking to. She had read somewhere that men preferred side-to-side talk, because face-to-face signaled confrontation to them. As she thought about this, she realized that the only man who ever asked for her full face was Alex. But then again, he was an empath.

"Steven," Ethan was saying, looking ahead rather than at her, so that she could only see his classically sculpted profile, "would like to live in a totally rational world, based on a totally rational system of order."

"I'm very rational," Jaguar interposed. "What I tell him is absolutely reasonable."

He held a hand out, "No," he said. "You're integrated. Emotionally and intellectually, and I suppose you'd call it spiritually, too. That's rational, but it's more than rational, too. Steven wants the rational. That's all."

"Is that why he's so invested in the antiempath movement?" she asked, keeping her voice neutral.

"Probably." Ethan turned his face to her and smiled. "Emotions in general terrify him. That's one reason why he's so terrified of you."

In the low lighting of the room, the shadows were soft and diffuse, merging with his eyes that had gone deep blue. She saw nothing of the empath in their surface or their depth. He was a very physical man, she thought, but not a man of passionate emotion. Always cool and self-possessed. Perhaps that's why Steven was drawn to him. Perhaps that's why she was, too.

"I'm not sure I understand," she said.

"You don't?"

She shook her head.

"Jaguar, he's got a crush on you. His physical desire terrifies him as much as his emotions. And I must say, for all his problems, Steven has a very good eye."

Jaguar lifted her glass and took a long sip. Somehow, that hadn't occurred to her.

Ethan chuckled. "I wish you could see yourself right

now. I believe it's the first time I've ever seen you flustered. But now I've made you aware of it, and you've closed down again. You're very good at staying closed, aren't you?''

Her hand jerked, and wine spilled onto her wrist. Ethan grabbed a napkin from the table and made a swipe at her wrist. She pulled back quickly, spilling more wine. She didn't want him to see the glass knife. Didn't want him to feel it under her sleeve. Suddenly felt unsafe.

No contact. Stay closed. No contact.

She stood and went over to the fire, wiping the wine from her wrist into it and watching it sizzle in response. Ethan stood and joined her.

"Here," Ethan said, handing the napkin to her. "Please. I didn't mean to intrude in any way."

She took it from him and mopped at her sleeve, then smiled apologetically. "Sorry," she said. "It's just—I didn't know how to take your question. There seems to be so much suspicion about someone who's from the Planetoids."

Ethan grinned. "Would you be relieved if I told you my interests are merely and only lascivious?"

She grinned back. "Probably. If that was the truth."

He lifted a hand to her hair and stroked at it lightly. "I believe you'd rather go to bed with me than talk to me," he murmured. "How unusual for a woman."

"Maybe," she said, "you've been hanging around with the wrong women."

And then his doorbell rang.

An expression very like rage passed over his face and was quickly traded in for his usual cool reserve. Talk about your closed books, she thought.

"Aren't you going to answer that?" she asked.

He scratched at his head. "To be honest, I think I know who it is, and I'd rather not."

A face appeared in the living-room window, then disappeared.

The doorbell rang again. Oh well, she thought. Oh well.

She walked over to her coat, put it on. "You go ahead," she said. "I'll just let myself out the back way."

Planetoid Three, Toronto Replica

There was something wrong with his bed, Alex decided. He turned onto his back, and his neck tensed. Rolled onto his stomach, and felt knots. Tried his side, and got pressure in his shoulders.

"Dammit," he said, and pushed himself to sitting. No more.

He swung his legs down off the bed and made his way to the light switch. No more dreams, thank you. He'd go get some work done.

He went over to his computer and opened it, looking for something to do. There were the monthly expenditure reports to file. And he needed to update some yearly reviews. But his mailbox was flashing at him. Message from the home planet. Must be Brad, he thought, and opened that.

Alex read, noting that Brad had already managed to get to a meeting of the antiempath group, who were busy plaguing all suspect teachers with anonymous e-mail, articles on empath bashers, and other equally mature responses to their fear. They'd be stuffing office doors with memos soon, and from what Brad said, their prose was as dense as their reasoning.

"Sounds like fun for Jaguar," Alex murmured, and felt guilt well up. He'd sent her there. Hadn't lifted a finger to stop the assignment. No wonder he couldn't sleep, and was plagued by dreams of cellars filled with angry cats, ready to scratch his eyes out.

He scrolled through Brad's report, and saw that he'd also been following Jaguar to see if he could tag the people she spent the most time with. She seemed to be on very friendly terms with the dean, Ethan Davis. He'd watched her leave campus with him, seen them laughing together in the halls while he was waiting to speak with an adviser. That was the good thing about this campus, he said. You always had to wait, which gave you a lot of time for watching.

Alex drummed his fingers on his desk and scowled. Ethan Davis. Okay. One for the list of lookups.

Brad also saw her spending time with Leonard Peltier, temporary faculty from Lakota country.

"Leonard Peltier," he mused. "Must be related." That would bear looking up too.

She also recently had lunch with George Norton, seen a movie with Harold Smith, gone to a lecture with Samitu Laki.

"Aren't there any women faculty?" Alex muttered at the screen.

Apparently, there was one. Emily Rainer, whom Brad had consulted about a course for the spring semester. Alex read on and learned that Emily was definitely involved in the antiempath movement, that Brad's opinion of her was that she was doing drugs or something, by the look of her eyes, and that she didn't like Jaguar.

"Great," Alex said. "Thanks a lot."

The report went on, and Alex grew a little concerned when he realized the game Brad was playing, trying to get Emily to contact someone to help him "cure" an empath. That could be dangerous, especially if they bothered to trace Brad back to the Planetoid. He made a mental note to get Rachel first thing in the morning and make sure she coded all of Brad's records.

He had a brief moment of speculation as to whether the Board sent Jaguar to the home planet to be cured of her empathic itch, but dismissed it pretty quickly. They knew better than that. He hoped. Still, what Brad had turned up was valuable, and he'd taken risks to get it. "Good for you," Alex muttered at his computer. "Compensation will be forthcoming."

The report ended by Brad giving his opinion that the student group was largely harmless, but he included a list of names of students involved. There was one—Katia Stone—Brad wasn't sure of. He couldn't tell if she was in the group, or just there because Steve Haigue, the Private Sanctions guru, was her boyfriend. She was a slippery one, he said. Had something she was sitting on pretty hard, he thought.

Alex sent back a message advising Brad to go slow and careful with Emily, and asking him to stick as close as he could to Jaguar without letting her know. Great job, he told him. Keep it up.

Then he worked his profile catcher on Leonard Peltier. The first thing he noted was that Leonard, born Thomas Bear Hand, was ex-army. He'd spent two years as a soldier in the Killing Times, and another two years in the psychological research unit. That, Alex knew, was a euphemism for psi work.

He requested a more complete record.

His computer worked it for a full minute, and then told him the information was not available.

"State reason for data unavailability," Alex requested.

The screen flashed back at him, "Information Classified."

Okay, he thought. That was interesting.

"Organization code for classified information," he said.

"Coded Red." Pretty heavy, but not impossible, Alex thought. Classified information was not necessarily unavailable if you knew how to work the system. Red was a mid-level code, signifying research that was hot, but not about to get anyone killed. And Peltier's involvement was more than twenty years ago, so it could mean nothing at all.

He leaned back from his computer and turned this over in his mind. Then he moved on to Emily Rainer, whose history was what he might have expected. Smith educated. Dissertation blameless and dull. Spent many years in the Middle East researching texts before she came back Stateside to teach again. Nothing to write home about.

He worked his way through the other faculty members and found more of the same. Lives that followed expected tracks from birth to tenure to emeritus status and probably to grave. The only blip that turned up was an absence more than a presence. The dean, Ethan Davis, had two years practically unaccounted for in his file. Listed only as work abroad.

He thought this one through and shook his head. Could mean anything, or nothing. Missing information. Lines that didn't get filled in between that country and this. He poked around it some, trying to establish a connection between that time and army work, intelligence work, sick time, anything. Nothing much came of it.

"Okay," he said. "Let's try the university itself."

Since he had at least one known ex-army here, and the faculty had the same, maybe those dots would connect. He went to a board that collated information from unrelated sources, and hooked in the University's code, which was public property, and the code for Pentagon psi work, which was not. The computer worked it for a while, then blipped out the names of the officials who approved the grant for the empathic-arts course.

He knew that already, and it was no help. He needed to know what wasn't made public. He needed to know something he didn't even know how to ask about yet. His hand twitched. Something. There was something here, he knew. Jaguar was in the middle of something, with a man who used to work for the army, and a University that was linked with the army, and faculty that wanted to cure empaths.

He needed to make contact with her, just as a check-in. A brief brush against her consciousness, polite and unobtrusive.

He settled himself into her signals, using the surface contact considered courteous when one empath was seeking another, and waited for a response, even if it was get the hell out of here.

"Damn," he said, when the static nipped at his brain. "Now, that's new."

It wasn't the rippling, unseeable lines of a mind that was cloaking itself, or the hard feel of a closure. This was static.

He tried it again, and got the same feeling. Static. A sort of interference. Perhaps having to do with her location on the home planet? Satellite energy? He didn't think so.

It was too highly charged and complicated, circling

the outskirts of her thoughts. Was it something that sought a way in, as he did? Or did it merely seek to keep him out? Maybe she'd come up with a method of blocking he didn't know. She could be so resourceful with blocking.

His hand rested over the side of his chair, and felt fur. He petted it absentmindedly, thoughtfully, and was rewarded with a purr of contentment.

It took him a full minute of petting to remember that he didn't have a cat. And if he did, it wouldn't be that large.

When his eyes followed to where his hand rested, he stopped its motion.

She was powerful, beautiful, and cryptic. She could take his hand off in one bite, and finish off the rest of him before he had a chance to cry out. If she was going to kill him, she'd go for the back of his skull and crack it with her teeth. If she wasn't—what was she doing here?

She turned her eyes up to him, light from an unknown source reflected in gold pierced with black slits that gazed serenely into the center of his mind.

I choose you. I choose you I choose you.

Then she stood and stalked from the room, through the door, and into the night. From somewhere far away, laughter reached him, human and knowing.

"Jesus, what are you?" he whispered after her.

No answer communicated itself to him.

BREATH.

It felt like breath to her.

Being breathed into the night. Being breathed in, and the night your skin and the moon your eyes.

The trees, all the branches were coated with a diamond sheath of frost that caught the glow of the full moon and cast it back in phosphorescent blue. Mist rolled across the earth like laughing silk. She glided across the grass soundlessly, and the feel of her legs moving was pure pleasure.

The scent of the moon. The scent of the moon was sweet as hibiscus blooming out orange curved into white at the center. The scent of the moon was a liquid prism. Quartz running liquid and heated to molecular dispersion. She stopped, glanced up, breathed in.

This is what chant-shaping was like.

Being breathed in to the heart of radiant sun. Breathed in to the source. Breathed in.

Like finding the absolute center of the universe, and kissing it. Like having it kiss you back.

She rested, breathing in what breathed her.

Then she considered her hand. The scent of the moon

was on her hands, and she brought her mouth down to taste.

Enough.

Enough pleasure. There was work to do.

Her feet down on the earth now. Moving now. Going. Going faster for delight. For the feel of it, muscles that would never stop and legs that never knew fatigue and going for delight. For the feel of it.

She raced the speed of the turning earth, every muscle an invocation to grace. She raced like fire coursing the hair of a sorceress. She was water. She was liquid fire burned into her own core and racing her heart to nowhere.

Liquid fire. Fire, singing her this song.

Like kissing the center of the universe. Like having it kiss you back.

She glided to herself. Breathed out.

Breathed out.

She breathed out to herself, and let go with a long sigh.

She tilted her head back and sang her song, let it begin in her, singing her where she needed to go next. The skin of the night would take her and she would let it.

Show him.

Words left her and she fell into this beauty, this ecstasy, this opening of time and space. Fell into the skin that was slippery as daylight on water, elusive as the shadow of moon on snow. She breathed out. She breathed in. There, where space curled into corridors of time, she ran like light.

Show him. Like kissing the center of the universe, and having it kiss you back.

Motion brought her into darkness, through thought and dreaming, through the pupils of an eye, and into the corners of a heart. Motion brought her forward, where she needed to go.

Energy skipped a beat in its natural flow. She licked the air, and let the energy she tasted become a river she could ride.

A sweet river. A way from here to there. Into dreaming. Into time and space.

Where he waits. Show him.

She let it carry her through dark places, through stars, through no air, through air again, and into the room where he sat, waiting. Waiting for her.

His hand brushed her back and encased her like fire. Her breath brushed his hand, like kissing the center of the universe.

Thought like motion filling her. Her breath rolled over his hand. She drew a rough tongue across his skin.

Chosen, marked, and mine.

That was all.

She slipped back down the river, back through the tunnels she'd crossed, and into a more familiar skin.

When Jaguar saw that she was drinking tequila, she assumed she wasn't at Cutters, which only served beer. She took the shot, licked the salt, and sucked the lime. Then she looked around.

This was a downtown bar, and pretty deserted except for an old man who sat down the way from her. When he turned a grin to her, she noticed the distinct absence of teeth in his mouth. But as she checked the state of her clothes, which were uniformly bedraggled and wet, she didn't blame him for thinking she was someone who'd like to spend time with him. In the large mirror that hung behind the bar, she saw that her face was streaked with mud. There was something wild in her eyes, and her hair had a mind of its own.

She looked awful.

She raised her hand in the direction of the bartender. ''Another one of these,'' she asked.

One more, and then she'd try to figure out where she was so that she could go home.

8

"COOL," GLEN SAID, LIFTING A GLASS OF beer to his lips and drinking. "I mean, this is a really cool thing to do, Dr. A."

"Thank you for completing the sentence, Glen. Don't forget what you're here for, though." She turned to the cluster of students gathered around the wooden table in the food service area of Cutters Bar. It was a wings-and-things night—free wings with two beers—and crowded.

She decided to hold class here so that the students could get an idea of what ritual was from observing their own rituals, in their most familiar ritual setting. She thought that might help them connect the dots of learning and life, and she was also damn glad not to have to run a class. The chant-shape was making it hard for her to focus. Tonight all she had to do was make sure they were here, and that they didn't get too rowdy.

"Your job is to observe," she told them when they arrived. "Look as if you were studying a foreign culture. Notice gestures, and what they mean. Particularly notice gestures that are repeated, and see if they're repeated for the same reason. And don't drink too much, okay?"

"Would we do that, Dr. A?" Jesse Goodman asked, nudging her with an elbow and spilling some beer on her shoulder in the process. "Sorry," he said, taking a swipe at it.

She watched it soak into her white cotton shirt. Every good idea has its drawbacks, she thought.

"All right," she said, waving her money card at Jesse. "Make up for it. Go get me a Guinness. I could use it. And the rest of you—disperse. We aren't under siege here, you know."

"Sure—hey, anyone wanna play holodarts?" Joey pulled at Glen's arm, and they moved through the crowds toward the game area.

The others mulled around in tight knots of friends, not sure if it was really okay to enjoy themselves this way during classtime. Some wandered off toward the VR room to play Glendarrow. Others made for the empty bar seats. They'd get over their wariness in about another beer and ten minutes, she thought, and when Jesse brought her drink to her, she sat back and watched the show.

Steve was standing, stiff and unsmiling, next to Katia, who sipped carefully at something that wasn't a beer, and peered out over the rim of her glass wistfully at the people around her. Someday, Jaguar thought, Katia would learn to look to her own needs first, and then she'd be quite a woman.

A group of young men she didn't know stood laughing with some of her students, and she noticed the gestures made toward her. One of hers—was that Joey? Yes, it was—turned and waved. She wiggled two fingers at him, and nodded. He raised his beer and shouted over the din of the soundjuke to her.

"Hey, Dr. A. Does it count as a ritual when a guy wants to pick someone up and he's checkin' her out from across the room?"

This, followed by a punch in the arm from a young man in black clothes and dark glasses.

"It counts, Joey," she shouted back.

At the bar, Selica, Taquana, and a few other young women clustered in what looked like a deep discussion. But Jaguar knew better. Probably nail color was as deep as it was getting. Pretty soon they'd rise and visit the bathroom together like a flock of young quail. They emerged from their huddle and screeched in laughter, waved at her, then returned to whatever they were whispering about.

She hoped they'd get something out of this besides a hangover and a night off.

Jaguar let her gaze pass over the variety of faces and costumes and postures at the bar, and as she did so, she saw that one man's eyes stayed with hers. He sat at the far end of the bar, opposite her trio of students, and he was staring at her. She returned the stare, waiting for him to drop it first.

He didn't.

Okay, she thought. I can play that way. She continued to stare at him, making no motion with her body or her face. She could do this all night, especially since he was a rather fine specimen of maleness to consider so closely. Classic chiseled face, broad shoulders, blue eyes fringed with dark lashes. Not a bad view as far as she could see.

"Hey, Doc—oh, shit, look out."

She turned reflexively, in time to see a glass of beer arc over her head and splash across the table where she sat.

"Oh man. I'm sorry, Doc. I'm really sorry. Lemme get it, okay?"

She stood in time to avoid the trickle that ran directly

toward her chair, and grinned at Ivy, a tall and gangly woman who hadn't yet learned to control her length.

"It's all right, Ivy. I'm just glad they give you guys plastic cups. No, really. I was just getting up anyway. Was there something you wanted?"

Ivy looked at her blankly. "Oh, yeah. But I forget."

"Maybe you'll remember later. I'll be over there." She indicated the bar, which she walked toward, working her way around a pack of people who had jammed themselves in front of it, reminding her of a herd of cows clumped together in front of the feeding trough.

She leaned on the bar, waiting to get the bartender's attention, tapping her money card against the plastic-coated wood. It did not surprise her when a softer, older male voice spoke somewhere in the vicinity of her left ear.

"Pack animals, aren't we?" it said.

She twisted around and regarded the man who had been staring at her.

"Some of us are," she said.

"And every once in a while you find someone who's not," he commented, letting his gaze slide up her long legs, her slim torso, her breasts.

"I like your opening line," she said. "What's next?"

He laughed, and tossed back the remainder of his drink. "Nothing half so impressive. Just a little chatter. My name, then your name. What you like to do, what I like to do. Your job, my job. That sort of thing."

"And then?"

He took in a slow breath and put his empty glass down on the bar next to her. "I buy you a drink. Or I offer to."

"So far so good. Anything else—or just more chatter and an exchange of phone numbers."

He rubbed his chin thoughtfully, then turned to look around the room. "You wouldn't know it from in here, but there's a pretty moon tonight."

"Is there? And does that signify?"

"I think it does to you, Jaguar," he said.

She would be damned if she would let him see her surprised. She smoothed her face, and let her gaze run from the top of his head to his shoes. It was in the vicinity of his belt that she saw the transmitter and the sensor, both army style.

Shit, she thought. A brat. That was what she and Alex called army. Brats. And he knew her name. She saw no weapon, but he could have something small and interesting palmed. The army did like its toys.

"How do you know my name?" she asked.

He laughed again. "That gaggle of gigglers at the other end of the bar. I saw them wave to you, so I went and talked to them. They told me all about their assignment."

He raised a finger and ran it down the side of her cheek. "I like it. Shows style. By the way, my name's Phil."

"Nice to meet you, Phil," she replied, taking a very small step back. He was cute, but he was also army.

"How about a walk in the moonlight?" he asked. "I'm sure your students wouldn't miss you."

"But, Phil, you haven't even done the chatter part of the evening, much less the part about buying me a drink," she said disapprovingly.

"We could skip it. Or, we could do the chatter under the moon and the drink a little later."

"I don't think I'm interested," she said, and turned back to the bar.

A hand on her shoulder told her he wasn't taking it

well. She shrugged it off, twisted her neck around to face him, and said again, "I'm not interested."

As she turned, she could see Glen and another young man she didn't know watching from across the dining area. They seemed fascinated by the interaction, and she wondered if they had bets on what would happen next.

"Hey," the man said, "it was just an idea. I don't intend to push it if it feels that heavy."

"That's good," she said, and grabbed the bartender as he soared past her, ordering another Guinness, which he brought to her promptly. When she turned to find her way back to her seat, Phil was blocking her way. Across the bar, Glen nudged his friend and whispered something behind his hand. Great, Jaguar thought. What an example to set. In the corner to their right, she saw Katia staring openly, eyes wide with something that might have been anger. Anger?

No, she thought. Must be misreading that one. Katia never got angry. Then she saw that behind Glen was another man, tall and broad and blond, attending to her and Phil. She ran her eyes down his outfit, and saw the same sensor, the same transmitter at his belt.

And as she saw this, Phil reached over with his left hand and grabbed her by the wrist.

She didn't pull back, but only looked down at his right hand, cupped loosely open, and realized that she had approximately three more seconds to call this one. Did he have a stunner in his hand, and would he take her out of here unconscious, or was it all her paranoia? His grip tightened.

She called it.

Pressing the button at her wrist, she released the blade into the palm of her own hand and brought it slicing down the inside of his arm. Sleeve and skin parted like water, and he released her with a small cry of surprise rather than pain. It would take a few seconds before the blood appeared and he felt the rending of tissue. She sidestepped around him and would have been out of his way except for a very sodden student—not her own— who stood swaying and leering directly in front of her.

Behind the student, Phil's friend had planted himself.

She pushed at the semiconscious young man, who stumbled and knocked against Phil's friend. As he fell, he reached out and grasped her shoulder, almost bringing her down, and causing some commotion around her. At this point Glen waxed chivalrous and shouted, "Hey—leggo my teacher," as he came rumbling across the room like a heavy storm.

Drinks were put in pause between tables and lips while heads turned her way. By this time Glen reached her, pulled back his meaty arm, and swung.

The punch landed.

"What the fuck is this?" someone shouted.

"Mind your own fucking business," someone else shouted back. Jaguar slipped her position and found a place to stand away from the possibility of entrapment, remembering to take her Guinness with her.

When she could turn and watch, she saw that Phil was down and out, but his friend was still punching, and Glen was punching back. Taquana had jumped his back and was pummeling it soundly, but another young woman she didn't know was trying to pull her down.

"Odd," Jaguar commented to her brew, "I wonder if she knows Phil." Checking the young woman's outfit, she saw the standard army belt. She sighed. They were after her.

Taquana seemed to grow tired of being pulled at, and jumped off the man's back to turn on the young woman, ripping with gusto at her blond hair. She came up waving a handful and howling gleefully to her friends, who were trying to make their way across the floor, which had gotten slippery with spilled beer. Selica got there first and rammed the blonde in the back with a head butt sufficient to bring her to her knees.

It was then that the pileup began in earnest.

Jaguar took a long draw off her Guinness and considered what she ought to do next.

She saw that most of her students—or the parts of them she could distinguish—were taking joyous part in the fracas. Peripherally, she saw Steve trying to hustle Katia to the door, and Katia resisting. That figured. She supposed she'd get in trouble for this, but right now she was primarily concerned that her students come out relatively unscathed, and who could tell what other weapons might appear in the now bar-wide struggle?

And then she heard the call.

Old friend, running to her.

Her skin tingled as she was pulled into the energy of the chant-shape, its power filling her, taking her over.

Now? she asked. *Here?*

But what choice did she have?

She relaxed. Breathed in beyond the din of Rank music combined with howls, screams, and hoots, breathed in to the space where events flowed around her and were not part of her, taking a moment, she welcomed her friend. She let go of herself and let herself be all of who she was.

In the bar everyone simultaneously experienced the distinct impression of a presence not normally associated with a bar fight. They heard the growl, saw the flashing eyes, felt the hot breath, the pulsing heart, the body in motion.

In a click of time all fighting ceased in surprise and fear.

"Jesus, Mary, and Joseph," someone whispered reverently.

Then it was gone. Whatever they saw receded into shadow, but the momentum of the fight was lost, and the security people from campus opened the door and looked around.

"Okay," one said. "What's the problem?"

Jaguar walked over to him to try to explain.

Planetoid Three, Toronto Replica

"Who is it?" Rich Forrest asked sullenly and groggily. He glanced at his bedside clock, noted the time was very late—or early in the morning, depending how you looked at it.

A voice barked at him on the other end of his line, and he sat up. "Yes, sir. I'm listening." He absorbed the information, processed the questions. "No, sir. I didn't give any instructions to take her. Of course not, sir. I'm following the agenda."

He listened more. Fools. Idiots. But so was Durk, for putting nonintelligence people in the project at all.

"All right, sir. I can meet you at 0900. Will he be there, too?"

No, of course he wouldn't. He stayed out of it, and took care of his own business.

Rich nodded, agreed again, prepared to sign off. But there was one more thing. He listened more.

"A—what, sir?"

Durk repeated his words.

"No, sir," he said definitively. "I have no idea what would cause that. Maybe—nerves?"

Durk's voice rumbled something to him, but he barely heard it. He was still chewing on the last sentence.

The three people assigned to Jaguar all swore they had been attacked by a great black cat.

9

"BUT, DR. ADDAMS, YOU CAN'T POSSIBLY expect these students to create their own learning in a— in a bar, can you?"

Jaguar regarded Emily coolly. "Actually, that's where they learn most of what they know. About how to be in the world. About how to be. And the legal drinking age in your state is eighteen, isn't it?"

"Emily," Ethan said, "it's quite all right. Really it is. I've spoken with Ja—Dr. Addams about University liability in these matters, and she understands the difficulty of our position when trying innovative pedagogies. It won't happen again, I'm sure."

"No," Jaguar said, "it won't. They've learned what I wanted them to learn from the experience, and we'll be moving into a new study unit."

"What?" Emily asked.

Jaguar shrugged. "We have other material to cover."

Emily began to look shocked, then turned grim. She stood and smoothed down her skirt, moved toward the door. "I guess I was foolish to expect better from you," she said. Then, to Ethan, "See you around seven?"

He nodded, smiled. She returned the smile and left. After she was gone, Jaguar tried to suppress her grin, but gave it up when Ethan threw his head back and laughed long and loud.

"Jaguar," he said when he'd recovered himself, "you really shouldn't torment her so. What has she ever done to you, after all?"

"I'm just telling her the truth," Jaguar insisted.

Ethan wiped at his eyes. "You're a wicked woman, but I suppose you know that. And in all seriousness, you must not bring your students to bars anymore. Or to— well, what would be worse? To strip joints, or to cy- bersex houses. If there's anything else, I can't think of it offhand, but you get the idea, don't you?"

"I believe I do. By the way, do I need to do the honorable thing with Emily and explain that I have no designs on you? Or did you take care of that after I left?"

"I wouldn't lie to her, Jaguar," he said. "I was hop- ing we could try another dinner. Soon."

She opened her mouth to answer, not sure whether she was about to accept or decline, when a tap on the door interrupted them, and Samitu stuck his head in the door. "Giving boxing lessons, Dr. Addams? Rumor has it—"

"Rumor has it she's a karate expert hidden among us to make bad martial-arts films, Samitu. Is there some- thing you wanted?"

Samitu chuckled, and waved a hand. "I just wanted to see if she had any bruises or whatnot."

"Not her. Better check the opponent, though. For signs of life."

He ducked back out, still chuckling, and Jaguar turned her hands palm up. "I suppose I'll never live it down," she said.

"Never. It is now inscribed in University legend."

And in student legend, too. They'd shown up at her office en masse that morning, to work off the lingering adrenaline.

"Did you see Glen?" Jesse kept saying until she listened. "Did you see him? I mean, he just went for the guy, and the guy went *down*."

"I saw him, Jesse. Glad I did, too."

Glen had flushed from forehead to neck and probably, though she couldn't see, beyond. "That guy was a real asshole, Dr. A," he mumbled. She had to agree.

"Glen, hell," Selica had retorted. "Did you see Taquana dancing around with that hunk of hair in her hand? I swear, she's making a trophy out of it."

Jaguar kept waiting for one of them to talk about the moment when something large and startling had appeared to stop the fight cold. Not one of them said a word. Either it had faded from their memories, or they were embarrassed to mention it. Whichever it was, she was relieved.

"Well," the dean said, "the important thing is that no one was hurt."

"Of course."

She rose to leave, and as she did so, he held up a finger to halt her. "Wait—are you aware that the rumors of the incident include reports of a very odd phenomenon?"

She shook her head. "What do you mean?"

"I heard from a student that what stopped the fight was the intrusion of a large black panther running in their midst."

Jaguar raised her eyebrows. "I thought serving hallucinogens at bars wasn't legal anymore."

Ethan turned his eyes up to her, and said nothing.

"Who reported that?" she asked.

"Steven," he said. "And Katia."

"Do they always act as your eyes and ears?" she asked.

His face went tight, and then he smoothed it out. "You know nothing of this," he said.

Not asking. Telling.

"Nothing. Maybe it's just hysteria, and given my name . . ."

He rubbed a finger up and down his nose thoughtfully. "Yes. Of course. But these rumors, once started, are most difficult to quash."

Jaguar moved toward the door of his office, then turned to speak before she left. "I'm sure," she said, "you'll do what you can to take care of it."

"Jaguar," he said. "Dinner again?"

She smiled. "Soon," she said, and slipped out the door.

She left Ethan's office and made her way toward the library, where she hoped to serve the dual purpose of hiding and getting some research done. She was continually greeted by faculty who never bothered to raise their heads in her presence before. She'd attracted attention to herself now, and she'd have to live with the consequences. As she entered the library, she felt a large hand descend on her shoulder, and instinctively she grasped it hard at the wrist. A deep rumble of laughter was the response. She turned and saw Leonard. She relinquished her hold.

"Sorry," he said. "I should know better than to do that—especially today. Surviving the aftermath?"

"Oh, Leonard. It's good to see *your* face, at least." And though she didn't know why, it was. Something comforting about him. Something solid and real, and suddenly she felt starved for that. "I'm surviving, but my reputation is shot to hell."

He grinned, and stuck his hands in the pockets of his down parka. "That's good. Now you don't have to worry about it anymore. So you wanna talk about it?"

"Not much to say. Rowdy kids. Flying beers."

He let his eyes focus in hers. "I thought you were gonna walk soft. Low profile and so on."

Keep it light, she told herself. He knows more about you than you want him to. More than he should. Don't show him more.

She tried on a grin. "Not my path, I guess. I'm going upstairs to look up a few references."

He gave a quick nod. "I'll come along, if you don't mind." He regarded her solemnly while she thought of different ways she could get rid of him, then gave it up. He came from a family of stubborn people. She knew the look. He was sticking, and she might as well get used to it.

They ascended the stairs and she turned toward the computer bank that carried abstracts and reviews of articles.

"What'd you need?" Leonard asked.

"Funeral rituals," she said. She chose a computer and Leonard found a spot at an empty computer next to her and stood leaning against the table as he watched her work.

"Davidson," she requested. "*Etiquette of Empaths*."

"Thought you were doing funeral rites," he said as he watched.

"Leonard," she said, "I don't know what the hell I'm doing and that's the truth."

He rubbed his chin thoughtfully, "I can see this," he commented.

The title appeared on the screen, and she flipped through chapters until she got to the section that she apparently wanted.

"*Tzok-ol,*" Leonard muttered over her shoulder. She ignored him and read.

> *The theft of empathic gifts remains a danger throughout the time it takes the spirit to pass entirely from the body. The Mertec name this soul theft, and their funerals guard against it. When a shaman dies, for instance, drumming and singing must continue for twenty-four hours after death.*
>
> *There is speculation among scientists who study psi capacities that it is possible to transfer empathic gifts from a living empath through the use of esper or telekinetic reading. How this would affect an empath is unknown, though Mertec tradition indicates that the practice is potentially deadly.*

"Esper," Jaguar muttered, staring at the screen, "and telekinesis." A form of reading. Easy for people with the touching arts. They run their fingers over the right parts, and read it. Stay open if they want to take it in. Her hand moved, and pushed the off button. She continued to stare at the screen.

"Esper and telekinesis," Leonard said. "That's a lot different from chant-shaping."

She twisted around to face him.

"Why do you know so much about me?" she demanded.

He surprised her by laughing in response.

"What? Did I say something funny?"

"No. Not really. It's just that if you put a thousand people right here in your place, not one of them would ask that question. They'd all want to know *how* I know. Not why.''

"I asked the right question," she said quietly. "Why do you know so much about me?"

He didn't hesitate. "Because of Katia," he said. "You're gonna help her. So I'm told."

She ran her hands roughly through her hair. She knew what that meant. He'd had a vision to ask for her help. But she wasn't doing anything blind. Not here. "That needs explanation."

"Yeah," he said. "I guess it does. You understand I don't have the complete picture, though."

She understood. She'd worked with an Adept for the last six years. "Give me what you can," she said.

He sighed. "She's in a tangle. Doesn't want to be what she is. You know what she is, right?" She gave him a neutral look, and he continued. "She's an empath, and she's scared. Somebody's scared her, and I don't know who, because she won't talk about it."

He stretched his hands out in front of him in a gesture that was familiar to her. Empaths did that when they were trying to remember what their hands had taught them in some encounter.

"What's it to you?" she asked. "Why're you involved?"

He blinked at her. "Because I'm here," he said.

Shit, she thought. He expected her to say the same. But she would not get involved, and didn't know that she could trust this man, even though she kept acting like she could.

"I'm not in a position to help anyone," she said coolly. "You asked why they sent me here, and the truth is I was sent by people who want to punish me. Maybe even get rid of me."

"Yeah," he said. "Like my great-grandfather got put in prison. And you're all pissed off about it. Especially at your supervisor, since there's no secret what you did for him. But you're here now, and you never know where your work is until you get there, do you?"

He let that sit in the air for a while, and she figured he knew that he was echoing Mertec philosophy. Keep walking. Your work is wherever you find it. He continued speaking.

"All kinds of people came to old Leonard's funeral. My grandmother told me about it. She said she didn't know most of them, but they all knew about Leonard Peltier. Some of them said he saved their lives. Said he was an inspiration, because he chose to stay alive, keep doing his work, even in prison. He didn't have to do that, but he did. He kept faith in faithless moments, they said, and that kept them alive. Just sitting in prison, he kept people alive."

Leonard was quiet, and Jaguar let the story settle in.

"Now that you're here, what're you gonna do?" he asked.

She looked away from him. What would she do? She'd chosen that when she accepted the chant-shape. She would take the ride and hope for the best. Beyond that, she hadn't a clue.

"When someone tells me the answer to that," she said, "I'll probably be the second person to know."

Planetoid Three, Toronto Replica

Brad's bright young visage on Alex's telecom screen looked amused.

"A brawl, sir. In a bar," he said. "I've been trying

to get you since yesterday. I didn't want to relay the message secondhand.''

Alex wiped a hand over his face. Brad thought it imperative to use the telecom for this. The line was easier to secure than e-mail, and he wanted personal delivery on it. Alex understood why.

"Give me the particulars," he said.

Brad hesitated. "You're secure?" he asked.

"I am."

"Okay. There were brats involved. I spotted three."

Brats. Their word for army. Three of them. Alex nodded. "What else?"

Brad looked a little chagrined, an unusual expression for him. It took a lot to knock him off his boat, which had a very even keel. "I didn't stick until the end," he said carefully, "so I didn't see this, but everyone's talking about it."

"Talking about what?"

"There's some rumor that a cat came in."

"A cat," Alex repeated.

"A big cat," Brad said. "Like, a panther. Some of them think it was a shadow. Others say they felt its breath."

A big cat, his mind repeated to him. In a barroom brawl. With Jaguar. He chewed on this thick piece of meat for a while.

Jaguar in bar brawls with brats. Big cats wandering bars. Big cats wandering his apartment. He tried out a variety of interpretations for these events, and found that only one would fit. He just couldn't believe she'd be doing it.

She was chant-shaping. She was walking in her power.

In a bar brawl, for God's sake.

Maybe she'd finally gone mad, after all. But he knew that when she appeared most off center, she was actually spinning directly toward some hidden goal. But what goal, and why?

This art, one he did not share with her, was the one that most defied description, and perhaps the most carefully protected by the few people who used it. Those who chant-shaped were calling on their essential being, pulling something from another energy level into this one. It was an energy undiluted, unbounded by space and time, surfacing from unsounded depths, and curling itself to the contours of matter. To use it required a willingness to give yourself over totally, relinquishing all notions of control, and the strength to bear up under a fierce and unwavering core of energy, direct from the realm of the spirits.

It would feed you. It could eat you. It was Jaguar's art.

"Imagine," Jaguar had said to him once, "that you can find the absolute center and origin of the universe, and kiss it. Now imagine that it kissed you back."

That, she told him, was what it felt like.

She was too respectful to use such a powerful art just for the fun of it, too knowledgeable to treat it lightly. And, she knew it was the height of folly to expose herself as someone who had such capacities, on campus where an antiempath movement was going strong. Where brats were watching her, which she must know if there was a brawl.

This was a lot to chew on. A quick rap on his door interrupted his meal.

"Thanks, Brad," he said. "Keep the telecom use to a minimum, okay?"

"Sure," Brad said. "Just thought you should hear this one straight."

"I appreciate it," Alex said, and clicked off the telecom. "Come in," he said.

Rachel's face appeared in the doorway of Alex's office.

"Some things you should see," she said.

"Walk it over," he said, gesturing her inside. He was about to tell her to close the door, but he didn't have to. She took a quick peek down the hall, shut them in, then pulled the inside lock.

Then she handed him a folder, which he opened.

He read, then swore softly. "He's still army."

"This is correct," Rachel noted. "I can't get at anything else about him, though. Classified Deep Red."

"That figures," Alex mused. He tapped his finger on the folder. Rich Forrest was still with the Pentagon. Consultant. What the hell was going on?

"Thanks," he said to Rachel. "What's the other thing?"

She reached into her pocket and fished up a printout, handed it to him.

"What's this?"

"Just look at it. It came in over my line, but it was addressed to you."

He stared at the printout, which bore the return address of the University library. It was addressed to him, and it had only one line.

See Davidson, Etiquette of Empaths, *pp. 25 forward.*

He stared up at Rachel. "Jaguar," he said.

He turned to his computer, where he had Davidson's book stored.

"Don't bother," Rachel said. "I looked it up already." She handed him another piece of paper, which had the text written on it, and waited while he read.

"Soul thieves," he said out loud. "Shit."

"I agree," Rachel said. She hesitated, then spoke in a rush, "I think you should go there and see her. Maybe she was right about the assignment being a setup. I think you should go."

"Rachel, you know I can't," he said.

"Well, why not?"

That was a good question. And the answer was—because.

"Brad's keeping an eye on her," he said, staying professional. "I have to keep track of our soldier boy."

Rachel frowned. "Alex, I don't want to pry into what's not my business—"

"Then don't," he said bluntly.

She flushed, then pulled herself up to stand straight and stare him down. "Is there anything else you need, sir?" she asked formally and coldly.

Great, he thought. Another woman pissed off at him. As if he'd done anything wrong.

"What the hell am I supposed to do?" he asked. "Spend my life chasing after her? I've got other Teachers, and a helluva lot of work here, where I belong. And if she continually gets herself into trouble, is that my problem?"

"No," she said, "but something is."

"What? What's my problem?"

"Your problem," she said, "is that you can't face your problem. Maybe when you do, you'll see that you should be down there with her."

She turned, and walked out the door.

"Rachel," he said in the wake of her absence, "you've been learning far too many lessons from your mentor."

He waited to make sure she wouldn't return. Then he reached for his telecom and dialed the research offices, requesting Rich Forrest. But he wasn't there. Out of the office, expected back in late tomorrow.

Dammit. Delays. Just when he didn't want them. He picked up his telecom and punched in Forrest's code again. This time he left a message on his primary voice mail service.

"Rich," he said, "Dzarny here. Let's talk about what research I can help you with beyond prisoner profiling. I think you'll be interested. Give me a call."

That should do it. He wouldn't be surprised if he got a call back by the end of the day. The army loved Adepts. Adepts, and Telekines. And if he could get into their computer files, he might find something out. That made more sense than Rachel's advice. Although he had to admit she was right about one thing.

There were some problems he wasn't quite ready to face.

10

"IT WAS ABOUT AS STUPID A STUNT AS I could imagine," Durk said, tapping a wooden finger against the highly varnished conference tabletop. Here, where he always sat, the varnish was worn from his years of tapping in the same spot, with the wood of a hand that others said he had cut off himself in order to evade capture by his Euromarket equivalent. Intelligence General Lieutenant Matt Durk was head of special operations for the psychological investigation unit of the army. He had held this post for almost fifteen years.

"You said we should tag her," Phil Dormantof said, remaining surly days after the events at the bar. He'd been treated badly by the local police, and his arm hurt, and he supposed his neck would be in a brace for weeks. Damn kids.

"I said you should follow her," Durk barked. "And I said that if you saw the opportunity, you should initiate relations with her. I didn't say you should knock her down and drag her out into the streets by her hair. Christ, it was stupid."

"It was those kids," Phil insisted.

Durk dragged his hand across the table, making a sound reminiscent of nails on chalkboard. "Keep your hands off her. Let the situation develop. Understood?"

He turned to the others who were seated around him. Three men and two women who would replace the now defunct surveillance team, along with Rich Forrest and Sabrian Lisboa, who were coordinating with the Planetoid people on the project. They all nodded.

He waved his hand in dismissal, and all three rose, saluted, and left the room.

Durk turned to Rich Forrest, who stayed behind.

"Sir," Rich said, "I'm concerned. I don't see why we have to cater to him this way."

"Then," Durk said, "you haven't worked with him long enough. And if you keep going this way, you won't ever. He's agreed to handle the Almadin business for us, by the way."

"Cleaner than he handled the last one, I hope," Rich said. "We had trouble covering him on that. And on those girls he likes to use as personal toys."

"He handled it," Durk said, raising his eyebrows. "He got the job done. And that's what you need to know about him. He always gets the job done. Do you understand?"

Rich shifted uncomfortably.

"Do you?"

"I understand."

"Good. How's cooperation on the Planetoid?"

Rich took in a deep breath and let it out. Here he felt on more solid ground.

"I caught a fish," he said. "Big one."

Durk's hand went *tap tap tap*.

"He called the office," Rich continued. He smoothed the papers in front of him, remembering their conversation, and a smile grew on his face. "Left a message for me, offering himself for research. I called him back a little while ago. Asked him what kind of help research, and why. He said, whatever we wanted, because he's gotta think ahead. After what the Board did to Jaguar, he said he figured he better make sure his ass is covered."

Durk lowered his head. Thinking through the possibilities, Rich knew. If he didn't know better, he'd think the old bastard was an Adept, but he'd seen his testing run and there was no sing of psi capacities. He was just expert at keeping his cards close to his chest.

"Okay," Durk said, "Go ahead and run the tests on him. The specialist'll want the results to study. But don't go any further until you hear from me. And be careful. He's slippery"

"I'm not an ignorant rookie," Rich commented.

"I know," Durk said, "but sometimes you seem to play one on TV."

Emily Rainer threw open the door to University President Carol Johnston's office and strode across the carpet to her desk, with a nervous secretary hot on her heels.

"Get her out of here," Emily hissed.

President Johnston nodded her steel-gray head at the secretary, who left, and closed the door behind her.

"Not her," Emily said. "Dr. Addams."

She leaned back and pressed her hands together on her lap. "What's wrong, Professor Rainer?" she asked.

"What's wrong? Oh, what could possibly be wrong?" She leaned her hands onto the sleek and clean surface of the president's desk. "You know what's wrong. You've got to stop this. Get that woman out of here."

"Emily, please—"

"Look," she said, "I've been playing it your way. Watching the students, diverting attention from him, but it's getting out of hand. Do you have any idea what she is, and what she can do?''

"Stop it," President Johnston snapped. "Shut your mouth now."

Emily drew back and stood staring, eyes glittering sharply. The president regained her calm demeanor, her deeply lined face drawing itself into an expression of confident authority. "It's true that you've given good service up until now, and that will be remembered in your tenure process, in spite of your limited publications. But you must not be speaking of these matters to me or to anyone. Do you understand?''

"Do you know what she is?" Emily repeated. "And do you know what he's doing?''

"I know she's a qualified professor, and her presence is an important part of our progress in some crucial matters. There's nothing else I need to know.''

Emily looked at her as if she was lower than a flea on a bloodsucker. "Never mind," she said. "I'll take care of it myself. She won't hang around long if she knows she's just a rat in your lab.''

She turned on her heels and left, banging the door shut behind her. President Johnston picked up her telecom and punched in a code.

The face that appeared on the other side belonged to Matt Durk. "We've got trouble," Carol said. "Emily Rainer.''

"Tell me," Durk said, and Carol did.

"She's buckling, Matt. I think he's doing something to her. Her eyes—they look like those other girls. It's something he does to them and he does too much of it.''

He said only, "I'll report it.''

She hesitated. "What will he do?''

Durk shrugged. "What he thinks is best.''

"You don't have control over any of this anymore, do you?"

"I have what I need," Durk said.

"And your ass isn't hanging out naked over the line. How about getting me what I need?"

"Your funding source is secure."

President Johnston clucked at him petulantly. "I recommended against letting her know any of this in the first place. She was not my choice."

"She was the best choice because she's got the most at stake," Durk reminded her. "And she's been doing her part just fine—until lately. If you ask me, she's jealous."

"Jealous? Now, there's a sexist mind at work."

He shrugged. "I know what I'm talking about, and I know what I'm doing."

"I just wish," Carol said, "you'd let someone else in on the secret now and then."

Planetoid Three, Toronto Replica

Alex looked around the new equipment the Ivory Tower people had brought in and estimated its cost. Three new Teachers and another shuttle were his results. Between the Pentagon and the University, they were doing okay. He turned a tight grin toward Rich.

"Where do we start?" he asked.

"We'll do the standard interview then move on to some of the physiological stuff," he said.

"I'd bet the omega wave scan is first," Alex noted, running a finger across the smooth laminate of the lab table and enjoying the sensation.

"You got it," Rich agreed.

"So," Alex said, "what if I fail it?"

It was then Rich's turn to grin. "We'll probably kill you, and then ask for our money back. In that order."

"That's what I thought," Alex said.

The omega wave scan was the most accurate detector of lies that either the army or the criminal justice system possessed. It could spot a misplaced word within a sentence, if that word created a lie of the whole, based on a scan of the waves that the amygdala, organic keeper of fear, produced as the lie was told. He knew he'd have to take this test, and he knew he'd fail it utterly. It might, he thought, prove to be a problem.

When Rich returned to the Planetoid, they met for lunch and Alex told him he was looking to get out of Planetoid work and into something new. He'd gone on to express an interest in returning to the army. Rich looked at first shocked at Alex's knowledge, then relieved that he wasn't going to blow the whistle on him, then pleased that Alex was in.

"We'd make it worth your while, Alex," he said.

The army, he thought, always showed its appreciation. He'd grant them that.

"So let's start," he said to Rich. "Might as well, right?"

"Might as well."

Rich led Alex to a computer and called up the standard interview and life-history-information form, which Alex began to fill out. Rich said it would take him about half an hour to finish it, and then they'd start hooking up the machines. That didn't give him much time, especially since he wasn't sure what he was going to do.

"You hang around and watch?" Alex asked as he began keying in codes.

"That's my job," Rich admitted.

"Dull," Alex said.

"It shouldn't take too long."

Rich went to his desk and sat while Alex continued his task and tried to think through his next set of moves. He couldn't decide anything ahead of time, because he had no idea what the setup would be until he saw it. And now here he was. He assumed that Rich, who worked directly with a variety of psi areas, wouldn't be particularly susceptible to empathic tricks, and would probably spot any attempt pretty quickly. A convenient emergency phone call would be nice, but he had no way of arranging for that now.

He looked down and considered his hands. There was that. And, he supposed he could implant an empathic suggestion during unconsciousness. He sighed, stood, and stretched.

"Hey, Rich," he said, "got anything like coffee around? I had a late night."

Rich looked up from his desk and indicated the pot tucked in the corner behind him. "Help yourself."

"Thanks. I will."

Alex walked to the pot, poured into a mug, added sugar, and stirred.

"Sorry," Alex said. "Don't mean to bother you, but—milk?"

Rich straightened, turned toward him, and reached toward a small refrigerator unit under the pot.

"Perfect," Alex said, put out a hand, and grasped the appropriate nerve at the base of the skull. "Many people," he said as Rich's eyes rolled back, "prefer the nerve that runs through the shoulder, but this one that I'm utilizing has the advantage of a longer period of unconsciousness. In fact," he added as Rich went down, "it should last at least half an hour."

Alex propped his friend over his desk and went

through his pockets for clearance keys. He found two. One for this room and another that was unlabeled. He let it rest in his hand, giving himself time to sense the relationship between it and the doors within this building. Giving himself time to see the web that wove itself around this item.

"All right," he said after a while. "I'll give that a shot. And one more thing."

He did something empaths are particularly warned against doing. He dove into Rich's memory banks, stole a bit of information, and exited. The entry code for the program he wanted. Later Rich would develop a fierce headache, but he'd recover, so Alex wasted no guilt on that.

He left the room and turned left, found a set of stairs, and took them up two flights. At the top of the stairs was a door, and the clearance key slid into it easily, with no click announcing that someone had arrived. Rich's office.

He made for the desk and went through the drawers until he found Rich's personal computer. Then he went to work. First he had to shift the scanner's mix so it responded to his face and voice, since it was keyed only for Rich. Fortunately he'd spent enough years in the army to know how to adjust volume and visual codes for a temporary fix. Then he asked the computer for information on Peltier, who turned up listed as deactivated for at least twenty years.

Okay, he thought. That says something, anyway. He checked his time. Not too much of it, and he had many directions he could go in.

"Shit," he said. "Let's try the main problem."

He collated university and army to a third element. Jaguar.

The computer flashed at him. *Information unavailable.*

He typed in the code requesting reason for the unavailability, fully expecting to be told the information was classified. Code Blue if there was no current activity on her. Red if there was. He knew how to access both.

But the answer came: *Unrecognized element. Jaguar Addams unrecognized.*

Unrecognzied. Jaguar? The Pentagon had a file on her as thick as a brick. For her name to come up as unrecognized, she'd have to have been wiped out of their banks completely.

"That's not right," he mumbled. He ran the program again. Waited. It came up the same. And every move he tried to make gave him the same results.

As far as the system was concerned, she didn't exist. He stilled a moment of panic as the implications became clear.

"Shit. She's in Blackout code," he said. That was the Pentagon's deepest cover, for work that literally did not exist in any recorded fashion because it was too dangerous to record it.

He stilled a moment of inexplicable panic. She was right in the middle of an operation they weren't even running as far as any records would ever tell. And he couldn't break a Blackout code because there was nothing to break. No information available. She no longer existed, and that meant they could do anything they wanted to her.

He had to let her know.

He rose and exited without anyone taking note, made it back to the office, and regarded Rich's form. Before waking him, he went over to the files he was supposed to be filling out and made use of the send command.

The clerical staff might wonder at receiving a blank form, but it would take them a while to get to that point, and they'd never know it was his.

He returned to Rich, placing two fingers on his forehead. There might be more information here than in any computer, and aside from a headache, there's be no long-range harm done from scanning his mental files.

At the surface, he found meandering thoughts of lunch. A woman dressed in tight blue pants. A television show. He pressed in deeper, looking specifically for information on Jaguar.

Not much. Something about a fight with Durk. Matthew Durk. Alex knew about him. Durk wanted—what?

Don't think it's a good idea, sir. She's got a reputation for being difficult. I think our specialist bit off more than he can chew.

Then, a different presence. Different voice.

Leave it to me. You know nothing, and you'll continue to know nothing.

Alex pressed in deeper. Something here. Something.

Then, nothing. Like the information on the computer. Blackout. That same circling static that he found around Jaguar.

"What the hell?" he asked, and pulled his hand back, stared at it as if it had an answer for him. "Army got some new tricks?" he asked. No answer.

All right, then, he thought, keep it simple. He brought his fingers back to Rich's forehead and spoke into him.

You sure were tired, he said to the inside of Rich's brain. *So tired. You really needed to lie back and recharge your batteries. It was a good idea. Now you feel so refreshed, and Alex is done with his work, so you can move on to the next step.*

Good idea, that nap. Hope Alex didn't see it.

When Rich opened his eyes, Alex was sitting at his computer with his back turned. "Finished," he said, "and sent." He swiveled his chair around. "Now what?"

Rich rubbed his face, blinked twice, and stared at Alex, who sat kicking one leg against the leg of his chair.

"Oh. Done? That was quick—wasn't it?"

"I'm fast, Rich. You remember that about me."

"Right. Omega test is next," Rich said, and pushed himself to standing.

Alex, knowing what was coming, allowed himself a very broad grin. It would take them twenty-four hours to get the results, and he would be laughing all that time, thinking of the expression on Rich's face when he discovered he'd been played for a fool.

HE SENT HIS THOUGHTS TOWARD THE ASHTRAY, and it flew across the room, shattering against the wall.

A pointless exercise, but it felt good.

It expressed some of what he was feeling, though what he really wished was that he could take the damn army fools who attacked her and fling them against this wall. Take them, and then send a few other people after. Emily Rainer, for one.

She seemed to be going over the edge in a determined way. He lifted his hands to the light and looked at them. Maybe he'd created some long-term damage in the delicate unbalance of her mind. Molecular dispersion could have subtle results that took a while to show. There was something about the glitter in her eyes, and something about a similar look in Katia's, that he didn't like. Maybe it was time for her to go away altogether. Maybe that would help send his cause forward, because things seemed to be stalled pretty effectively.

Dzarny wasn't moving, and he should be. What kept him? Durk's idiots were acting like—like idiots. Emily was losing all control. She was terrified just because some boy from the Planetoid showed up in her office wanting contacts. It meant nothing, he told her, but even if it did, didn't she realize how easily he could take care of it? But she was panicked.

And now Jaguar was walking in her power, dangerous and beautiful.

A shudder ran through him, starting at the lowest vertebral neural synapse and spreading outward, upward. He blinked hard and reached out a hand. Felt for the source of the energy, which seemed to swim in the air around her. Elusive. Unique. Beautiful and hers.

"She is walking in her power," he muttered to himself. "She is walking."

He could feel it, pulsing through his hand, but he couldn't touch it, couldn't wrap himself around it the way he wanted to. Patience, he reminded himself. Walk slow and walk soft. This is all new. If he moved slowly into understanding, the pleasure of that could all be his.

If she didn't eat him first.

In her power, she might be capable of that. It was so hard to find out what a chant-shaper could actually do. They were so rare, and kept themselves so hidden.

He would like to feel her living body dance with his. Perhaps he could sing to her. There were many songs he knew that might work. Or, he could simply explore her with his own art. Touch her in places she hadn't been touched.

She would bring him what he wanted even more than he wanted her. Though he had to admit that the more he knew her, the more his desire for her grew. The means had become an end in itself, and he anticipated a great deal of enjoyment in achieving his goal.

His hand, aching for her, dropped back down onto the table. He'd have to consider what to do about Emily first. And perhaps it would be best to remove the boy who came to see her. He had a few ideas about that already.

11

''SHIT,'' JAGUAR MUTTERED WITH FEELING as she simultaneously caught the toe of her brown suede boot on a loose piece of tile and let slip a pile of papers from her hand.

She stooped down to pull the heel from the floor and retrieve the papers, stood, and straightened herself. Did a visual scan of her clothing. She was having a hard time keeping track of her mundane self. Her clothes. Her work. Did the students notice she looked distracted? Did she have her sweater on inside out? Did she have her sweater on?

She knew she was walking at night, because she woke in the morning disheveled and exhausted. Or she came to in odd pockets of the tunnels that she didn't recognize. At a faculty meeting, she'd felt the energy surge that presaged the moment, and had to excuse herself quickly.

She'd gone to her office, laid her head on her desk, and waited to see if it would pass, or lead her on.

Whispers spoke in her, thick as night. The information accumulated during night walks translated itself slowly into waking words. She was gathering information, some of it available to her waking self, and some of it not.

Katia needed to be watched. There is a soul thief waiting nearby. Make no contact.

But that was all.

Her people were riding her hard. It left her confused and liable to fall and hurt herself. She straightened herself, took a step forward, then stopped.

Slow darkness moved through her, then was still.

The strident sound of an angry female voice was coming from one of the offices. She heard it with preternatural clarity, as if it was next to her left ear.

She concentrated, locating the sound two doors down, and walked carefully toward it, minding that her heels didn't click as she went.

Then she stood very still and listened.

". . . chances are slim? How can you base *anything* on odds like that? I told you he's asking questions."

Both the office and the voice belonged to Emily Rainer.

"You might trust him, but I don't. And that girl's not stable."

Then a low rumbling male voice. She couldn't distinguish either the words or the person who spoke them. She moved closer, and found that it did no good. Emily's voice rang clear as a bell. The male voice was distorted, rumbling thunder that made no words.

"Let her go," Emily said, "That's what I suggest. You don't need her, even if you do want her—"

The male voice, interjecting.

She lifted a hand and put it out in front of her, trying to hear with her hand, then, just as quickly, she pulled her hand back and rubbed it.

No contact. Don't make any contact.

In her hand she felt a tingling, as if she had touched a humming wire, and nothing else. Somewhere on the other side of that door was someone who was using the arts, and setting up a cloaking that she had never encountered before.

The sound of Emily's laughter, and again her voice, this time quite loud. "I have *nothing* to lose by talking. Not anymore. You just *remember* that."

That sounded final enough to Jaguar. She quickly exited the scene, turning a corner, where she stopped and waited, listening as heels clicked toward her, then receded.

Jaguar waited to see who would come out of Emily's office next. This wasn't safe. None of it. But she had to know who, even if she couldn't know what or why or how.

The door to Emily's office stayed closed. She could wait longer, or she could knock on the door and see who opened. She sniffed the air for knowledge, and found none. Only a rippling in her skin, disturbed electrochemical responses, and the slip of night her only cloak, her only protection. Here we go again, she thought.

You are being watched. Walk now.

She straightened, glided silently down the hall, noted that the walls were a vision in infrared and she could feel her pupils dilating to read it.

Now. In time to the sighing, it emerged from her and not from her. Old friend. Circling slowly. Space curved back in on itself and walked in circles. She curved her body around it and let the curl of time she had become carry her down the halls, scenting the air for knowledge.

Go. Down the stairs. Go now.

Down the stairs and through the doors, into tunnels that were dimly lit, tunnels she saw in the leached infrared of vision available to her.

She scanned the corridor she was in. Saw it as familiar. She'd walked here already, knew the layout, where corner met door, where trash went, where great canisters of Arcon and Lacro were stored, where pipes became warm as heat flowed through them. She'd seen it with night eyes, in the darkness of reduced lighting. She'd walked many places, understanding them through scent and the infrared edge of vision. And the knowledge she gathered from these walks existed inside her without words, and was accumulating. It would be there for her when she needed it.

The corridor seemed to roll on with no breaks for quite some time, snaking Escher-like toward nowhere, or perhaps back toward itself. An optical illusion of unchanging landscape, giving you the feeling that you were going nowhere. That you were standing still.

She opened one of the black doors and walked on, toward what she knew were the dormitories. The tunnels narrowed here, and there were no lights because they weren't supposed to be in use. She walked, and quickly realized that someone walked behind her.

She heard footsteps trailing her, and she walked on.

The presence had a smell that was slightly familiar. A student? Katia? Steve? No. A smell she didn't associate with this place.

Hide. Now.

The directive propelled her forward, and to the shelter of a pile of desks waiting to be carted away for repair or recycling.

She sat, listening, feeling her own vision return to her. She swallowed, felt at her hands and arms. Put her hands to her face. All present and accounted for. And waiting for company.

There. Footsteps drawing closer. Closer. She could smell the human presence, sense when to leap and—

Now.

Her long arm reached out and grabbed a chunk of flesh, flung it to the cement floor, and held it there. She put her body on his back, holding one of his arms back, and with her other hand pinching hard at the back of his neck.

She waited for him to speak.

"Um, Dr. Addams," he said, "do you mind letting me explain this?"

She frowned at the body under her. She recognized that voice. Someone from Alex's office. She stood and flipped him onto his back. Stared hard.

"Brad?" she asked.

He sat up, rubbed at his arm. "Yes, Dr. Addams," he said. "It's me."

"Oh, for fuck's sake," she said. "What are you doing here?"

She put a hand down and helped him to his feet, then stood with her hands on her hips and tapped a foot. "Go on," she invited him, "explain yourself."

He breathed in and out deeply. "I'm keeping an eye on you."

"For whom?"

"Supervisor Dzarny," he said, and held a hand up to protect his face when he saw hers.

"Alex sent you? To watch me?"

"He was worried, Dr. Addams. He's—worried."

Alex was worried. Alex was worried. She was going crazy, and he was worried. In her fury, she turned glittering eyes like blades to Brad, stuck a finger in his face.

"Tell him," she hissed, and then she stopped.

Tell him what?

Something she needed to tell him. She listened. In her and around her, the swirling energy of the chant-shape moved. Alex had to do something. She had to tell him.

She raised golden eyes to a very surprised Brad.
Spoke into him and around him.

*Go back and tell him he must choose. Tell him. GO.
NOW.*

Within the vision that was filling her and becoming
her, she saw him retreat down the tunnels, running away
from her. Very fast.

Planetoid Three, Toronto Replica

Alex went directly home after the omega scan and tried
to telecom Jaguar. He tried five times, in five different
places. Each time the connection failed, not even allow-
ing him to leave a message. He debated leaving a message at the department office, making it sound urgent,
but was reluctant to make that public a move. Then
Brad's most recent report came through, and he was glad
he waited.

He'd had nothing new to report in the last week. No
one had tried to contact him about curing empaths. Nothing was new with Private Sanctions. He continued to
follow Jaguar, who was teaching, spending time with a
student named Katia Stone, with Ethan Davis. Yesterday, she went with Leonard to the local Serials memorial
and put flowers in the snow. She seemed a little distracted.

He thought of her, putting flowers in the snow. It had
snowed there. Somehow, he'd gotten through almost
three months without her. Somehow, the great gaping
holes she left in his life carried him through time anyway, though they still felt like great gaping holes.

Then, today, Brad reported that she'd spotted him following her in the tunnels. All was not well. Brad de-

scribed her as agitated. She said things he didn't understand. Something about Alex had to choose. She didn't say choose what. Implicit in her words was the command to stay away until he did choose.

Words spoken in the chant-shape were always the truth. Actions always had something true in them. That was the nature of the beast. Alex would like to pretend he didn't know what she meant, but he couldn't. Choose. Choose the truth. Stay away until you do.

He made dinner for himself, then found he was too tired to eat. A darkness folded around him. A malaise of almost sorrow. He went and sat in his rocking chair, stared out at the lake, and tried to think of nothing. Time moved around him slowly, carefully. His hand twitched in his lap, and he watched it twitch. Adept space, curving around him, unsought.

All right, he thought. Okay.

He waited for the falling to begin, relaxed into it, feeling boundaries dissolve around him as he was washed away into what would be. Into what would be.

Into rain forest, thick and steamy. Click and buzz of wings and call of birds. A river, and a log in the river that he stepped onto.

Wait. That's the past. Not right.

Stepped onto the log, and as it carried him downriver, he saw the great golden eyes of the jaguar, seeking him. Seeking him as his ancestors sought light and heat and sun.

Give me your eyes.

He turned to her, saw the golden fire she promised.

Her eyes pulled at him. He was already chosen. That was the truth. But he could refuse it. He had a choice, too.

As if I ever wanted one.

He felt her laughter resonate within him, saw her float away down the river as he swam up into normal time and space, opened his eyes, and blinked at his own reflection in the darkened window.

"What?" he asked, a short prayer to the deities that swarmed him. "What?"

And like their namesake, the jaguar people made no response.

He pushed himself up from his chair, and walked into his living room.

Choose.

He couldn't make the vision go away. He could only make her go away, as he had.

He took a deep breath. Walked over to the part of the living room where a dart set hung on the wall, and opened it, pulled out the darts, and stood back from the board.

He hefted a dart in his hands, felt the weight of it, let it rest on his finger in perfect balance.

Okay, he said to himself, so you want her. You want her in your bed. That's no surprise. She's beautiful and compelling and wild. What man doesn't look at her and feel a yearning? It's nothing to be ashamed of. But you've never made her pay for your unkempt desire.

He'd been willing to work with her in a growing cloud of unresolved sexual tension. He hadn't said a damn word to her about it, never plagued her with what he considered to be his problem.

What a saint, he chided himself. Saint and martyr. As if she needed his protection in that. She wasn't a child, and she wouldn't take offense at honest desire. She might not necessarily take advantage of it, either, but he wouldn't be harming her by telling her about it. So why hadn't he talked to her about it?

He closed his eyes, tossed the dart, and it stuck on the outside ring.

All right, then. Maybe it's more than that. More than lust. But he wasn't about to act on it even if it was. He was her supervisor, dammit, and he wouldn't breach protocol with her.

He tossed another dart, eyes shut, and it bounced off the board, fell onto the floor.

"Hell," he muttered. "I've never been her boss. Nobody has."

And that was the truth. When they worked together it was as a team, and an excellent one. She told him once that she didn't worry too much about getting in trouble, because if she had to quit her Planetoid job, she could always sign on with Moon Illusion full-time. Or go back to Jake and One Bird. Or teach at a college. She knew how to take care of herself, and never gave him more power than was his by innate talent or experience. His title meant very little to her. Even in this situation, she could have refused to go, resigned, walked away. That she hadn't was significant, though he wasn't sure what it signified.

He closed his eyes, stood swaying in the internal darkness, darts in his hands.

Tell me what, he asked himself. The part of me that knows. Just say it.

Choose.

He was chosen long ago. Soul work beyond his control. Spirits wandering, seeking sun and finding each other, waiting for the knowledge to become action and words. He had seen long ago. Now he was being asked to live it.

How can I? he asked, desperation in his belly. How can I?

How did you love something wild without either domesticating it, or being eaten by it?

Somewhere inside him, he heard laughter. He knew the answer to that.

Feed it.

You could live with something wild, as long as you kept it well fed.

He knew that. That was how he'd worked with her so successfully all these years. But no matter what he chose, she would always be wild, raw, untamable. What he found most valuable in her was what made all of this such a risk. Because even if he chose her, there was no telling what she'd choose. The stakes were too high, and the odds were too damn low.

Like stone hitting stone and making sparks, his words slammed into truth at last, and he knew.

He was afraid of losing her.

Afraid of trying, for fear of losing. Afraid of losing her entirely, to the wilderness she would always be. To the nature of the beast. Afraid she'd get herself killed, sleep around, reject him. He was afraid he'd have to live without her, and so he'd sent her away. It had, at least, given him the illusion of control.

He breathed into himself and let go of fear. Let go of his last shred of resistance to those golden eyes that pulled at him in the dark. Let the truth be named. Face it. Have done with it. It didn't matter what she chose. It didn't matter if he lost her. What mattered was that he chose to speak his truth, admit what was in his own heart.

It might end up hurting like hell, but his continued denial could kill her.

I choose you. I choose you, Jaguar. I choose you.

With his eyes closed, he drew back his arm and threw

the last dart, heard it catch with a thunk in the board.

When he opened his eyes, he saw it stuck firmly in the center.

Bull's-eye.

He leaned forward and covered his face with his hands.

12

JAGUAR JERKED HER HEAD UP FROM THE MASK
she was making and looked around at her students.

"Does someone want me?" she asked. Heads rose
above work in progress, but nobody said anything.

She'd heard someone calling her. Asking her—no.
Telling her something. But what? She shook herself.
Gone. It was gone.

The most recent studio effort of the group Moon Illusion was on the disk player and the students, in their
groups, were chatting, cutting out pieces of paper and
plastic, gluing together string and feathers and leaves.
She felt herself floating in and out of real time and space,
but the students didn't seem to notice.

They were busy making masks.

She set them up in small groups, each of which would
design its own brand of spirituality and ritual. They had
to learn what their options were before they made
choices. They had to see how their beliefs were inter-
connected with other systems of belief, see the overlap
between practice and belief. They had to argue with each
other, learn from each other, examine their backgrounds,
and get the feel of the sacred as it lived within them.

So she had them make masks of what they saw as

sacred in themselves, because how could they understand the multitude of ways people named the sacred and lived within it if they couldn't find where it lived in them?

She realized that for good or ill, she was conducting class very much as she conducted her work on the Planetoids. The students couldn't sit passively and listen to her talk. They needed to get their hands and hearts into the learning. And they were integrating their learning, too. Tonight, as they sat in their groups and worked on their masks, she could see that.

Jesse was making a mask of eyes. All eyes, with something like wings around the edges. Jesse, who wanted to work in movies. There. That was his version of the sacred. Very nice, she thought.

Glen's mask was a large and meaty hand gently cradling a hummingbird in the palm. He worked slowly, taking the utmost care as his own fleshy fingers carved out the image he sought.

When the class had discussed the idea of spirit guides, trading stories of interactions they'd had with wild animals, Glen told that once a hummingbird buzzed his ear in Grand Central Station.

"That was weird," he said. "A hummingbird, like trying to drink out of my ear."

"Not so strange," she said, "If you want to be a writer."

His jaw dropped open. "How did you—did someone tell you that?"

She shook her head. "The Aztec say that the hummingbird puts the song in the ear of the poet. That's their spirit guide. You want to write?"

A slow grin had spread across his heavy face. As it turned out, he did. It was a nice moment.

And then, looking over at Taquana's work, Jaguar saw that indeed she had kept the hair from the fight. She was using some of it to make herself a warrior woman's mask.

Katia's mask was a drifing of black cloth over a face that kept its eyes and mouth closed. She told Jaguar she'd painted something else under the surface, but she wouldn't say what it was. She just looked nervously at Steve when Jaguar asked. Katia was trying to please him and Jaguar at the same time. It was an impossible task, and one that made her lose sight of what might actually please herself.

Complicated kids, she thought. The first generation after the Killing Times. She had read that children of Holocaust survivors had borne the weight of generational fear, and assumed these young men and women had, in some sense, to do the same. Their parents' fears worked around and in them.

She walked around the class, looking at the work they were engaged in, commenting here and there.

"How you doing, Steve?" she asked, stopping at his seat. As he always did, he paused before answering, keeping his face turned from hers for a moment while he considered.

"Fine," he said. "Though I'm not sure this is what you want." He held up a piece of thick white paper with a human face on it. No surprises here. What you saw was what you got. She laughed, and moved back to the front of the class.

"Anyone need help?" she asked, turning the music down. "Ready to wrap it up for now?"

Maria, at the back, called out, "What do we do with these things?"

"You talk to them," Jaguar said. "Ask what they have to say about you."

"We can't," Steven said, shaking his head. "In our group's religion, that would be idolatry."

She gazed over at him. "Really? How so?"

He did not quite roll his eyes at her, but she could tell he wanted to. Katia spoke up.

"That's not true, Steven. Idolatry is when you worship something false."

Steve looked at her, surprised. "It's a false image," he said, pointing to her mask.

"Mine's not," she replied. "Is yours?"

Someone in the back of the class said, "Ooooh. Cut him down."

"That's an interesting distinction you're making," Jaguar noted. "How a group defines idolatry says a lot about how they'll run their lives."

She turned from him to Katia. "What makes your mask real, Katia?" she asked.

Katia stared down at the face she'd created, then back at Jaguar. "Because this is who I am?"

"That's not fair," Steven said, voice loud and high. Katia startled.

The room became hushed. Jaguar turned a neutral face to him. "Why not?" she said.

"You're asking us to assume a belief in spirits and soul and all that crap. What if we don't believe that? It's not fair to make us believe it."

"I'm asking you to name what's sacred in you, and make it into a mask. For a grade," she reminded him. He subsided into silence. Katia leaned toward him and put a hand on his shoulder. Jaguar, watching, sighed.

"Hey, how do you like this music?" she asked as an idea occurred to her.

A ripple of approval went through the class.

"Would you like it if I brought the musicians here, to talk to you about music as a container for the sacred?" It was, she knew, the one area where they felt the spirit move them. Inside music.

"How about if you just get them here to play?" Tony suggested.

"That, too," she said.

When class ended, she stayed behind, packing up materials left over from the mask making. As she worked, she heard soft footsteps coming back down the hall and toward the room. She stooped and picked up a ball of yarn from under a desk, then lifted her head to see who it was.

Katia.

"Hello. Forget something?"

"No. I—I just had a question."

"Okay. Here I am. Ask."

She moved her head this way and that, as if checking the room for hidden cameras. She brought her face close to Jaguar's and said, very softly, "How do you know?"

"How do you know what?" she asked.

"If you're an empath."

Katia's eyes were glittering. Her eyes were almost drugged or—like Emily's eyes.

Jaguar let the question rest a moment, then, as gently as she could, replied, "Most people know when they have to ask the question."

Katia's pupils dilated, and she sucked in air. "How can you say that?" she asked, quick and breathy. "How do you know that sort of thing? You could be wrong, couldn't you?"

"Couldn't she what?" a voice said from the doorway. Katia startled and spun around. It was Steven.

Jaguar intervened. "Katia was asking if someone couldn't make more than one mask, because sometimes you're more than one thing at a time," she said. "I was saying I think you can, as long as the masks agree not to fight with each other too much."

This last she said looking toward Steven. He strode over, grabbed Katia with one arm, and pointed at Jaguar with his other hand.

"You think you got it all figured out," he hissed. "You don't know shit. Wait and see."

He tugged on Katia's arm. "C'mon," he said. "Let's get the hell out of here."

Jaguar went to her office after class to sit and collect her thoughts. As she entered, she stepped on a piece of paper someone had slid under her door.

A note that read, *I need to talk to you. Meet me in B39, nine-thirty.*

No signature. Katia, trying to hide from Steve? Someone less friendly?

Jaguar read it over three times before she realized it would tell her nothing other than exactly what it said. She wouldn't know more unless she went.

She looked at the clock. Quarter of nine. Time to attend to a piece of business first. She'd promised her students Moon Illusion, and she knew Rachel could arrange it for her. She calculated quickly, to figure what Planetoid time would be. Working hours still. Then she punched in Rachel's office number and waited.

To her surprise, when the pickup came on the other line, it wasn't Rachel's face she saw.

It was Alex.

He moved toward the screen, eyes wide with surprise, face looking tired and tense around his surprise. They stared at each other, waiting for the cognitive dissonance to settle. It had been almost three months since she'd seen his face.

"I'm calling Rachel," she said at last.

Alex relaxed back into himself. "I know," he said. "She's out on a team assignment. I had her calls forwarded to me."

She was about to ask why, then realized she didn't have to. She was a big girl. She could figure out the answer on her own. He was hoping she'd call Rachel if not him.

"You look awful," she said.

He leaned back in his chair, placing a finger across his lips.

"You don't," he said.

"A little home rest leave does wonders for the complexion. How's everything there?" she asked.

He took the finger from his lips and tapped it thoughtfully against his chin. "Quiet, Dr. Addams."

"Enjoying it?"

"Not particularly. I miss you."

He could not see her hands, but he imagined them in her lap, clenching and unclenching, as the expression on her face darkened.

"Everything okay with you?" he asked.

She grinned at him wickedly. "Hey, how about them Jaguars? Going to the Super Bowl this year to beat the Packers."

"I don't think so," Alex said. "The Packers'll take 'em early and often."

"Wouldn't be too sure. You know how Jaguars are. Relentlessly wild."

"I know," Alex noted. "I know that. But the Packers have a little more patience. They can stick to the task.

Did you call Rachel to discuss the football pool?''

She backed off and returned to business. "No. I wanted her to help me get Moon Illusion here. For my students. I can call back.''

"No," he said quickly. Then, more calmly, "I can take care of it. What did you need?''

She tilted her head at him, questions forming themselves and dispersing in her eyes. She stuck to business. "What would the funding resources be for transport and payment and so on?''

"There's the prisoners' opportunity fund for transport. For fees—maybe Arts for Earth. When do you want them?''

"The last week of classes, or a little before. A few weeks from now. I know it's short notice, but I just thought of it tonight.''

That's all right. I'll take care of it. You have class Tuesday and Thursday, right?''

"Brad tell you that?''

A jab at him, and it hit home.

"No. I knew it before I sent him. Why?''

"Because I want you to stop playing Supervisor," she said acidly. "I don't work for you anymore.''

He kept his face quiet, took her anger full on. I deserve it, he thought.

"Jaguar, would it help if I said I'm sorry. That I owe you in a big way, and I'm here to pay up.''

She startled, and drew back. Alex pressed on. "There's something you need to know, and I don't want it going over the lines. Can we find another way to speak?''

"No," she said curtly. Bluntly. No explanation. But her eyes said not safe. No contact.

He frowned. That wasn't good. "I'll come to the

home planet. Tomorrow. We can talk then.''

"No," she said. "Don't."

"Why not?"

"I'll be out."

"Out?"

"With Ethan. We have plans."

"Jaguar—this is important. This is about—"

"I'll be *out,* Alex," she said. "Or, didn't I mention that Ethan's courting me assiduously? Leonard might be cajoled along those lines, too, if I put my mind to it. The room'd get a little crowded with you there, too."

He stopped, and looked at her hard. He noticed how carefully closed she was keeping her face as she spoke. This was more than anger. This was caution in the face of an unknown danger. Was she trying to keep him away, tell him something, or just keep him quiet?

"We have to talk," he said. "You need to know—"

"No," she snapped.

She leaned toward the image of his face and opened her mouth to speak, then, unexpectedly, gave a short gasp. She pressed a hand against her eyes.

Jesus. What was that? He held out a hand, as if he could touch her through the screen.

And he saw it. The energy flow, as visible to him as if someone had poured a bucket of water around her. There, circling her, and becoming her. She, becoming that other self, and yet not changing. The shifting of space and time around her, like light, like water, like fire.

"Beautiful," he murmured. "So beautiful."

And a voice speaking to him directly. Not over the wires. Not empathic contact. Something else. As if it strolled in the room with him, rough fur under his hands, golden eyes pulling at him, hot breath on his face.

Not safe Don't talk don't tell nothing don't say not safe.

"Okay," he said quietly, "Okay. But how can I—dammit, don't cut me off."

This last in response to the sudden blurring of the screen. It flickered, and her image was gone. He stared at his telecom.

"Dr. Addams," he said, and noticed that the machine was still registering for sound. He couldn't hear her, though. Where was she?

"Dr. Addams, if you can hear me, put this in your mental file—you've been coded by the—dammit, Jaguar, answer me."

He brought a fist down on his desk, making the telecom jump, but doing absolutely no other good in the world.

She flipped off the telecom and sat staring at the blank screen while she rubbed her temples with her fingers. What had happened?

She could hear his voice, but she couldn't see his face. Did he cut her off?

No. Something else did. She knew this. Knew this.

But there was something else she was supposed to do. Tonight, before she went home. Something to do with—with whom? Her brain was suddenly void of the capacity for thought.

You're exhausted, she said to herself. Walking in power and playing pretend don't match. There was an elemental truth being spoken in her, and it took too much energy to engage with it and hide it at the same time. It was wearing her out. And there was something else she had to do tonight. Something.

She looked around the room as if the answer would

be there somewhere. It was. The clock on her wall told her she was fifteen minutes late for her meeting, and how the hell did that ever happen. She cursed prolifically, pushed herself up from her chair, and without grabbing her coat or turning off her lights, left the office, shutting the door with a bang.

She jogged down the halls and deferred use of the elevator in favor of the stairs, which she took two at a time. She might still make it, she thought as she hurtled down the hall toward the basement level.

Then she was at the door to B39, staring down the empty hall, standing still.

Nobody was there.

''Dammit,'' she exclaimed, and then stood, breathing hard.

The sound of motion down the hall caught her attention. She moved toward the door to the tunnels, stood, and pressed her hand against it. Someone in there. She pushed it open.

She walked a few steps down the tunnel and stopped again. She walked slowly, stopped to listen, then walked on. She walked, stopped, listened. Walked. Stopped. Listened.

Someone else was walking with her. Someone behind her, walking in time with her steps. They stopped when she stopped, only a faint echo of presence remaining. Brad again?

Not safe. Not safe. No contact.

The chant-shape moved inside her like a perturbed cat rolling out of dreams. She walked forward, past broken desks piled by the side of the wall, past cans of garbage heading for recycle or burn. She walked past a row of canisters labeled ARCON: HIGHLY VOLATILE. The footsteps behind her stayed their distance. The path rolled sharply downhill ahead. She walked under the tubed lighting that seemed to dim here.

Her foot slipped under her. The slope was steep and the cement worn smooth. Behind her she heard laughter and resisted the urge to go faster. To run. The lights flickered. Something wrong.

She stopped at the crest of the downslope. Darkness clicked in. Absolute darkness. No ambient light available.

Not safe. Not safe.

Her eyes peered through the dark and saw the colorless figure ahead of her. Someone. Someone walking. Now stopping and standing, looking at her. Staring at her. She made her way delicately down the cement slope. It was Emily, her starched white blouse the only visible light. She stood at the bottom of the slope, staring, eyes wide with terror, her entire body quivering.

Emily. Not safe.

"Emily?" she asked. Behind her she heard laughter. She turned to it, saw nothing. Turned back to Emily.

"Don't," Emily hissed. "I have to tell you. I can't hide for them anymore."

Jaguar walked toward her, whispered, "What is it?"

Emily shivered. Her skin began to ripple, as if each layer of molecules adjusted itself slowly, shifting in directions they weren't meant to go. A gurgling emerged from her throat, which she clutched with her hands. Blood appeared on her white blouse, a growing stain across her chest, and Jaguar ran, not sure if she was in her chant-shape or just herself, not sure if she was followed or not. The lights undimmed, flickered on and off strobelike, showing her Emily's form falling over and over, continuing to fall and bounce off the wall and bounce into a garbage can, against it, slouching onto it, falling behind it.

Jaguar slipped and came down hard on her knee, unable to sound for depth in the flickering lights. She stayed down and felt her way toward the sound of expelled air, a sigh that kept repeating itself. Emily Rainer lay hunched behind the garbage cans, her lungs working against all laws of differential pressure as she tried to breathe through the great slash across the front of her chest. Jaguar pressed her hand against it.

"Emily?" she asked. "Emily?"

Her hands moved over the pool of blood and someone was talking, trying to whisper and shout at the same time.

"Dr. Addams?"

She looked up. A young man emerged from behind the row of Arcon canisters up the slope.

She frowned.

"Dr. Addams," he whispered urgently. "It's Brad. You have to get out of here. There's someone following us. I saw—"

He stopped speaking, in response to the low rumble that began behind him. The canisters were moving. Rumbling. Shaking. Arcon. Volatile and explosive.

"Brad, *run*," she screamed, but instead he twisted slowly around to see what was happening behind him, twisting under the flickering lights as she heard laughter and saw the canisters fall, saw the ball of flame explode out toward him, through him as he exploded with it, and she flung herself over the body of Emily Rainer, into the only protection offered by the garbage cans against the wall.

13

Planetoid Three, Toronto Replica

ALEX WAS ALMOST AWAKE WHEN THE TELECOM next to his bed buzzed. He picked it up and saw Rachel's face.

Stricken would be a good word to apply to it.

"What?" he asked.

"Trouble," she said. "Big trouble. There's been a—a murder on campus."

Alex felt the blood leave his face as his hand clutched for the edge of anything to hang on to. "Rachel," he said, and could find nothing else to say.

"They found her in the tunnels," she said. "Alex—her heart was—gone. Just gone."

"Rachel," he said again, unable to squeeze out anything else.

"She was a professor. In Jaguar's department. Emily Rainer," Rachel said, then she blinked at Alex. "Oh, God. Did you think—you didn't think it was—oh, God. I'm sorry."

Alex felt oxygen return to his brain, his heart begin to beat again. She wasn't dead. Not dead. Not murdered. Not too late.

Adrenaline raced around his body, and he let it. "Is Jaguar—okay?"

"Sort of. She was at the scene of the crime and there was an explosion of some kind. I don't have all the details. She's not hurt, I don't think, but she's being held for questioning."

"Shit," he said. "Figures. Did she call for an attorney?"

"No. The cop shop called here. She gave my number. Alex, there's more."

He waited.

"Another body was found at the scene. Pretty badly burned. They couldn't ID it, which is why they called. To see if it was one of ours. I guess they found a code chip they thought was Planetoid material."

Brad. It would be Brad.

"Hell," he said. "Hell." He glanced up at the shuttle schedule on his wall. Next one out wasn't until four in the afternoon. He'd have to get a special requisition.

"Get get Jill on it. She's Jaguar's usual legal counsel, and about the only woman I know who isn't flustered by this sort of shit. Apprise her of the situation. Tell her I'm getting a special rec and we'll leave in an hour."

He hung up on Rachel and called in his seat reserve.

Lieutenant Durk tapped a wooden finger against the table, pressed his face to the computer monitor, and read.

A murder on campus. Dzarny was on his way. Forrest wanted to know how long they should stick around, or if the project could be called complete at this point.

Twitchy man, Durk thought. The murder threw him. Granted, it wasn't in the plans, but it wasn't out of the reach of probability either. And it made sense. She was getting out of hand. Going out of bounds. Something had to be done. Pretty high profile, but it could be covered. Forrest was twitchy about it, though. But then again, he'd worked research for a lot of years. That tended to make people twitchy.

He understood why. Working with people like their specialist made him want to twitch. If he was naturally inclined that way, he was sure he'd be nervous. But he wasn't. He sent a response: Stick, but prepare to move out quickly. Await notification of status change.

That was all. For Durk, the most important factor to consider was Dzarny, who was on his way. Durk leaned away from the computer screen and considered it.

Dzarny would arrive by the afternoon. Probably he'd be busy for a while. Durk would let him take care of business before contacting him. Then they'd talk. Durk would find out Alex's plans and make his accordingly. He knew all his options, and the consequences of each one.

The only thing he didn't know was what the Addams woman would do next. He wished she was a little more predictable, but he'd have to work around that. He didn't trust her to cooperate, or else he'd talk to her directly. He considered it again briefly, wondering if she'd do it for Dzarny's sake. No. She wouldn't trust anything the army had to say, and he couldn't blame her. Not even a little bit. If he was in her position, he'd have a good laugh at any proposition the Pentagon threw at her.

No. He'd trust his first instinct. She'd have to come through, whether she wanted to or not.

"Look, I'll say it one more time in English, and then I go to Mertec since you'd probably understand that about as well as you understand your mother tongue. I was in the tunnels because I got an anonymous note from someone asking me to meet them. The blood on my hand is Emily's. I got it trying to press her chest closed.''

Jaguar held out her left hand, which was lightly stained. They hadn't let her wash it until they took any number of pointless samples.

A large and rather corpulent man named Keene stared down at her and said, ''Sure, sister. C'mon. Why'd you kill her? And what did you do with the heart?''

Jaguar rested her head in her hands. ''I ate it,'' she muttered.

''What?''

She brought her face up to stare at him with fiery eyes. ''I ate it,'' she said. Keene's eyes widened, the pupils dilating. She held out two fingers and began to growl.

''What the—you some kind of fucking witch?'' he stuttered, backing away. ''Cut that shit out—hey, Dolaski, get in here, would ya?''

Keene backed toward the door and exited, locking her in the interrogation room.

That was better. At least she could get a few minutes alone. They'd been at her all night, holding her as a material witness in the local cop shop. She knew she could make them either arrest her or release her after a certain point, but she figured she might as well stay here and see if she could learn anything. It might even be safer.

She pulled up the only other chair in the room and rested her feet on it, slumped back as far as she could in the other chair, and closed her eyes. Maybe she'd practice sleeping. See if she remembered how.

She was burned and bruised and shocked and splattered with blood. Bruised and charred and wild-eyed from being overtaken by her chant-shape. Her chant-shape, which was keeping her alive, protecting her from whatever sliced Emily's chest open and dissolved her heart.

She shuddered.

Telekine, esper, Adept. Who was on campus, capable of doing that? Someone working for the army? Telekine, esper, Adept. It had to be a Telekine. She didn't know of any other art that could shred flesh in that precise and layered way. Telekine. Precise. Accurate and fast as lightning.

But who?

It could be anyone. A Telekine could operate from anywhere on campus, could be moving parts of her she didn't even know she had, if they were good enough to get through her closing. Of course, when she walked in her power, she wasn't closed. Just elusive. Slippery as a shadow.

And alive. Still alive, if she could stand the ride. As she began to feel the soft drifting of sleep encompass her, the door opened, and someone cleared their throat.

"Flu season's such a bitch," she commented.

"Funny," a familiar voice said, "that's exactly what these fine officers keep saying about you."

She drew herself up in her seat, and let her feet fall hard on the floor. Alex walked across the room and pulled up the chair she had been using, and sat down facing her.

He wondered how she managed to look exhausted and radiant at the same time. It must have been the chant-shape showing in her eyes, in spite of smears of blood and soot and fatigue on her face.

"Hello, Alex," she said, leaning back in her chair, relaxing. "What's the matter? Bored with the Planetoids and want a nice fat cop to deal with for a change, or am

I your assignment when I'm sentenced to Planetoid Three for murder?''

Okay, he thought. At least he knew what mood she was adopting for him. He decided to sidestep the bullshit.

"Was Brad in the tunnel with you?" he asked.

He saw her shoulder twitch. "You should know. You sent him."

"I did," he confirmed. "Now I have to ID what's left of him."

"You must feel like shit about that, too," was her only comment.

She was right. He did.

She picked at a torn nail. "Go away, Alex," she said.

"Why, Jaguar?"

Her eyes, hooded and closed, told him nothing. She pushed her chair away and stood, turned her back to him, arms crossed at her chest, staring at the wall. "See Davidson," she said, "*The Etiquette of Empaths,* pages twenty-five forward."

"In spite of my recent stupidity, what makes you think I'd leave you alone to face that?"

She didn't move.

"Jaguar," he said, "look at me."

"No," she said. "I want you to leave."

"Then look at me and tell me that."

She turned around and her face twisted into motion, but no words emerged. She made a sound of frustration and turned back to the wall, gave it a kick. He felt some sympathy for her. It was difficult, that truth thing. But right now he would work the advantage.

"I came to tell you two things," he said. "First, the army's got you listed under Blackout. You're in the middle of an operation."

She went very still, which was her way of expressing surprise. Then he saw her shoulders lift and fall. "What's it to you?"

"That's the second thing I came to tell you," he said.

He felt her absorbing his words, knew she read his tone as well. Her body tensed as if for a fight, and she swung around to him, her face painted with soot and blood, hair wild as a solar storm, eyes a holocaust of flame, unwilling to yield to any power except the one she walked in now, clear as the night sky.

Jaguar, as she really was. In her power. Beautiful and dangerous.

I choose you. I choose you.

He stood, pushing his chair over.

"I'm not leaving," he said. "I came here because I should never have let you go."

He walked toward her, and he kept his eyes with hers. She held a hand up as if warding him off, holding him back, but he kept walking.

"Stop it," she hissed at him. "You don't know. It's not—you can't be here."

"Jaguar," he said, "I *am* here. Where I belong. With you."

The truth. There it was. He had chosen, and felt the relief of that.

"Stop it," she said. "Stop it. You can't. You don't know. You are not to *think* of me that way."

He took one more step, wrapped his hand around hers. "I already do."

She stood poised inside his thought, and he waited to know what she'd do next. Push him away. Hit him. She could do anything and it would be fine. Anything, if he could stand here with his hand on hers for one minute more.

She breathed in, and her breath emerged from her as a moan, a fury of longing in her eyes. She moved her hand to his face, exploring it as if she'd never seen it before. Then she pulled him to her and kissed him.

I choose you. I choose you.

Her lips were warm, the length of her pressed into his flesh was a fire barely contained. He twined his fingers in her hair and held her here, in this moment, tasting her, tasting the essential power she was walking in, tasting all of who she was, to the bottom of her wild soul.

Like finding the center of the universe and kissing it. Like having it kiss you back.

He knew now what she meant by that.

Then, abruptly, she pulled away and stared at him hard. When she spoke, her voice sizzled like the edge of a star.

"And what would you do with all *that* in your bed?" she asked him.

He opened his mouth to tell her, specifically and in great detail, but never had the chance to speak.

The door opened, and Keene returned with his partner in tow.

"Addams," he barked, "we're releasing you."

"Dammit," Alex said under his breath. "Fucking cops."

She closed her eyes and pressed her hand to her face, swaying as she stood. When she turned her face up, she was herself again. The moment was gone.

"Was it something I said?" she asked brightly.

"Your attorney called. Said we'd better. For now," he said, looking disgusted. "Go to the desk and one of the women'll take you downstairs so you can wash and get the rest of your things."

"*What* a disappointment to be leaving. I so hoped we

could continue our discussion of Kafka's metaphysical
approach to pain as it relates to effete ineptitude in the
criminal justice system.''

"Yeah—well, don't leave the city. Got it?''

"I got it. Wish I could get rid of it.'' She patted Keene
on the back and turned to Alex, wiggled a finger at him.
"Bye-bye now.''

He grabbed her arm. "I'll go with you.''

"You can't,'' she said. "No men allowed where I'm
going.''

"Then I'll meet you back at your room. Do you hear
me?''

She tried to jerk her arm back but he held on. "Go
away,'' she growled at him.

"No,'' he said sharply. "Meet me back in your
rooms. Will you?'' She said nothing, but looked as if
she wanted to say a lot.

"Will you?'' he repeated, and she nodded at him,
once. He let her go.

As she swung the door open, he was given a clear
view of an attractive man greeting her, putting a sym-
pathetic arm around her, and leading her out the door.

"That man with Dr. Addams,'' he asked Keene,
"who would he be?''

"That guy? Some kind of dean or something. Yeah.
Ethan Davis. We got nothing on him.''

"That's unfortunate,'' Alex said. "It really is.''

Alex went through the grim task of identifying Brad's
remains, calling his family and letting them know, making arrangements for transfer of his body after autopsy.
Then he'd gotten into his rented wings and headed back
toward campus and Jaguar.

Although he would never convince her of this, Alex

thought there was something to be said for using wings instead of wheels. For instance, they made it easier to tell when you were being tailed.

As he skimmed the tops of buildings where he could safely and legally cruise at two hundred and fifty, he saw on his instrument panel that someone was too close behind him. They approached and pulled back, approached and pulled back. He slowed to one fifty, then one hundred.

They slowed with him.

A visual check showed him a current model Eagle, gold. That was a machine made for speed. He slowed just a little further, to seventy-five, hoping the hover capacity on his older Thunderbird would kick in and hold the line. The Eagle actually had an advanced hover, but his reading on this model taught him that if it was pressed, it would stall out.

"Surprise," he commented to his readout, when it indicated that the Eagle was not landing. In fact, it was putting on speed, and no longer hiding. The chase was on.

He kicked his wings to three hundred and got out of their airspace, but they kept pace, as he knew they would. He gave the situation a moment's thought and assessed his chances of evasion at about zero. That was all right, since he'd like to know who was chasing him and what they wanted to tell him, but he wanted to at least give them a little run for their money first.

Just because. Just because he didn't like them much. Just because he considered that what they did was rude, he punched in to four hundred and veered a sharp left to nowhere. It was a random move, and these sorts of people usually didn't deal well with the random. Order was more in their line.

The Eagle faltered behind him, then turned wide, started to catch up.

Alex remembered a cute trick he'd learned in his early lessons on wings. It was something an ex-prisoner showed him, about looping under an oncoming vehicle. There was a way to do it without dropping your power level, if you just—ah. That was it.

The Thunderbird about-faced and went careening directly into the path of the Eagle. Head-on, they sped toward each other, and both had a split second of knowing that whichever way they turned, the other might turn the same way, resulting in a sudden dispersal of body parts for all concerned. But Alex was an Adept.

He grinned, pulled right as the Eagle did, then shot under them, headed in the other direction.

That felt good.

He sighed deeply in satisfaction, and in the realization that he'd have to land sooner or later, at which point someone would pick him up. There was no escaping these boys. He might as well, he supposed, get it over with.

Scanning the groundfield plan, he saw a lot about a mile east, and pulled in to make the landing.

As he got out of his seat, rough hands put him face-down on the ground and kept him there.

"Hello, boys," he said. "Where to now?"

"Shut the fuck up," one of them said, and he was cuffed, and a blindfold wrapped over his eyes. When the Eagle he knew he was occupying took flight, he heard the ping of a computer-driven speedometer that had been stressed by the quick shift of their recent chase.

"That ping," he said. "You oughta have someone look at that. Sounds like someone who doesn't know how to shift very well stripped the overdrive."

"Shut the fuck up," the other one said.

"Anything you say," he replied, and sat silent for the rest of the fairly short trip.

When they landed, roughly he thought, and he felt himself pulled up and out of the vehicle, he asked, "Will Rich be joining us? Or am I important enough to rate his boss—that'd be Matt Durk, general lieutenant, wouldn't it?"

A hand pushed at his back. "Shut the fuck up," a voice said.

Then he was shoved into a darkened room, onto a seat, and the blindfold was removed.

When the room didn't get much lighter without the blindfold, he blinked. Not totally dark, but shaded. What fools, he thought. Did they really expect him not to know whom he was with, or were they just trying to set an ominous mood?

From a corner, he heard a tapping as of wood against wood. A voice that had been hollowed out by years of the need to stay in the duck-and-cover position spoke to him.

"Supervisor Dzarny," it said, "you've been playing games with us."

Alex sighed. "That's true, Durk. I have."

He heard a low chuckle.

"I know where I am, too. You didn't honestly think I'd miss the most obvious cues to people and place, did you?"

"With your training? I suppose not." This said with something like fatigue. Whatever he wanted from Alex, it bored him. He had something else on his mind of greater import, Alex suspected. Alex saw his hand rise, and the room empty, except for the two of them.

"How about we try this?" Alex said. "Since I'm

here, why don't you tell me enough so that I don't bug the hell out of you, and I tell you enough so that you don't bug the hell out of me."

Silence. Then, *tap tap tap tap.*

"There is an operation in progress which is of a rather delicate nature. A specialist is involved. We need to complete it, and hope to complete it soon. In order to meet our schedule, all blocks to progress must be removed. *Must* be removed."

A long silence.

"Do you understand?"

Alex said nothing.

More silence, and a sharp, sudden crack. Alex couldn't stop the reflex jump, and knew Durk had seen and enjoyed the moment. Good for him, Alex thought. He knows how to run his show.

"I don't understand," Alex said carefully. "While I have no wish to interfere with Pentagon activities, I'm as you see me. Sitting in the dark. How can I avoid interfering when I don't know which of my actions will create interference?"

Tap tap tap.

"Let's say you have options," Durk suggested. "Limited options. And we want to know which one you'll choose."

"Tell me what they are."

"You can stay here with Dr. Addams. Or you can leave. Go back to the Planetoids and let her run the game on her own."

"Game?" Alex asked. "What's the game?"

"Go fish," Durk said.

Alex was silent. Go fish. What the hell did that mean? Jaguar had a game with the big boys? That seemed eminently unlikely.

He shook his head. "What happens if I stay?"

Durk tapped. "You'll probably end up dead."

"What about Dr. Addams?"

Alex saw the shoulders lift and fall. "Both of you."

"What if I leave?"

"You'll be safe," Durk said.

"Dr. Addams?"

Silence.

Alex assumed that was the lot. He took his time in mulling it. Sitting there in the dark, cuffed and not happy about it, he remembered how very much he hated the army.

Okay. He would try one test.

"Do you want me to pull her out of there?"

Quickly, too quickly. "No. That is not an option."

"Why not?"

That tapping. "She's gone fishing."

Silence.

"What kind of empath is the specialist?"

He saw the shadow of Durk's wooden hand make a quick gesture. He hadn't expected that. Something Alex wasn't supposed to know. Now he was trying to figure out how much more Alex knew, how much he should keep hidden.

"No mention has been made of psi capacities. None will be made. Our specialist is singularly expert, and attached to anonymity."

"Expert at what?"

"Long-distance work."

Alex let the euphemisms settle in. Esper, or Telekine. Or both. Shit. Powerful, if he was any good. And Durk didn't like the specialist. Or somebody didn't. Someone wanted him removed. Jaguar was—what? Working for Durk? Or dancing in the dark? Tricky.

Alex tried another stab in the dark.

"He's getting out of hand, and you can't deal anymore, so you want him taken out. Is that it? Is that Dr. Addams's function?"

"This is a situation with options. My preference in this matter may not coincide with the preference of others involved."

"You're on your own in this one, aren't you? And Dr. Addams isn't behaving as expected, is she?"

A grunt. Maybe an affirmation.

"She never does," Alex said. "What do you need from me?"

"To know which option you'll pick."

An easy one. "I'm in," he said without hesitation. "Up to my short-lived neck."

The wooden finger tapped, and moments accumulated. "You won't leave?"

"No."

"Don't you want to think about it?"

Alex shook his head. "Nothing to think about."

Durk made another gesture, and a man emerged from the shadows, put the blindfold back on, and led him out.

He was shoved back into the Eagle, which pinged even worse as it lifted. He felt the motion of landing, hands clutching his elbow and pushing him out the door into a noisy place. Hum of engine all around.

That wasn't right. He landed in an empty field. A dead lot. There shouldn't be engine noise.

"Where are you taking me?" he asked.

"Back," a voice replied. He was pushed forward.

He pressed his heels into the ground. "No," he said.

"Yeah," a voice said. "Right."

He felt the displaced air before he felt the fist, but it was a good one when it hit, because he felt, saw, and knew nothing more for some time.

14

EMILY'S FUNERAL WAS HELD THE DAY AFTER Jaguar was released from custody, in order to have some closure before Thanksgiving. It was packed with students and faculty and friends who all agreed on one thing: her death was horrible.

The students looked frightened and angry. The faculty looked confused, and ready, at a moment's notice, to run away. Leonard stood at the back of the church, and Jaguar didn't greet him on the way in. For all she knew, that was the worst thing she could do. She noticed that he slipped out the door before it was over.

In his eulogy, Ethan focused on Emily's contributions as a teacher and a scholar to cover the fact that in the past semester she'd become an emotional wreck. Nobody wanted to talk about that. To give him credit, Ethan kept his talk short, and allowed others to speak.

A few students came up and spoke about how much time she took with their papers, with them. She was tough, they said, but she was fair. Jaguar was glad to hear them speak well of her. It was horrible to leave the world without adding something to its share of good, and she was glad that in spite of everything, Emily hadn't done that.

But when Ethan raised his eyebrows to offer her a chance to talk, she shook her head. What could she say? Here lies Emily, who asked the system to be what it could not be. Or perhaps, here lies Emily, whom I did not kill. Or more accurately, Emily whom I did not protect.

That would be her burden, and she felt it heavily. Two people dead, and maybe she couldn't have prevented it, but maybe they'd died on the altar of her need to stay uninvolved. For her, that knowledge was much worse than the suspicious eyes she met everywhere. She didn't need to be an empath to know what they were thinking. The trouble started when that strange woman arrived from the Planetoid, where empaths sucked children's blood at night. Of course she killed Emily, those eyes said. And Jaguar, in a very different way, found it hard not to agree.

She walked from the Episcopalian church to the cemetery where they'd lay Emily down for eternity. Intermittent sleet pelted the back of her neck, but she wanted to feel the awfulness of the weather. It matched her mood. As she stood by the grave, waiting for the ponderous funeral procession to catch up, Leonard, who had also chosen the footpath, made his way toward her, head bent to the wind.

"Hello, Jaguar," he said. "Nasty day, isn't it?"

She jerked her head up at the sound of his voice and looked at him with cold eyes.

"Stay away from me," she said.

His face furrowed in confusion. "Jaguar? What is it?"

She waited to see what she would say. "I can't do what you ask," were the words that came out.

She jerked her head toward the students that were get-

ting out of cars, heading their way. There was Steven
and Katia. Leonard looked toward them.

"Why not?" he asked.

"Because it's a trap," she said.

He closed his eyes and rocked back on his heels as
he absorbed these words. "You know the difference between being connected and being trapped?"

She drew in breath and let it out as a hiss. "Yeah,"
she said. "When you're trapped, you have no space.
When you're connected, you have no time."

Leonard's eyes stayed closed, but his head swung
back and forth in a negative. "No, Jaguar. It's the difference between love and fear. What you're afraid of
traps you. What you love connects you to everything
else that's alive." He opened his eyes and smiled.
"Maybe that's the lesson you came here to learn."

He put his hands in his pockets and turned his back
on her, walking slowly toward the group of approaching
students.

She pulled herself farther into her coat and stared
down into the hole in the earth where Emily Rainer
would soon reside. This was her family plot, Jaguar was
told. It had been purchased for her on the day of her
birth by her grandparents. Even the state of New York's
new laws requiring cremation except in cases of religious taboo couldn't negate previously purchased property.

The sound of feet walking hard brought her up sharp,
and she saw Steven and Katia coming toward her.
Steven was in the lead, and Katia was trying to pull him
back, but he yanked away and took great strides across
the slippery grass to reach her.

When they stood face-to-face, he pointed an un-
gloved, chapped finger in her face.

"Murderer," he spit out. "You have no right to be here."

Too much, she thought. This was too much.

"Steve, I didn't kill her," she said softly. "You know that."

"You—you did," he said, punching his finger in the air. "You did. I know you did because of what you are. Because people like you—that's what they do."

She didn't feel like she had an ounce of fight or an ounce of compassion in her to meet this. It was all pretty dried up inside her right now.

"No, Steven," she said evenly. "Not people like me. That's not what you mean. You mean people like your father."

He brought his hand back and would have slapped her, but she blocked the swing and wrapped her hand around his. He struggled against her grasp, but she held on. "You know what empaths say, Steven? Before they go into someone's mind," she said, her voice low and harsh. "They say, see who you are. Be what you see. Try it sometime. You and Katia."

"Stop it," he cried out, his voice suddenly young and very frightened. "You're hurting me."

She looked at her hand, horrified to see she was twisting his fingers. She let him go. Then she turned and walked away.

Jaguar didn't return to her rooms. Instead she wandered around the old part of the cemetery reading tombstones and staring at the relentlessly gray sky. When she tired of walking, she picked a flat stone to sit on and considered some more. She was still in this state, her thoughts going somewhere she couldn't seem to follow, when she felt a hand gently touch her hair.

"You'll catch your death out here," Ethan said.

She looked around at all the names, all the graves, all the forgotten lives she walked over so carelessly. "Doesn't everyone?" she said.

Ethan laughed heartily. "Dr. Addams, that's what I like about you. You never let sentimentality get in the way of truth. But you should know enough to come in out of the sleet. How about if we go to my old mausoleum of a house, and I'll make some soup. Would you do that for me so I don't have to worry about losing you, too?"

She huddled farther down into her coat and considered. "How was the remainder of the party?" she asked.

"Pretty awful. I still don't quite believe it. My relationship with Emily had its troubles. I know I could have treated her better, but I can't imagine that she's really gone. It seems so unlikely."

"Death is like that," Jaguar said. "Death and departure. There was no further trouble?"

"There never was trouble, Jaguar. The hysterics of a student in supreme stress will not be held against you. Everyone knows you didn't—"

"No, they don't, Ethan. No more than they know Leonard didn't kill the Gone Girls." She uncurled herself from her huddle and stretched her face skyward, feeling the pellets of ice bounce off her eyelids. "It doesn't matter. Not at all."

"My dear woman—" Ethan started to say, and she waved him to silence.

"Let's skip it. I'll go have hot soup and sympathy at your place, but only on one condition."

"Name it. I'll agree."

"That we don't talk about murders or empaths or Planetoids or death of any kind. Agreed?"

"Absolutely. We'll talk only of gourmet cooking and the higher arts."

He kept his agreement not to talk about Emily, though the feeling of her presence lingered as a sustained bass note under the preparations of food and surface talk of weather and upcoming end-of-semester tasks.

Jaguar distracted herself by watching his hands slice mushrooms and onions for the soup, focusing on her awareness of how soft they looked, how finely tuned were all the gestures he made with them. When he brushed his hand against hers, she noticed that it was still very cool to the touch. A blazing fire in the living room where they brought their food kept her very warm, but his hands soothed and cooled her. Ocean cool on a hot day.

After they ate, he sat on the couch next to her, brushing his hands against her cheek, soothing her, cooling her. Ripples of hunger warmed her skin under his cool hand, and desire rose up from her belly and groin.

"You need some tender attention," he whispered into her hair, his leg pressed against hers. "A return to feeling and life and desire."

She couldn't produce a word. She could only feel his hands on her face. She lifted her eyes to his. His eyes were very large. She sensed no pull from them, no empathic ability, but his eyes could hold her beyond her will.

"You are an inspiration to desire, Jaguar," he said.

Every inch of her skin danced with lust, sparkling neurons singing of the body's deep contentment, the joy of flesh and hands and mouth. He kissed her, his mouth delicately playing against hers, taking her lips into his and savoring them.

She leaned into him, hungry for this. Hungry for touch, and kiss and flesh. Hungry for desire and feeling after death. Longing for the feel of a live body participating in life, held close to her. And Ethan was perfect. Detached. Cool. Not riling her emotions as Alex did, though why his name should come unbidden into her thoughts right now was beyond her. Why should she see an image of his face behind her closed eyes now, while her desire grew and she had a place to satisfy it.

Alex? Had she kissed Alex like this? Why would she be foolish enough to do that? She had a memory of it, but it seemed to belong to someone else. And he was gone, wasn't he? She could give herself here, where her body was treated kindly and her heart was left alone, in peace.

Something like smooth, easy laughter rippled through her thoughts, followed by words entering her just as smoothly.

I will squeeze him from your mind.

The heart of the universe washed into her, wrapped around her, told her what to do.

Stop. Now.

She pulled away from the kiss, and without a break in the flow of her motion she was standing, looking down at Ethan, not sure why she was standing or what she was to do next.

He blinked up at her, his face the model of courtesy. "Have I offended you?"

"No," she said. "Not at all. It's just—" She ran a hand through her hair, and lifted a palm up, unable to complete the thought.

"Ae you afraid?" he asked solicitously. "Does this frighten you?"

She resisted the urge to laugh. Who did he think he

was? Alex? But she couldn't keep the amusement from her voice when she answered, "No. I'm not afraid of you."

A shadow of anger passed over his eyes and was gone. "Sure of that, Jaguar? Maybe this felt a little out of your control, and I believe you like to stay in control, don't you?"

"No," she said, thinking of the last few weeks and how very out of control she had consented to be. "I like to stay with my power, but I don't confuse power with control. Not ever."

"Power belongs to you only if you control it," he said, speaking with the cool tones of the philosopher. He stood up and faced her, closing her eyes with the tips of his fingers. At his touch, desire spiraled through her mercilessly. She pushed his hand away, opened her eyes.

She grasped his fingers and took them from her face, opened her eyes.

He studied her in his detached way. "What is it you're not telling me?" he asked softly, "I know there's something. All semester I've known. Won't you trust me as your friend, at least?"

She shook her head. There was no way for her to tell him who she was, what she faced, the nature of the chant shape and how a kiss given from the heart of the universe overrode this temporary desire. She wanted to tell him simply, I can't.

Instead she leaned on the mantelpiece and stared into the fire. "It's Alex," she said.

"Who?" Ethan asked.

She brought her face up, hoping her confusion didn't show. "Emily," she said, recovering herself. "I can't so soon after she—Ethan, it isn't right."

Ethan sat down on the couch, spread his hands out

across his knees, and stared down at them. "I see. And I understand. I hope you don't think I was being disrespectful to her, but it seems that the force of life will prevail, particularly after a death."

"I know. And if I stay here any longer, I'll take you up on it, so I'd better leave."

He stood and took her hand, patted it, and let it go. "Thank you for that, even if it's flattery."

Jaguar turned her open smile to him. "Oh," she said, "I never flatter. I don't really know how. What I said is just the truth."

And it was, though she still didn't know why.

Planetoid Three, Toronto Replica

Alex came to in an empty shuttle outside the Zone 12 shuttleport.

No blindfold. No people. When he ran his hand across his dry mouth and felt the growth on his face, he figured he'd been out for longer than it took to get him to wherever he was now.

He kicked the seat in front of him. "Fucking army," he said.

He climbed out of the shuttle and stared blankly into bright sun. The street sign at the corner gave directions to downtown Toronto. He was alive and well and on Planetoid Three. He tested his legs for walking and found they were up to the task, so he walked. A man walking a dog passed by him and he stopped him.

"Could you tell me the time?" he asked, holding up his empty wrist. Like Jaguar, he couldn't wear a watch. They blew out at every empathic encounter.

"Sure," the man said. "Five after three."

"Thanks and—um, is today's date the twenty-third?"

The dog at the end of the man's leash growled, and the man reined him in. "Twenty-fifth," he said, eyeing Alex a little oddly.

"Right. Thanks," Alex said, and walked on. Two days. He'd lost two days.

He grabbed a taxi—wheels, not wings, feeling he'd had enough flight for a few days—and took it to the Supervisors' Building. He asked himself to be as low profile as he could and got down the hall and to his office without being observed. Once inside, he picked up his telecom and punched in Rachel's code.

"Goddammit, what the hell is this?" he asked her face when it appeared on-screen.

She opened her mouth and gaped, then stopped gaping. "I'm on my way," she said.

In a minute she arrived and tapped on his door.

"Come right the hell in," he barked.

Rachel slid in, closed the door behind her, and pressed her back against it. "You're back," she said.

"Not for long," he said. "The army brought me back, and why the hell Paul let them drop me off here is something I'd like to find out, but that'll wait until I get back. The next shuttle out is mine."

"No," she said quietly.

He stopped and frowned at her. "No?"

"No. You can't."

Alex looked like a volcano about to erupt, and her eyes grew wide. He leaned across the desk and pointed a finger at her. "Do you have any idea how much danger Jaguar's in?"

"I know."

Alex sat down hard at his desk. "Can you explain what's going on around here?"

She sighed, and took a chair across from his desk.

"Not really. All I know is I got a call from Jaguar. She said keep you here. She said at all costs, keep you here. If you talked to her, you'd understand. There was something about her words. Like—they were the truth, and there wasn't any other truth in the world."

Alex pulled back and considered. Jaguar called Rachel. Walking in her power. In that place where only the essential truth remained.

He leaned back in his chair and rubbed at his temples. "Rachel, do you know anything else about this?"

"No. But I think Paul does, if you can get hold of him. I heard he was on the home planet and couldn't be reached. Vacation, I think."

Christ, Alex thought. Payback's a bitch.

"All right. I'll go looking for him. Are you game for a little fishing?"

"What?"

"I want you to get into a Pentagon site for me. I'll give you some program codes that might help. Find anything you can about fishing. Or Go Fish. Gone Fishing. Anything like that."

Rachel blinked at him. "Fishing?"

He explained his conversation with Durk. As much as he could about what he'd learned.

Rachel shook her head a number of times. "It'll be tough."

"It will. But fish long enough, something's bound to get hungry and go for your hook."

15

JAGUAR MET WITH THE UNIVERSITY PRESIDENT
the day after the funeral. Each member of the department
would be given a similar audience when classes resumed
after the break, to discuss how they had been affected
by Emily's death and strategize on damage control. She
would be addressing the students in a general assembly
when they returned, and letters had gone out to all parents.

No wonder she looks tired, Jaguar thought.

Her office was large and sunny, with banks of windows on two walls and a desk with a gleaming dark
surface that stretched a mirrored vista against another
wall. A soft and intricately patterned Oriental carpet covered the standard institutional carpeting, and the paint-
ings on the wall were originals. Mary Yates's pastel
vision of poetry in motion. Monica Miller's *Origin of
Voices* in oil. Krisin Noonan's watercolor of Freya. They
were beautiful, and quite expensive, as was the bone
china Jaguar sipped her tea from.

''You like the artists?'' President Johnston asked, seeing Jaguar study her walls.

''Three of my favorites. Miller, in particular. I understand she lived nearby.''

"Yes. In a little town about forty miles south of here. Her home is open to the public. You can go and view some of her later works."

"That would be lovely," Jaguar said. "It might be nice to get off campus for a day."

That was the opening Dr. Johnston was waiting for. She put her cup and saucer down on her desk and leaned forward, folding her hands on her desk. "How are you weathering the storm? I would imagine you're bearing the worst of the gossip."

That was a good piece of understatement, Jaguar thought. Though forensics had officially cleared her, the police called her office three times a day with more questions, except for Ethan the faculty avoided her like the plague, and her students—she'd see about them when they returned from Thanksgiving break.

"It's bad," she admitted.

The president let her head rise and fall slowly in a sagacious nod, her steely-gray eyes exuding wisdom, sedate and imperturbable. Jaguar wondered if University administrators were trained to nod that way, as if they had the answers. Of course, in this case, she probably did.

"I'll make sure to mention your guiltless status in my speech," she said. "You shouldn't bear the burden of this, when you're here as our guest."

"I don't know that anything you say will stop the whispers," Jaguar noted.

"Perhaps not. But maybe your students will help. I understand they like you very much. They seem to get a lot out of your nontraditional teaching style."

"Oh, my teaching style is very traditional. Mertec tradition."

Unruffled, the president pondered her remark. "Of

course. Your background. I've heard of your grandfather, you know. An admirable man. Quite remarkable."

Jaguar breathed in, and, with her breath, called in a part of herself she had hoped not to bring to this meeting. The words were out of her mouth before she thought them. "He's quite dead, too. Which is what I'd prefer not to be. I'm not sure I'll get my preference, though."

President Johnston's hands, folded neatly on her desk, went white at the knuckles, but her face didn't change at all.

Jaguar continued speaking. "You've got a funding deal with the Pentagon. It's about the course. You're scratching each other's backs, maybe using the course as an arena for future Pentagon research on psi capacities. Or maybe there's more to it that I don't know. But I do know that Emily made the wrong move and got someone's nails in her chest. And whoever killed her is after me, too."

The white at President Johnston's knuckles was now matched by a blanching at the edge of her lips, which she pressed together tightly. "Have you reported your speculations to any authorities? The police or your Planetoid people?"

Jaguar laughed. "What if I did?"

The president unclenched her hands and picked up her tea, no discernible sign of trembling in her hands as she lifted and sipped. When she spoke, her voice remained imperturbable. Jaguar was impressed.

"Dr. Addams," she said, "although I know you're aware of why I wanted someone with your specific talents in the cultural studies department, I had requested that we never meet, and that my involvement in your work here be strictly academic. I almost changed my mind about that after the incident at Cutters, but decided to wait. Now, with this, we need to speak about your assignment. If your work here is connected to this tragic murder and you have evidence of that, you must tell me, and then report it to the police.''

Jaguar placed her teacup on the desk and leaned back in her chair. ''Bullshit,'' she said.

A small muscle below Dr. Johnston's left eye twitched once and was still. ''What do you mean by that?'' she asked.

''I mean, the army's spent years poking at willing and unwilling empaths, or looking for drugs and technology that would induce psi states—particularly telekinesis and precognition. Now they're on your campus, and I think one of them is Tzok-ol.'' She let the two syllables fall harshly from her lips.

''I'm not familiar with that word.''

''Soul thief,'' Jaguar said. ''And I doubt that I need to explain that term, but in case you're stupid enough to let the Pentagon keep you ignorant, that's someone who uses their psi capacities to steal empathic gifts from others, usually killing them in the process. Emily knew about it, and got herself killed because of it.''

The president kept her face from revealing either belief or disbelief. She only asked, ''And do you also know who this—um—soul thief is?''

The question, tossed casually into the air between them, was at the heart of the matter. Jaguar suspected it was what quite a few people wanted to know. Did she have a name?

Somewhere in the room Jaguar scented the ethereal perfume of the full moon, saw a young woman walking into the door of a dimly lit house. She knew. Some part of her knew. If only it would tell the rest of her.

''I know,'' she said. ''Tell them I know.''

Dr. Johnston lowered her gaze and asked, without any emotion at all, "What will you do?"

"That's my business. You just tell your army buddies to watch their backs. And stay the hell off mine."

She stood and turned her head down toward President Johnston. She lifted two fingers and pushed them against her forehead, letting the energy flow into her. The soft growl of a friend could be heard. The breath of the universe was warm and moist on her face. The president gasped, her hands struggling against the edge of the desk.

Jaguar laughed.

"Tell them there are some powers even the Pentagon can't control," she said.

She covered the floor between desk and exit, and at the door she turned and bowed her head to President Johnston. "Thank you so much for the tea. It's been such a pleasure to meet you, after hearing so much about your work."

Then she was gone, and President Johnston sat alone in the room. She reached under her desk and pressed a button. She heard a short buzzing sound in the adjacent suite of rooms, and the door that led from their to hers opened. Lieutenant General Durk walked in.

"You heard?" President Johnston asked.

He nodded.

"All of it?"

He nodded again.

She slapped her hand against her desk, her face going hard and sharp. "Say something, you supreme idiot," she barked at him.

Durk sniffed. "We'll take care of it."

"I suppose that's what you told the last president after those girls started disappearing."

"You'll get your funding, if that's what you're worried about. We won't back out."

She lifted her chin high and regarded him as if he were an inferior specimen. "It won't do me any good if the University continues to be a locus of scandal. I want to know what you plan to do to keep that woman under wraps."

Durk smiled. "Do you? Do you really want to know?"

Her chin dropped, and her demeanor followed.

"Whatever it is," she said coldly, "this time, see to it that it's done off campus."

Planetoid Three, Toronto Replica

"Alex," Rachel said, her eyes wide and frightened as she stared at him over the telecom screen,

"Rachel—are you okay?"

"Alex," she said, "they killed my bird."

Alex held her gaze and spoke with her subvocally.

Be still, Rachel. Tell me what it is. Are you safe?

He saw a shudder run through her, and then she spoke, words drawn out with difficulty, but making sense. "They—someone's been in my apartment. It's wrecked. They killed my bird."

Jesus. She must've found something. But what?

"Rachel—what was in the files I asked you to research?"

She shook her head, pressed a hand against it. "You."

"What?"

"You, as—as operative something. Operative goal. Not your name. Your army ID. Under a larger file. Operation School of Fish." Rachel looked around her. "I didn't understand a lot of it. It was Deep Red code, so

I couldn't download. I could only save it to the internal drive—you know how I do that sometimes? But my computer's smashed.''

"Do you remember anything else about it, Rachel?"

"Just what I said. Alex, they killed my bird."

"Listen, I want you to leave there. You have a key to Jaguar's place? Stay there. I'll find out what I can."

Alex was an essentially nonviolent man. He knew how to respond in self-defense, but he carried no weapons except his hands. For an Adept, he'd found, that was enough, as long as you kept your hands connected to your art, and used them sparingly. Tonight, though, he wanted to kill someone. At first just about anyone would have been fine. After a while he grew a little more specific. He wanted to kill Rich Forrest, and Matt Durk.

By the time he got to Rachel's apartment and started looking through the rubble, he wished it was possible to kill them each more than once.

"Fucking hell," he commented, walking through the apartment, stepping over the stuffing of couch cushions and around strewn papers. This was more than looking for something. It was wanton destruction, just to scare her. Broken disks were everywhere. Besides her computer, they'd smashed her telecom and her stereo and a bunch of plates.

Then two items caught his eye.

The first was a parrotlet, neck bent, dead, lying on the windowsill. Someone had slit it open from throat to legs, and disemboweled it.

The second was the shards of a small clay bowl that had once held a red feather. Jaguar had made the bowl and painted it with the signs of her people. The red feather, traditional offering to a desert deity she felt particularly close to, was included in this gift to Rachel.

She had given it to her when they'd returned from Israel, as a sign of friendship and trust.

The bowl was smashed. The feather was crushed.

"Fuckers," he shouted, and fire surged from the back of his head, coursing through his retinas to the back of his eyes. A rapture of rage filled him, and he was off and running with it, knowing where it wanted him to go.

He had no memory of getting his wings. He had no memory of driving them anywhere. He had no memory of walking into the army's new building. The next thing he remembered of this day was slipping the lock on the door to Rich's office and going inside.

The office was empty.

All signs of life vanished.

A breeze blew through open windows. He stood in the emptiness and tried to understand it. As he stood, he became aware of another person entering the room. He whirled, and saw Paul Dinardo standing there.

"They're gone, Alex," he said. "Cleared out yesterday. Said their research grant was pulled and they had to go home. They were through."

"And so am I, if I don't start getting some answers."

Paul grabbed a chair out and sat. He pulled in as large an amount of air as he could, and expelled it loudly. "I stopped at your office and I figured you'd be here. I came to—Alex, I want you to know I had nothing to do with the shit they pulled on you."

"It might help if you were specific. Names, for instance, are useful."

"Anyone ever tell you you're overeducated, and snotty with it? You know who I mean. Durk and his buddies. I didn't know about it, and I had nothing to do with it."

Alex found a chair and sat down. It was a swivel chair, so he swiveled. Made a triangle with his index fingers and thumb, pushing it in and out.

"And the stuff with Addams. I didn't know about all that, either."

Alex continued to consider the triangle of his fingers.

"I've got a team going to the home planet to pull her out," Paul continued. "You call her and let her know she's coming back."

Alex swiveled and said nothing.

"Well?" Paul asked.

"Well what? Her assignment is classified as mandatory rest leave, and I won't have supervisory discretion until she's officially reinstated. You know the procedure, Paul. You wrote it."

"Forget the procedure," Paul said. "We didn't expect this to happen, and we can't afford to have it go any further. Get in touch with her and tell her to cooperate."

Alex swiveled back and forth, back and forth.

"No," he said. "I'm not her supervisor."

Paul ran a thick-fingered hand through what was left of his hair. "Listen," he said, "She won't answer my calls. Won't call back. You gotta tell her to get her ass back here before—"

"Before what?" Alex stopped swiveling. "Before she discredits you, or gets herself killed?"

"Jesus. We never meant for her to—" Paul stopped. Turned away.

"I guess I'll never know," Alex commented, "which verb you were about to choose."

"What do you want?" Paul asked.

That was better, Alex thought. Paul was getting the hang of this.

"I want a reinstatement letter for her, signed by you

and the Board president. And I want it by five o'clock.''

"You and old man kangaroo," Paul said. "Want us to clear her records, too?''

"Yes. And she's overdue for a pay raise.''

"You mean this, don't you?''

"Mean it? Get that letter to me, or she won't be the only employee you've lost. I'll be right on her heels, Paul.''

Paul eyed him suspiciously. "When I get it to you, what'll you do?''

"Get on a shuttle and bring it to her. If we're lucky, and she accepts the apology I'll offer, I'll bring her back," he said.

Paul shook his head. "You can't.''

"Then forget it. I'll quit and join her.''

Alex waited while Paul sat and stared, his knuckles white against the arm of his chair. After a few minutes he pushed himself up and stood staring at Alex.

"Okay," he said. "Okay. Listen to this, Dzarny, because I won't repeat it. O'Brien's on his way to get her. You tell her to get her ass back here with him. And you aren't going anywhere.''

Alex pushed the heels of his hands against the arms of his chair and lifted himself up. "Much as I enjoy chatting with you, I've got a shuttle to catch.''

Paul jabbed a finger at him. "Try it. You'll be arrested before you hit the streets. Your shuttle pass is suspended, for security reasons.''

"Security reasons?''

"Yeah. Your security. Because your sweetheart Jaguar isn't who they want. She's just the bait.''

Alex frowned. "Who's the fish?" he asked.

"You are," Paul said. "*You* are, asshole. Get it? So stay the hell away from the hook.''

Alex sat back down. "Paul, whatever this is, you'd better tell me all of it."

"I am telling you if you'd shut up and listen. There's somebody on campus working for the army. A specialist, they call him, and whatever he does, it isn't pretty, because even the Pentagon is scared of him. They give him what he wants, and don't ask questions. And his affiliation is very unofficial, so the uniforms can all stay nice and clean. Look, Alex, there's more and you won't like it, so just get used to being pissed off."

Alex settled into this expectation. "Go on," he said.

Paul found a chair and sat in it. "It was like I told you. Someone on the Board set up this exchange program idea. It seemed pretty harmless. Drew funds, created good PR. What's wrong with it? Nothing, as far as anyone can see. When we start picking people for the University, the president explains about their situation and asks for someone with experience in—you know—someone like you or Jaguar. Specifically, she named Jaguar. So I sent her, like I said, thinking it'd be good for her. Good for me. Maybe even good for you. You weren't throwing out any objections, so I figured it was okay."

Alex stifled a profanity. Paul was right. He hadn't objected.

"Then," Paul continued, "when she gets all settled in, I get a call from Durk."

Alex sat up and began to pay attention in earnest. "General Lieutenant Durk?"

"This is right. He says he wants Addams to do a job for him while she's there, and he doesn't want you interfering. Says it's a matter of national security, highly classified, and I'm to keep you the hell away from it."

"What?"

"You heard me. He says it's something to do with their specialist, but he can't say what. And nobody is to know, especially not you, because you'd blab it to her. Then he calls me yesterday. Says he has you and he can either hold you or send you back. Which would I prefer? I told him to send you back and he said fine, as long as I held you, because Jaguar was playing bait, and you were the fish."

Alex blinked, and waited for the world to come back into focus. "She didn't know? She *doesn't* know?" he asked.

"Durk said he was handling it."

"Christ. She doesn't know. She's been working blind the whole time she's been there."

"Look," Paul said reasonably, "there's no reason for you to think—"

Alex stood up and slammed a fist against the wall. "Somebody has to think around here," he growled. "Somebody has to do something besides flap their goddamn lips and suck air."

"I kept you out of it, didn't I? I don't see you saying thank you for it, either."

"You'd cover my ass and let her be chum for the sharks," he said.

"Yeah, well, I feel sorry for the sharks if they eat her," Paul commented. "They'll get more of a bellyful than they expected. Anyway, I'm pulling her out. It's getting too messy. I told Durk I'm pulling her."

Alex shook his head. "If you told Durk, it's probably too late. He'll push the game to the end. Besides, she won't come," he said. "Not unless I go get her. Even then—"

"Then she's just gonna have to take her chances, because I'll lock you up at the first sign of flight. Jesus,

Alex. Do you have any idea how hard it is to get good Supervisors?''

Alex was appalled—at the system, at the army, at the University, at Paul—and at himself. Jaguar was right. She wasn't white enough, male enough, quiet enough to merit protection.

He wiped his hand over his face. Stood up, and left.

"Hey," Paul said. "Where you going?"

"Anywhere," Alex said. "Except here."

THEY MET AS A GROUP AT THE SAME BAR where Jaguar had unwittingly started the brawl. Glen had called the meeting of the class, and the others had agreed to it. They sat around a large table in relative quiet, during the off-hours between lunch and happy hour.

"She's dangerous," Steven said decisively. "She'll do something to us, I know." He looked over at Katia. "She already made us fight."

"Steven," Katia replied, "you made us fight. Not Dr. Addams."

"I wouldn't have fought with you if she wasn't putting ideas in your head. Empathic arts—shit. I should grieve her for undue influence. Fucking murderer."

"Look," Taquana said. "She's not a murderer. They cleared her. That's why we're here, isn't it? To figure out a way to show her we know she's okay."

"And to see if there's anything we can do to help her," Glen added.

"What do you suggest? A greeting card? In sympathy at your arrest—that'd be nice."

Joey Bursky slugged down a beer and put the mug down hard. "If you don't want to be here, you don't gotta be,'' he said. "And that goes for anyone who feels like you.''

"Stop it. Just *stop* it," Katia said, her voice edged with hysteria. "I can't stand all this fighting." She stood up and walked away from the others, and Steven followed.

"Let 'em go," Glen said when Jesse rose to go after them. "They got something of their own going on. They wouldn't be any help anyway."

"Steven," Jessica said, "is a major jerk."

Nobody disagreed, and they moved on to more important matters.

Steven followed Katia out the door and to the crossing, where he reached her and grasped her firmly by the arm, turning her around.

"Why'd you leave?" he asked.

She turned her dark eyes to him. "Because we know what we have to do. Just—let's do it without all the talk." She pulled away from his grasp. Sometimes, she thought, his hand felt as desperate as a drowning man's, clutching at her. It made her angry, and then guilty for her anger.

"Look, I have a responsibility to tell them what she is. If she hurts anyone else and I don't try and stop it, what does that make me?"

Katia knit her brows over her dark eyes. "What if she's not an empath? What if it isn't her making me feel this way, think the way I'm thinking? What if I'm just crazy or something?"

He laughed. "C'mon, Katia. You know better than that. You're not crazy."

"How can you be so sure?"

He put his hands on her shoulders and held her facing him. She looked down at the ground, and he lifted her chin so she would see his face.

"He warned us about that," Steve said. "She's very good, and she'll make you feel like she's telling you the truth. Make you believe all kinds of things, like my father did with me. That's what empaths do. But you know what she did. What she can do. He explained it all to us."

"And you believe him?"

"Of course. He knows all about her. He's studied her for years. Her and people like her. And he showed us how she did Emily."

She closed her dark eyes. "I never want to see anything like it again."

"And you don't want to end up like one of them. Like my father. Like her. Do you? Do you, Katia?"

"No," she said. "I don't. Only, I don't like the secrets. I like things to be up-front. And I don't want him to hurt her. If she can't help it, then it's not really her fault, is it? He shouldn't hurt her, should he?"

"He won't. He said he knows how to do this. We gotta trust him. So let's stick to the plan. You take care of your part, and don't worry about anything else. He'll take care of the rest."

16

JAGUAR STARED AT THE COMPUTER SCREEN, wondering if what was on it made sense. Her on-line students sent questions to her regarding their exam areas, and she answered them as best she could, referring them to other professors when she couldn't. Then she would send more questions to them to help them prepare for their exams.

This student had been asked to explain positive and negative uses of ritual space as proposed by J. Post in *Unparticular Magic,* and using this work, compare use of ritual space in the Serials with use of ritual space in the Lakota sweat ceremony. It was a standard question and the student had answered at length, but she couldn't tell if it made any sense. She turned away from the screen. Impossible to concentrate.

Tonight would be the first class since the funeral. The first time she'd see her students since the murder. And what would they say?

She wondered if Steve would show up, or Katia. Especially Katia, whom Leonard wanted her to guard. Katia whose eyes glittered like Emily's. Molecular dispersion. Coming apart at the seams. That's what she suspected happened to Emily.

Telekine. It had to be a Telekine. But who? It could be anyone on campus. It could be the one man here who she knew practiced the arts. It could be the man whose bed she had refused. It could be the president, or someone she hadn't thought of yet.

A phrase kept circling her thoughts, but wouldn't come to the front where she could hear it. A phrase she was supposed to remember that kept skittering away. She did not pursue it. It would have to find her. Along with the army, she thought grimly.

If she didn't trust her own art so implicitly, she'd be kicking herself around the block for what she'd said to the president. She'd given it all away, left herself no secrets to cuddle. She even let the president see the chant-shape, and she had no idea why. Maybe it was meant to bring the danger close enough so she herself could see it. Smell it. Deal with it. Was that it? Something—that phrase flitting about, not landing. What was it, and why should she remember it?

Her telecom buzzed, and she flicked the on switch, saw a face appear and disappear, and heard the crackling of static.

"Who's there?" she asked.

More crackling, then, ". . . hear me? Can you? If you . . ."

It dissolved into noise. "Who is it? I can't hear a damn thing."

". . . nothing. I . . . very . . . us they want . . ."

"They want? Who wants? Who is this?"

A snapping sound, and the disconnection was complete.

She frowned at her machine, stood and stretched out her legs, then went to look out her window at the gray and chilly day. A hawk skimmed the air above the tower dorms, looking for lunch. Two crows mobbed it, one from the top, and one from the bottom. She pressed her hand and face against the cool glass. Her hand felt warm against it, and her breath made a circle of steam. A phrase lingered at the edge of her consciousness, waiting to be let in. Her hand felt warm against the cool glass.

Her hand felt warm.

Ethan's hand felt cool. His hands were deft and cool on her skin. She felt the pulse of sexual longing just thinking about it. Big magic, that. And yet she'd refused it. Why?

There.

That phrase again, meandering randomly across her brain. The hand of something is always cool. The hand of something is always cool. She pulled back from the window. It was an old phrase, an old bit of lore she'd picked up from *The Etiquette of Empaths*.

The hand of the something is always cool. Something. No. It started differently. The hand of the empath is always warm. That was it. The hand of the empath is always warm. And the hand of the Telekine is always cool.

The hand of the Telekine is always cool.

As simple as that. Just a cool hand run delicately over her face.

The hand of the Telekine.

Ethan's hand.

Shit, she thought.

Telekine.

Planetoid Three, Toronto Replica

Alex sat in the middle of a great dark forest, where the trees were black marble columns reaching up toward a night that reeled around the sky. He tried to determine where the top was, peering up and up. They were, as far as he could see, endless.

He squatted at the base of a tree, listening.

There was silence.

There was the sound of breathing, a scooped-out sound like a respirator or breath within a cavernous chamber of echoes.

There was no sound of walking.

There was no sound of gliding motion as two figures approached, woman and shadow cat. He watched as she put her hand on the great black head, and the two merged, woman into shadow cat, cat into woman, two separate beings who shared the same soul.

They walked toward him.

Go. Go now. The Moon is waiting to carry you.

He sat very still, not sure what they were saying. Not sure what they wanted from him.

He sensed impatience.

Go. The Moon is leaving. She'll carry you.

"I don't know what you mean," he told them.

They lifted themselves and wrapped great hands around his shoulders, held him down with their eyes. The great teeth sank into his face, claiming him, and he pressed forward to let them enter even more deeply. He felt nothing like pain.

Wake up. Go. Now.

The dream dissolved and he was suddenly, fully, and urgently awake, standing at the telecom in his living room, his hand punching in the telecom code for Jaguar's office.

"Answer," he said into the screen. "Come on, Jaguar. Pick up. Pick up. I have to tell you."

He didn't even get a busy signal. Just static. He stared at the telecom.

"Jesus," he mumbled. "What'm I doing?"

Last thing he remembered, after he returned from his talk with Paul, he went and sat in his rocking chair, meaning to take a few minutes to clear his mind, expunge the emotional detritus of the day so he could figure out what to do next. But he'd fallen asleep and had this dream. About the moon carrying him somewhere he wanted to go.

"Damn," he said. "Moon Illusion."

The band was scheduled to go to Jaguar's class and play. They had a private shuttle booked. He knew, because he'd booked it for them after he spoke with Jaguar. And they were leaving—when? Today? Tomorrow? He looked around and saw that it was dark. It wasn't today anymore. It was at least tonight.

He reached for the telecom and punched in Gerry's code.

A groggy male voice mumbled something that was either hello, or fuck off. He couldn't quite tell which.

"Gerry," he said. "It's Alex. What time does your shuttle leave?"

"I didn't do it," Gerry said. "Honest to God, I didn't."

"Gerry," Alex said, "it's okay. You're not in trouble. It's Alex. I just want to know when you're heading out."

There was a pause. "Alex?" the voice said tentatively.

"This is right," he replied.

"It's—kinda late. You know that?"

"No. I don't have a clue what time it is."

"About—well, exactly three thirty-seven A.M."

"Thanks for the update. When are you heading to Jaguar's place?"

"Shuttle leaves at seven. We're there for Wednesday rehearsal and Thursday night class."

Alex swallowed his impatience. It was the best he could hope for, the best he could get.

"Great. I'll be riding with you," Alex said. "There's one thing. I don't have a shuttle pass."

He heard a long, drawn-out rasping sound, which he understood to be Gerry at thought. "You could have Casey's. He's not going."

"Then," Alex said, "I'll need his chip, too. Mine's Supervisor-coded. His would be—"

"Service. He's a garbageman."

Of course, Alex thought.

"I'm on my way to you," he said, and hung up.

Before he left, he punched in the telecom code for Jaguar's apartment. Rachel was staying there while her apartment got put back together. When her face appeared, sleepy and confused, he said simply, "Hear anything from O'Brien?"

"Nothing. He should've called in by now. Gail's with him, too. She's good."

"Not that good," he said. "They won't find her. Be lucky if they get back alive."

Operation School of Fish. Jaguar the bait. They'd use her to get at him. Soul thief, trying for his gift. Who's their man on campus? Esper, Telekine, Adept. No. Not Adept. If it was, why would they want him?

"Rachel, I need you to do something for me," he said. "Get into the ID codes and reset Casey Maloney's chip to my scan and prints. Can you?"

"Yes," she said. And he appreciated her more than

he ever had when she asked just one more question of him. "When?"

Not why. Just when.

"I'd kiss you if you were here," he said. "Now."

"Now is when you'd kiss me? Or now is when you need it."

"Both," he said. "And what size are you?"

At this she showed surprise. "What size is my what?"

"Like, skirts and whatnot. Would they, by any chance, fit me?"

Rachel cleared her throat. "I'm a small woman, Alex. Size three. Jaguar's about a ten, though."

"Pick something out for me and bring it over around six A.M., would you?"

"Anything in particular? Evening wear, day wear?"

"Try the category of something I can wear," he suggested. "Something that'll keep any surveillance off me if I want to take a walk alone."

"Oh. Right. I got it. Okay. I'll see you at six."

He signed off, and sat drumming his fingers against his desk. He realized that his hands were sweaty and his heart was beating hard. Once Jaguar had stolen a shuttle and blown it up to save his life. What had gone around was coming around, he thought. Which was certainly fair, if only it would carry them both safely home.

17

JAGUAR WAS RELIEVED WHEN BOTH STEVEN AND
Katia showed up for class. She had been afraid they'd
be absent, that it would be already too late.

Shit.

Telekine.

Katia was quiet and Steve looked exceptionally nervous, and a Telekine was on the loose. A Telekine who
had been toying with her since she arrived. Pressing the
neurons to release the memory of Alex's voice. Pressing
at her for sexual response. Pressing into Emily until her
mind snapped. And what damage had he already done
to Katia? To Steve?

Telekine. Damn and hell.

And why hadn't he killed her yet?

She wondered if he read her night walks. If he knew
enough to catch that graceful spirit in flight. No. If he
did, she'd be dead by now. Probably he was waiting to
learn enough to steal it from her.

Telekine, and a soul thief.

The Mertec and Maya called Telekines Lightning Fingers. You can't outrun lightning, her grandfather told her
when she was little. You have to curl up in a ball and
ground yourself. Or direct the lightning somewhere else.

Divert it. He brought her out during a storm and let her feel the crackle against her skin, showed her how to become small and smooth and unreachable. Showed her how to stay calm when she felt the lightning approach.

Telekine.

When she was wandering Manhattan after her grand-parents were killed, afraid to go back to the apartment where their bodies lay rotting, unsure where else to go, she'd seen one, without knowing how to name what she saw. A woman wearing diamonds. She remembered the diamonds, and the way the sun sparked off of them. She wanted to touch them, hold them in her hand like magic. She remembered the woman's eyes, which were large and ice blue. They had something of sorrow in them that Jaguar also wanted to touch, as if she could stroke out tears and let the running water melt that ice the sun sparked off like diamonds. She walked toward the woman, mesmerized by the diamonds. Then a man bumped into the woman.

She whirled toward his receding back and held up a finger. Cut a swath in the air with it. He spasmed as if he'd stuck his hand inside a transformer, blood pouring from his ears and nose.

Jaguar remembered how quickly she turned and walked away.

Lightning. You can't stop it. You can only divert it or ground yourself, stay close to the earth.

Poor Emily. She never had a chance. And Jaguar, not knowing, couldn't have saved her or Brad. But she wouldn't let it happen to anyone else. Now that she knew who, it was time to call a halt. If only she could figure out how.

She looked around the room. Steven, nervous and closed. Katia, quiet. Glen, relaxed behind a certain guardedness. Maria, drumming her fingers on her desk. Taquana, fierce and angry. Ivy, her eyebrows furrowed in thought. First, though, she had to deal with this.

"Okay," she said, perching herself on the desk. "Let's talk about Emily Rainer."

She looked directly at Steven, and waited.

"You killed her," he said, glaring at her. "You're one of them."

Jaguar looked to Katia, who lowered her head and would not meet her gaze. Then she let his words pass over her own lips. "One of them?" she asked. "Meaning what?"

He stared at her belligerently. "You're an empath," he said. "Katia told me."

"Perhaps," she said, looking directly at Katia again, "it takes one to know one."

Steven pushed himself up from his seat with such force that he knocked it over. He turned to the class and pointed a portentous finger. "I only came tonight to warn you," he said. "She's an empath and a murderer. She killed Professor Rainer, and she's fucking with your minds."

He clumsily gathered up his materials, papers and disks falling from his hands, and walked to the door. Katia cast one apologetic glance at Jaguar before she hustled out the door after him.

She watched their retreating backs, then turned to her students.

They were uncomfortable, unsure, afraid. So was she. She pulled a student's desk over to them, placing it within their circle. To her surprise, nobody pulled away from her.

"If you think I killed Professor Rainer, you shouldn't be here," she said. "You should walk out right now and not listen to anything I say because I'm not fit to teach you. I promise," she added, "I won't fail you for it."

Nobody moved. Nobody got up and left.

"Dr. A," Selica said, "I think everybody who believes you're a killer just left the room. I mean, the cops cleared you, and to my mind, it just doesn't seem like your style. I think if you killed someone, you'd stand right up and say it, because you'd have good reason."

Jaguar bowed her head, feeling somehow pierced by this. Trust. Such trust. It was frightening, and it humbled her. Two new experiences.

"Thank you," she said simply. "I appreciate that more than I can say. And if there's anything you want to ask me, well, I'm here. Don't be afraid to know something, or to say what you believe. That's how you learn. By—by facing the fear, and speaking to it."

A student raised a tentative hand. "What Steve said about you. Being an empath. Are you?"

That was direct enough, and to be expected, but of all the questions they might ask, for some reason this was the last she felt prepared to answer. Maybe because it was so true, and a truth she was so used to hiding.

"What would it mean if I was?" she asked quietly. "How would that matter to you?"

"It might mean that you could—like, control us?" Jesse suggested.

"That I could make you believe, for instance, I'm not a murderer when I am?"

Murmuring, and shifting. Yes. That was some of their fear. They might trust her, but how could they trust themselves to be putting their faith in the right place?

She nodded. "A shadowed empath will try to control you. Someone who's—sick with fear and power. But so will someone who's sick with fear and power and not an empath. They'll just try it in different ways."

"But this way—with an empath," another student said, "we can't do anything about it."

"Because why?" she asked.

"Because we don't know how it works?" one student suggested.

"Mm," she said. "Seems like that's a good reason to have the empathic arts course on campus. Or a good reason to learn from empaths what they really do and are."

A voice from the circle—a face she couldn't see—said some words.

"Can we learn from you?" the voice asked.

"Yeah," Jesse said nervously. "Are you an empath?"

Should she tell them the truth? They placed trust in her. Should she?

She felt danger, and smiled grimly at it. As if, she thought, this will put me in more danger than I am in already. No. It was just the epicenter where the new stories grow.

Are you an empath?

"Yes," she replied, "I am."

She ducked her head down, and brought it back up, her sea eyes scanning their silent faces. She had liked them very much, and they had liked her. She hoped that wouldn't change.

"I don't use it here any more than you do—for instance, when you look at me and try to tell by my face what answer you think I want to hear."

Some laughter at this, nervous and small. She smiled at them. "It's not bad. Nor is it necessarily good. It just—*is*."

She ran her gaze around the circle, holding her empty

hands palms up to them. "It just is," she repeated, hoping they would understand.

There was silence for a long time. Then, next to her, someone said, "Like wind."

"Or rain," someone else replied.

"Thunder."

"Trees."

"Black skin."

"Snow."

A chorus of voices suggested that which was in nature, uncontrollable, unbearably beautiful, and undeniably mundane. The shockingly everyday beauty of natural forces. The infinite humor of the divine. It just is. She sighed deeply. They would, she decided, be all right.

"Are there any other questions about it?" she asked.

Half a dozen hands shot up, and she took a moment to gather her thoughts so she could teach them something real about what she knew best.

When class ended, she left the humanities building and walked across the campus toward her rooms, her mind a jumble of student questions and her own concerns. She would go back to her rooms and call Alex, she decided. She needed help on this, and there was no one else she could trust.

As she crossed the quad, she heard a voice calling her and she stopped.

"Dr. Addams," it whispered hoarsely. "Here."

Katia. Katia's voice.

She turned back and walked toward the grouping of trees between buildings. She could almost see her.

"Katia," she said, keeping her voice low as she approached. "Are you okay?"

Katia gestured to her, and she walked into the trees.

Into the darkness. Katia's eyes glittered at her from the bushes like—like Emily's eyes. Emily's eyes.

Shit, Jaguar said to herself, catch a clue.

But Katia was looking at a point behind her and nodding, and Jaguar was aware of a sinking in her belly. Katia cooperating with the Telekine. She'd put on a good act.

"Nice piece," she said when she felt the muzzle at her back. "A 2010 laser fire?"

"Shut up," Steven's voice said behind her, low and intent. "Just do what I say."

He turned her around and walked her to an air runner that was waiting at the edge of the quad. He put her in it and pulled out a piece of black cloth, wrapped it around her head, and tied it tight as the air runner kicked into motion.

"Katia," she asked, "why are you doing this?"

"It'll be okay, Dr. Addams," she said. "He's not gonna hurt you. I made him promise not to hurt you. He's just gonna make you normal again, so you won't hurt anyone else."

Of course, Jaguar thought sadly. Of course.

"Is that what he's doing for you, Katia? Making you normal? Not an empath anymore."

A hand grabbed the back of her hair and shook hard. "Shut up. Katia, don't listen. He told us we shouldn't let her talk."

The air runner braked and came to a halt, and Steve pulled her out of it, pushed her ahead of him roughly. She counted twelve steps along a flat path. Three steps up. The sound of a door opening. They moved forward and she felt the shift from cold outdoor air to warm inside air. She heard the door click closed behind them.

"Good," Ethan's voice said. "Very good. You two

go on upstairs and wait. I'll take it from here. Your weapon, Steve."

A moment of silence, and then she heard Katia, her voice rising into hysteria. "What're you doing? Steve? Professor Davis, what're you—"

Jaguar jerked toward the sound, felt pressure pushing against her, heard a gurgling in the throat that subsided.

No. He couldn't. She couldn't let him. Couldn't stop him. Pressure wrapped her head. He pushed her forward without touching her. She felt her legs moving down stairs fast.

"What're you doing?" she asked. No answer. The air around her grew cooler.

"Stop," he said, and her legs obeyed.

"Where's Katia?" No answer.

She felt breath on her neck. Air on her eyes. She brought her hands up to her face and felt for the blindfold. It was gone. The darkness was around her, maybe in her, rather than something she wore. It washed against her in waves of impenetrable silence.

Was she alone? Was he watching? Had he already stolen her vision? Her hearing?

Danger. There was danger. How immediate? Like lightning. Soul thief, pressing close.

She breathed, feeling her lungs working air in and out, hollow space filling with empty air. She was breathing.

Danger. There was danger. Immediate danger.

She was alone in the thick dark and she could smell the Telekine gloating, waiting to steal her gifts. A Telekine like lightning. She couldn't run. She couldn't hide. She couldn't fight. But her grandfather had taught her well.

You can't outrun lightning. Can't outpower it. All you can do is find the earth and drop.

She knew what to do.

Dark.

Call darkness to dark, and let the singing be the shadow. Shadow cat stalked and she felt the wind in its wake. Old friend, finding her, circling her.

Dark. Drop into it. Solstice dark. Drop down.

She began to curl in on herself.

Slowly, like the ungrowth of a leaf, she furled her body in, folding matter over spirit over matter in the dark. All internal talk silenced. All energy focused into a sphere of light that she hugged to her center. All of her, layered in a protective circle around a small core. She curled in like a sleeping deity. Rolled herself inward as if her body was the atmosphere curving around a great blue planet, as if she were the wings of a great bird hugging the sun. Slowly, she rolled herself up and put herself away until she was only layers of thought curved over a song, which she began to sing.

This song, which would sing her into the darkness.

This song, which would hold her within it.

This song, which would fill her.

When she was small and singing, layered spirit under layered flesh that was still as ice, still as a rim of gold over a mountain, something like grace circled out of its spin through the solar system and came to rest near the spiraling song she had become.

Something like a tossing of light, protecting and protected by her song, as she folded into herself and the darkness, totally vulnerable, and totally enclosed.

Planetoid Three, Toronto Replica

Gerry eyed Alex hard. "I don't think that scarf's a good color for you," he noted. "Something about yellow washes you out."

"Thanks," Alex said. "The skirt's not really my size, either."

Gerry stepped out of the doorway, and Alex entered, closing the door behind him.

As soon as he was in, he took a deep breath of relief and let it out. Then he stripped from the skirt and scarf, pulled off the shades and coat, and rolled his pants back down over his boots.

"Um," Gerry asked, "is there something I need to know here?"

"Not a thing," Alex said. "We set to go?"

Gerry scratched at his head. "I guess," he said.

"Then let's move."

18

ALEX AND THE BAND MEMBERS FOUND JAGUAR'S apartment empty when they arrived that afternoon. When he searched for any lingering signal, any scent of her presence, it seemed as if she had been gone for some time. How long? And where had she gone to? He stifled his growing panic.

"Maybe she's in her classroom," Gerry said, still leaning on her buzzer. "Whaddaya think?"

"Go on and check," Alex said to Gerry, "If she's there, send her here. I'll stick around and see if she shows up."

"Yeah. Sure. Geez, it's not like Jag to stand us up. We gotta rehearse before tomorrow."

"I think there's probably a reason why she's not here," Alex said. "Try and keep things quiet. If anyone asks about Dr. Addams, tell them she was overcome by the flu or something. If neither of us shows up by to-night, call Rachel. She'll know what to do. Okay?"

"Sure. Yeah. Okay."

As soon as he was gone, Alex used a trick Jaguar taught him to open the door to her building. He ascended the three flights to her apartment and opened that door as well. Once inside, he tried to relax. Tried to focus.

Tried not to think about where Jaguar might be or how little time, if any, he might have left.

He just focused, and felt for anything that might give him a clue as to where she would be.

"Save it," a voice said behind him. "I can tell you where she is."

He whirled around and found himself staring at a very tall and broad man in his late forties, who wore his thick dark hair in a ponytail that went halfway down his back. Alex recognized the face from the files he'd read. Leonard Peltier.

"Where?" he asked.

"With Ethan Davis," he said. "And she's in deep shit. I'll explain along the way."

He was already heading out the door as he spoke.

"Wait," Alex said. "Why're you involved in this?"

The man turned back and grinned. "You ask questions like someone else I know. Because I was asked to be."

"You're Peltier. Ex-army. Another one of Durk's brats?"

Leonard shook his head. "I'm Lakota. Native, like this Mohawk student I have. Katia. Someone I was asked to keep an eye on. She's the one I'm going after."

"Why should I believe you?" Alex asked.

Alex felt the twinge that was a subvocal request to speak telepathically. There was one good reason to believe him. He asked permission.

Okay, Alex said. *Any other reason?*

None, Leonard replied. *But maybe you should learn to believe yourself.*

They stood and stared at each other. Alex read both fear and understanding in Leonard's eyes. He wondered what Leonard read in his. Every impulse in him was directed toward one goal. Find Jaguar. Find Jaguar. Find Jaguar.

"I'll tell you everything I know, which isn't everything," Leonard said out loud, "only I'm concerned about time. Maybe we should keep moving while I talk?"

Alex hesitated only one moment more. "Let's move," he said.

By the time they were down the stairs and Leonard had given him the basics, he was already sure they weren't moving fast enough.

Telekine, he thought.

Jaguar's caught herself a Telekine.

And he wondered if it could possibly get any worse.

"Get up," the voice said, and it wasn't pleased.

She heard it as if it was far away, but she responded as if it was very close.

She uncurled herself carefully, slowly, rose and opened her eyes a little at a time. How long had she circled herself in the darkness? Minutes, hours, or days?

There was dim light now. She saw that she stood in a large and open room. The air was cool and damp. A basement, she thought. As her eyes adjusted was able to make out shapes. Ahead were wide wooden stairs, outline of dark against light. Beyond that, a figure moving. The play of candlelight against a wall. A chair with a small table in front of it. Candle on the table. Someone sitting in the chair.

Ethan Davis.

She walked to him and he held up a hand. "I wouldn't if I were you," he said pleasantly enough.

"Are they dead?" she asked.

Ethan laughed. "Steve and Katia? No. Though why

you should care after what they did to you is something I won't try to understand.''

"Where are they?'' Jaguar asked.

"Upstairs. In a state of altered consciousness. I'll attend to them when I'm through with you." He ran his eyes up and down her with something like admiration. "You must know a thousand ways to avoid death," he said.

"A thousand and one,'' she said, "to avoid a thousand and one different kinds of death. Shall I tell you all about them, one at a time?" She took a step forward and he raised his hand again.

"No, Scheherazade. You shall not." He pushed his hand forward, and she felt a stabbing sensation in her legs. She stopped walking.

"Very good," he said. "What you shall do is be very careful to keep your eyes lowered, and your body still. I suspect that what I can do supersedes even your talents in terms of speed and efficiency. However, after the display of ingenuity you've just given me, I hesitate to lay money on it. Jaguar," he asked, "where did you learn that trick?"

"What?" she asked. "Earth curl?"

"Is that what it's called? That's one of the chant-shape practices you don't talk about in your dissertation, isn't it?"

"It's a variant I picked up from an old man I know."

"Fascinating. I could have sliced the skin from your bones without disrupting the space."

She nodded. "It would have killed me all the same."

"Mm. You were absolutely undefended and totally impenetrable at the same time. It was—quite beautiful. You shimmered like molten glass. Are you aware of that?"

"I am. Is that why you didn't kill me?" She stayed still, but lifted her eyes to meet his.

He gestured with his hand like an orchestra conductor. "Eyes down, please. Thank you. That was part of it. I wanted to watch. And I suspected that in that state your empathic integrity was inviolable. Even if I killed you, I'd never touch your gift. Was I right?"

"You were."

"I thought so. Tell me more about it. For instance, why you didn't use your chant-shape to just slip away."

She paused. "What will you do with Katia and Steve?"

"Empaths are self-sacrificing fools, I've always thought."

"And Telekines are always confusing control with power."

"Are we?" he asked.

He raised his hand and swept it down in front of her, and a shiver of desire ran through her. She closed her eyes and breathed it away.

"If you'd slept with me, Jaguar, we might have been able to work out the difference."

"I don't use the arts for sex. I don't have to."

"Is that supposed to be an insult?"

The desire turned into pain, sharp and jolting. Breathe, she told herself. Just breathe it out.

"Is it direct contact?" she asked when it dissipated. "Or are you using cerebral cortex response?"

"Both. It works better that way."

Jaguar asked herself to remain very calm. Telekine like lightning, and all you could do was divert it or ground yourself. She could ground herself, but it wouldn't save her life. Or Katia's, or Steve's. She needed a diversion.

She touched a finger to her wrist. The blade rested

cool and reassuring against her skin. He must know she still had it, but he knew he was faster. She could use her knife accurately in a second, but he worked in smaller units of time. Didn't matter. Arrogance or carelessness would kill you every time. Time. It was about time now. Buy time, and hope for an opening. She'd have precious little of it to act, if an opening should arise.

"How do you take gifts from people?" she asked.

He smoothed down the front of his pant legs and stood, folding his hands behind his back. This was his teaching position, she thought. Very alpha male. Very pompous ass. Why had she failed to see that in him before?

"Simple neural transfer. Telekines' nervous systems are slightly more permeable than others'. We can absorb and integrate changes from another pathway, under the right circumstances. There needs to be direct physical contact—preferably with exposed nerves, although that's not absolutely necessary. And the empath needs to be completely open. That's why the point of death is the best time. Then all gifts are laid bare. Except in your case, my dear."

Yes, she thought. He would want her open. He would bide his time until he could get her open. Time. Buy time, wait for the right time, act before he has time to react.

"Did you kill the other girls—the Gone Girls—for gifts?" she asked.

He curled his hand at her. "Two of them were slips of the finger, though there's always something to be said for tasting young death. One gave me esper, and the other a little unpracticed Adeptness. Not much use, but the real thing is only a touch away, and I have you to thank for that.''

"I'm not an Adept," she said.

"I know."

She frowned. Something wasn't making sense. Let it go, she told herself. Keep him talking. "Did you kill the dean, too?"

"Yes. For the obvious reasons, I'm ashamed to say. I wanted his job. And department politics being what they are, it was the only sure way of getting it. Also, I thought he would catch on if I let him linger too long. He was an intelligent man."

She tilted her head and considered him. "You've been poking at people for years, haven't you? How many bodies have you been through?"

"A few dozen, I suppose," he said, shrugging it off. "Learning anatomy from a book is pointless without hands-on experience. There was nobody important, believe me. But someday, when I have my gifts all in order, I'll explore broader seas."

"For yourself, or the army?"

"Whichever suits me," he said. "I suppose I'll stay with the army as long as they continue to cooperate. They do love a Telekine above all others. Telekines, and then Adepts. We're so good at managing the more delicate tasks."

"Assassinations?"

"And so on. Satellite work. Communications. Your telecom hasn't been performing as it should this semester, has it?"

She nodded. "And where do I fit in?"

"You are my reward. You, and the larger fish you bring to me."

Larger fish? She opened her mouth to ask what he meant, but he held a finger to his lips.

"My turn," he said. "I want to know more about the gift I'll be receiving from you. I've watched your night walks, but I can't seem to grasp what it is you actually do. I know that it's an energy source, but which one?"

Shadow moving in shadow. Dream and not dream. Shared soul, animal self, Old one. Not an energy source he would give credence to. She shook her head.

"You wouldn't care for it," she said. "You give up a lot of control for the power you get."

"Don't worry your pretty face about that, Jaguar. I know what I'm doing." He twisted his hand. A sudden pain in her head told her he was right. She turned it away.

"Beautiful Jaguar. You're very good." He sighed in deep satisfaction. He held up a finger and sliced it down through the air. She felt a sensation as of the edge of a blade moving along the outer rim of a vein in her arm.

She pulled in away from him, her muscles drawing in taut and ready. "I can sing all night, and all day, and all night again if I choose. I can make this very difficult for you, and in the end you'll have nothing."

He chuckled softly. "Oh no, Jaguar. I'll still get exactly what I want. And you'll bring him to me."

She jerked her head up and looked him full in the face. "Him?" she asked.

"The Adept," he replied.

The Adept. The larger fish she'd bring to him. She wasn't an Adept. But Alex was.

"Alex?" she asked.

As she said his name, she experienced a sudden and sure sense of his presence. As if she had heard footsteps approaching that stopped at the mention of his name.

"Alex," Ethan repeated.

This was about—Alex?

"He's not here," she said. "He's on the Planetoid."

Ethan smiled. "Do you really think he's capable of leaving you alone? I don't. That's why I wanted you here. Eyes down, Jaguar. Eyes down. I studied you both for a long time before I began this project. If you're blind to his devotion, then it's willful blindness. It's quite clear to everyone else."

She was here to draw him. The Telekine needed direct contact at the time of death, and he knew Alex would not be easy to kill. But if he was distracted, looking to her safety—

Understanding filled her, followed by rage.

"You're using me as goddamn *bait*?" she snarled at him. "Me?"

Ethan pressed his hands against his heart. "That pinches the ego, doesn't it? To know I've been playing you on my line for so long. But as you said, the chant-shape is difficult to manage. Beyond accessing the energy, what good will it do me, in practical terms?"

She put a hand to her hip, tapped her foot against the basement floor.

"The art of the Adept, however—imagine what I can do when I add that to my fund of power."

"You used me as bait for Alex, you petty fascist pig dog." She took a step toward him, glittering green gold eyes spitting fire.

He unfolded his hands, and her arm went numb. She stared at it, breathing hard, caught between fury and fear. Block it, she told herself. It's a simple move. You know how. She focused, and felt pins and needles signal the return of sensation. He pressed finger and thumb together, and she felt a stabbing pain in her chest. She struggled for breath in the moment before she remembered how to access the appropriate relief.

He was good. Fast and accurate.

Calm down, she told herself. Focus. Don't be distracted.

"Don't take it so hard," he said. "You've become a prize in your own right. Courting you, observing your art, the prospect of bedding you—just the challenge of planning and staging all this—well, it's been a gratifying semester."

Xipe Totec flay him. How insulting could he get? And did Alex know? Or was he stumbling blind, as she had been. Stumbling blindly into a trap.

She could feel him drawing closer, his presence unmistakable to her. He was nearby, and she had to warn him. But the Telekine would feel her open, would know what she was doing. Fast and accurate. Like trying to outrun lightning.

She raised her eyes to Ethan's and pulled at him. Distract him. Time. Buy time. She needed a diversion.

"No, no," he said, averting his eyes. "That's not good."

"Then kill me," she said, and took a step toward him.

"My dear, I'd rather wait until Alex arrives. Watching you die will distract him from any act of self-preservation he could bring to bear on the situation."

Time. That gave her time. She took another step.

"But don't think I can't keep you still while we're waiting." He lifted his hand and her arm began to tingle. The sensation spread across her chest and became thicker, heavier, as her arms went numb. He chuckled softly and walked to her, walked around her, saw her trying to move, saw that she couldn't. He stopped behind her and put his hands on her shoulder. She could see them, but she couldn't feel them at all.

She tried to turn and couldn't. Tried to speak and couldn't. She tried to push him out, and couldn't do that either. Dammit. He'd gotten in. Found a crack and slipped into it and Katia and Steve were upstairs and where was Alex stumbling blind to this death trap? Time. No time. She was out of time and she couldn't make it better, so she'd have to make it worse.

She caught air and breathed it in, then opened herself to empathic contact.

Open. Wide open. Let him feel what she felt. Let him know what she knew. Let him feel something besides the tips of his fingers slicing flesh and consuming chemicals.

And she felt Alex, seeking her, reaching toward her. She had to warn him. Time. No time.

Alex, she whispered inside herself, *Telekine. He wants you.*

Clear as bells she heard the reply: *I know, dammit. Shut up. Close down.*

"How very interesting," Ethan murmured, listening to the whispered circles of thought, the danger she felt, the consternation and joy. Alex knew all about it, and was there anyway.

Try to steal that, she whispered into him. *I dare you.*

Ethan stood behind her, very still, his breath on her hair. The paralysis receded from her chest and arms and neck as he turned his attention elsewhere, his icy fingers clamoring toward her brain, a slicing and clear motion.

Then all motion stopped. His fingers poised within her thoughts, he paused, listened.

The sound of someone walking down the stairs. Not running. Not trying for silence. Just entering.

Jaguar saw Alex, emerging from the dim shadow shapes, walking toward them.

Alex, walking toward them, black eyes filled with sparks, hand raised in the gesture of the empath. Alex, smiling. Fully open, with his hand out in the gesture of the empathic touch. Gesturing toward Ethan. Smiling.

Jesus, was he crazy?

He caught her eyes, and she felt the stab of his thoughts. *No crazier than you.*

The Telekine was momentarily amused.

"What have we here?" he murmured, his thought shifting toward Alex.

Time. No time. Alex was giving her time.

Buying it for her with his life.

She would use it.

She pressed the button at her wrist, felt the blade slide into her grasp, and whirled.

Time broke into its smallest parts as she spun like a dancer on one raised foot, arms out like gracious wings, her body taut and balanced in a moment of pure motion. Her knife bit into Ethan's throat and sliced it cleanly and deeply as a shadow slicing air. Rich fresh blood flew off the end of the blade, painting the side of her face. There was such stunning grace in her brief dance of death that Alex, watching, thought it would be a pleasure to have her kill you, if only she would consent to do it in this beauty.

"Bite that bait, asshole," she growled at him as she completed the circle and faced him again.

The Telekine's eye grew wide and he lifted a hand to his throat and fell to his knees.

Alex caught her by the arm and pulled away from him, pushed her down to the floor, rolling over her and shielding her mind with his own as Ethan, gasping out

life through his throat, reached a cold hand toward them
both. Jaguar lifted her head to look and Alex pressed
her back down against his chest.

Wait, he said into her. *Wait. It's not safe yet.*

They lay there, waiting, listening as his body fought
to reclaim itself, until they heard the last catch of breath
as it gurgled out with the blood that poured from the
gash in Ethan's neck.

"Jesus," she said when it seemed safe, "you're heavy."

"Sorry." He stood and reached a hand down to pull
her up. She stood and went for the stairs, but Alex pulled
her back. "Where're you going?"

"Katia and Steven. I have to—"

"No, you don't," he said.

Her face fell. "Are they—"

"They're fine. Leonard got them out."

"Leonard?"

Alex nodded. "He brought me here. I think I probably
owe him an apology for what I've been thinking about
him. But I owe you one first." He searched her face to
see if he could remember how to read it. All he saw was
relief.

"For what?" she asked. "For getting your ass here,
or risking your ass here, or saving my ass here?"

"It wouldn't need saving if I hadn't been such an
idiot," he noted.

"True," she agreed, "but if you hadn't been such an
idiot, I wouldn't have been here. And who knows what
would have happened to Katia or Steven or you."

He drew back from her and held her out at arm's
length. "You're taking this better than I am. There's
claw marks on my telecom from all the times I couldn't
get through to you."

He felt her speaking into him, swift and unexpected pleasure of her thoughts moving within his.

Match the claw marks on your conscience? she asked, and he could feel the mischief in her. He ran interference on it.

No, Jaguar. The ones on my heart.

He felt her surprise, and the way she tried to cover it, like a cat who tumbles off a counter and stalks away, pretending he meant to do that.

"At any rate," she said, withdrawing from his thoughts and speaking out loud, "I accept your apology." She looked down at her knife blade and observed the blood at the tip, the blood all over the floor. She wiped it on Ethan's pants, then retracted it.

She was so contradictory, Alex thought. She risked her own life so readily, guarded other lives so fiercely, and killed with such ease when necessary. While he worked his way into corners trying to find the right solution, she acted. Terrifying, the way she would cut through to that point of life and death, choose and act as quick as thought.

"Are you okay, Jaguar?" he asked. "No wounds that need tending?"

"Just the ones to my ego," she said. He raised an eyebrow at her.

She kicked at the back of the Telekine's leg. Bad form, Alex thought, but he bet it felt good.

"Bait," she muttered, "my ass."

epilogue

THE SNOW CAME DOWN IN EARNEST OUTSIDE HER office window. She kept her head bent over the work on her desk, ignoring the two suitcases packed and ready at her side, beckoning her to finish and get the hell out of there. To where, she still wasn't sure. Maybe north to look for the aurora. Maybe south to see Jake and One Bird.

The days of explanation, questions and answers, the tightrope walk across the politics of cleanup and cover-up had taken more out of her than the sustained chant-shape. Alex had been in top form, though, and she'd had the distinct pleasure of watching him throw Officer Keene around.

Keene hadn't even been very rude. Just made some offhand comment about women like her who usually slice a man a lot lower than this guy was sliced. Alex picked Keene up by the back of the neck and tossed him out the door. The local police seemed to run out of questions after that.

But there was still a contingency of military people to get through. Debriefings, they said. Which meant a chance for the army to tell them a series of lies about their relationship with Ethan and his death. Durk never made an appearance, but as they left the military offices for their hotel, she saw him sitting in an army vehicle parked across the street. He stared ahead, his wooden hand resting against the steering wheel.

When Alex and Jaguar passed, he turned his head toward them and removed his hat.

"Jesus," Jaguar said. "Are we dead and nobody told us?"

"No," Alex replied, grinning. "I believe that was his way of saying thank you. Tell me, would you still have killed Davis if you knew you were working for the army?"

She thought about that a minute. "It's probably a good thing I didn't know."

The next thing she did was sleep for twelve hours straight, and when she woke up there was a pot of coffee at the bedside stand, with a note from Alex saying he had to take care of something, but he'd probably be back.

She took the time to wrap up her academic work, and to see Leonard. "This time I'll ask how," she said. "How'd you know to go to Ethan's?"

He shrugged. "I stay connected. It helps."

"I guess I was born lucky as well as stupid. I'm sorry if I was rude at the funeral. I thought it'd be safer for you."

"I knew that," he said. "Katia's going to the Mohawk res for the break. She tell you?"

Jaguar shook her head. "I don't think she wants to talk to me yet."

"Give her time. She'll get it straight. The universe doesn't do waste. It even takes the shit and makes flowers."

"Maybe you're right," Jaguar said.

He wrapped one bearlike hand around hers and patted it with the other. At that moment she realized that he reminded her of a younger version of her grandfather. Large and safe and real. That was why she always felt a mingling of warmth and sorrow in his presence. She was glad she'd had the chance to meet him.

She looked at the snow falling outside her office window, sighed deeply, and turned back to her computer. One last onerous task to complete, and then she could leave.

She had been at it for no more than five minutes when she heard the knock on her office door.

"Come in," she said, and the door opened.

She pushed her chair away from her desk and looked up at Alex. "I'm grading," she said. "It's awful."

He came over to where she sat and perched himself on the edge of her desk. "Aren't you ever glad that you survive your own chancy life long enough to bitch about these irritating tasks?"

"Now and then," she said. "Or, rather, not now, but then I was." She considered him for a moment. "I understand the Telekine and the military involvement are both being hushed."

"Like water on fire. As far as anyone will ever know, Professor Davis was your garden variety pervert, and you're the brave citizen who helped the University stop him. They are laying claim to a plan, but the publicity's still killing them. And President Johnston will announce her early retirement any day now. Nothing to do with the trouble, of course. Just wants to spend more time with the grandchildren."

Jaguar made a sound of disgust.

"Exactly. I understand Katia's spending the semester break on the reservation."

"Leonard told me," she said. "He'll stay close to her. She's got a lot to heal."

"She will, Jaguar. Not to worry."

"I know," Jaguar said. She paused a moment, then continued speaking. "They're keeping the History of Empathic Arts course, you know. They've asked me to stay on and teach it."

"I know."

He did not yet ask her if she had accepted, and she noticed this.

"Universities are amazing. They co-opt what they like least, to drive themselves crazy, I suppose. Or keep it under their watchful eye."

He nodded. "Like all good bureaucracies. By the way, I have something for you."

He reached into the pocket of his jacket and pulled out a letter, handed it to her.

She stared at it for a moment, then opened it and read.

A reinstatement letter from the Board, flattering and fulsome.

"There'll also be a raise," he said. "And a new evaluation letter for your permanent file."

Her lips went thin and tight, and she tore the letter in half, crumpled the pieces, and tossed them into the recycle bin.

"Slimy bastards," she spit out. "They want me back so they can try to kill me again."

"Is that what you think, Dr. Addams?"

"It's what I think, Supervisor Dzarny."

"You could be right," he agreed. "Maybe this whole thing was a setup to get rid of you once and for all. An intricate plot devised by men with brains no bigger than the forms they have to fill out on your repeated excursions into regrettable behaviors. That's one possibility."

"What's the alternative?" she asked suspiciously.

"Maybe," he said, "they're just assholes."

She lowered her head, and let it rest in her hand. Alex watched her as he thought through his next words.

"If it means anything to you, I want you to come back," he said.

She didn't move. Didn't speak.

"I'd like to tell you why," he continued, and he saw her shoulders stiffen.

"Alex, I don't think we should—"

"I do," he said. "Unless you've forgotten what happened in your chant-shape?"

She brought her face up from her hands, frowned.

"You remember, don't you?"

"Some of it," she said.

"Just some of it?"

Her breathing marked a minute before she replied, "All of it."

"And what you do at those times, what you say—it's all true. Correct?"

She nodded. She understood, and at least for now, she was sitting still with it. He allowed himself to breathe.

"Jaguar," he said gently. "I sent you here because I thought I'd be safe, if only I didn't look at the truth. That was stupid. More than stupid. It was almost fatal. To you."

He reached over and brushed a finger against her cheek. She took in breath, but she didn't back away from the gesture. "The truth is, something happened between us. It keeps happening. I can't call it back, but I'm not sure where to go with it."

"Where do you want to go with it?" she asked carefully, looking carefully away from him.

Stick with the truth, he told himself. Just say it.

"To my bed. To your bed. Any bed as long as you're in it with me."

He watched her reaction, which would have appeared noncommittal to any eyes but his. She bit her lip. Lowered her eyes. Considered her hands. Was silent. But he could feel her breath quickening. Thoughts moving like fire behind the lowered eyes. He waited.

"It would change everything," she said softly, hands quiet in her lap, eyes quiet in her face. "You know that."

She turned her face up to his, and he read the jungle of fear in it. "It's like the chant-shape. What you feel, what I feel—once we let it out, there's no telling what it'll do."

"I know," he said. "And I can't guarantee safety. Either we give ourselves to it and hope for the best, or not."

She turned her hands up on her lap and stared into her palms. Looking for answers, perhaps.

"And you would choose that risk?" she asked.

"It chose me," he said. "A long time ago. I just stopped running away from it."

"What if I haven't?" she asked.

"Then you haven't. I won't try to stop you. You've got to choose for yourself. What you want. What you're willing to risk. Whatever choice you make, you're still the best Teacher on Planetoid 3, Zone 12, and I feel privileged to work with you."

She smoothed her finger against her lips, silent. Trying to find a way to quieter ground, he supposed. Her computer, tired of waiting, beeped at her. She smiled wryly. "I have to finish my grades," she said.

"If you want, I can wait," he said. He spoke deliberately so she would understand the full weight of his words.

"I wouldn't ask you to do that," she said, just as deliberately.

"You wouldn't have to," he replied.

She turned her face to his. "It might take a while."

"That's okay," he said. "I have time."

He felt the brief pull and release of her eyes. Then she turned back to the computer and began punching in letters. Conservative radicals. Radical conservatives. She'd had enough of them.

She punched in the letter A next to each student's name. Even Katia and Steve. When she was finished, she looked up at Alex.

"When can we go back home?" she asked.

He allowed himself a smile.

"Whenever you're ready, Dr. Addams."